ALSO BY DAVID HANDLER

FEATURING BERGER & MITRY

The Coal Black Asphalt Tomb
The Snow White Christmas Cookie
The Blood Red Indian Summer
The Shimmering Blond Sister
The Sour Cherry Surprise
The Sweet Golden Parachute
The Burnt Orange Sunrise
The Bright Silver Star
The Hot Pink Farmhouse
The Cold Blue Blood

FEATURING BENJI GOLDEN

Phantom Angel
Runaway Man

FEATURING HUNT LEIBLING

Click to Play

FEATURING STEWART HOAG

The Man Who Died Laughing
The Man Who Lived by Night
The Man Who Would Be F. Scott Fitzgerald
The Woman Who Fell from Grace
The Boy Who Never Grew Up
The Man Who Cancelled Himself
The Girl Who Ran Off with Daddy
The Man Who Loved Women to Death

FEATURING DANNY LEVINE

Kiddo
Boss

THE
LAVENDER
LANE LOTHARIO

THE
LAVENDER
LANE LOTHARIO

A Berger and Mitry Mystery

DAVID
HANDLER

MINOTAUR BOOKS

A THOMAS DUNNE BOOK

NEW YORK

A THOMAS DUNNE BOOK FOR MINOTAUR BOOKS.
An imprint of St. Martin's Publishing Group.

THE LAVENDER LANE LOTHARIO. Copyright © 2016 by David Handler. All rights reserved. Printed in the United States of America. For information, address St. Martin's Press, 175 Fifth Avenue, New York, N.Y. 10010.

www.thomasdunnebooks.com
www.minotaurbooks.com

The Library of Congress Cataloging-in-Publication Data is available upon demand.

ISBN 978-1-250-07611-3 (hardcover)
ISBN 978-1-4668-8749-7 (e-book)

Our books may be purchased in bulk for promotional, educational, or business use. Please contact your local bookseller or the Macmillan Corporate and Premium Sales Department at (800) 221-7945, extension 5442, or by e-mail at MacmillanSpecialMarkets@macmillan.com.

First Edition: February 2016

10 9 8 7 6 5 4 3 2 1

For the late, great Ray Bradbury, who kindly gave this aspiring author the single most valuable piece of advice I've ever gotten: "Write what you love to read."

THE
LAVENDER
LANE LOTHARIO

PROLOGUE

HE WAS A LUCKY man. Many, many people said so.

Except they didn't know him. They didn't know the gloom that lived inside of him, day and night. Didn't know that some mornings he could barely force himself out of bed. No one knew this about him. He didn't let them. He had responsibilities. There were people who depended upon him. They thought he was satisfied being who he was. Happy, even.

People, he'd learned, could be remarkably stupid that way.

It was the last Thursday in April. Not yet dark out, but raw and blustery. The temperature had never made it out of the fifties that day. There was a Citgo mini-mart on Old Shore Road near the corner of Pitcairn Avenue that was open. But Pitcairn Avenue itself was absolutely deserted. Everything south of Old Shore Road was deserted during the off-season. The flimsy wood-framed buildings weren't winterized.

Slowly, he eased his car past the boarded-up ice cream parlor and T-shirt shop, past Abe's tattoo parlor and John's pizzeria, past Patsy's fried everything takeout seafood stand and the Sound View Kiddie Arcade. There was, for him, something incredibly forlorn about Pitcairn Avenue in the off-season. The buildings looked so beaten-up and neglected.

The Pit stood at the very end of the avenue facing Sound View Beach. The ramshackle beer joint was plenty rowdy on hot summer days. The picnic tables out on the patio were packed with people.

After dark, it was an even rowdier dance club that was mobbed until 2:00 A.M. The summer people flocked there, most of them young. The Pit was their place.

Right now, it was no one's place. Sand drifts blew across the parking lot, which was empty except for one car. The person whom he was meeting had already arrived. He parked and got out of his car, sorry he hadn't worn a jacket. The wind was really gusting down at the water's edge, billowing his pant legs as he trudged across the lot. The water of Long Island Sound was slate gray and choppy. It was hard to believe that in a few short weeks people would be sitting out on this patio in their bathing suits drinking ice-cold Coronas.

A hand-lettered sign on the door read: WE'LL SEE YOU AGAIN MEMORIAL DAY WEEKEND! HAVE A GREAT WINTER! The door was unlocked. Inside, it was almost the same temperature as outside. The Pit had no heat, no insulation. It smelled faintly of beer in there. Spilled beer that had soaked its way into the worn wooden floorboards. It was a smell that never went away no matter how many times the floor was swabbed.

"Hello. . . ?" he called out. "Are you here?"

No one was there.

He made his way over toward the bar. There were some empty glass Budweiser pitchers on it. Nothing else. The cash register was wide open to show that there was no money to steal. The weathered wooden picnic tables from the patio were stacked in the middle of the room with their overturned benches piled atop them. The walls were adorned with electric signs from many different breweries. The Pit proudly carried eighteen beers on tap and another twenty-four in bottles and cans. Also hanging on display were dozens of brightly colored bikini tops and bras that had been shed, and autographed, by their wearers after drinking many, many of those beers.

"Hello. . . ?" he called out once again.

That was when he got hit.

He didn't know with what. Only that he'd been whacked incredibly hard on the back of his head, so hard that he let out a groan of pain as he sank to his knees, dazed. Then he got hit again. And again.

And then . . . then he felt himself tumble over onto his back. There were bright flashbulbs going off in front of his eyes as he gazed up at his killer, who was smiling at him. And saying something to him now. But he couldn't hear the words over the incredible roaring sound in his ears. And then he couldn't see anything, either. He didn't feel what came next. He was very lucky that way.

He was a lucky man. Many, many people said so.

THE PREVIOUS EVENING

Chapter 1

"I must say, Master Sergeant. This qualifies as *the* most unusual date we've ever been on."

"It's not a date."

"Are you sure? It feels like a date."

"It's not a date."

Des and the chronically overweight Jewish man in her life were sitting together in the darkness on a picnic blanket in Duck River Cemetery, not far from the marble tomb where the great Aurora Bing had been interred since her death in 1961. It was an elaborate tomb compared to the historic cemetery's older, simpler headstones, set apart by a stone retaining wall and adorned with intricate scrollwork as well as an inscription courtesy of Byron:

She walks in beauty, like the night
Of cloudless climes and starry skies;
And all that's best of dark and bright
Meets in her aspect and her eyes . . .

The night was foggy and damp. Des wore a Gore-Tex jacket over her uniform. Mitch had on his C. C. Filson wool packer coat. They'd brought a Thermos of hot coffee and a bag of ham-and-cheese sandwiches. The sandwiches were for Mitch. There are two types of people in this world, Des had come to realize—those who eat when they're on edge and those who don't. Which explained why she, Desiree Mitry, Dorset's resident Connecticut State Trooper, had zero fat on her leggy six-foot-one-inch frame and why he, Mitch Berger, bore an uncanny resemblance to the Pillsbury Doughboy. They'd been waiting here since darkness fell. It was nearly nine o'clock now and way quiet, aside from those mournful blasts of the foghorn from the Old Saybrook lighthouse across the Connecticut River.

"I'm on the job right now," she reminded him. "And you're keeping me company because I didn't feel like doing this by myself. Cemeteries weird me out."

"No problemo," he assured her, munching on either his third or fourth sandwich. "Although I do keep expecting vampires to show up. This really reminds me of one of those color-drenched Dracula movies that Hammer Films made with Christopher Lee. Would you believe that he played Dracula for Hammer seven times? Starting with *The Horror of Dracula* in 1958 and ending with *The Satanic Rites of Dracula* in 1973, which incidentally featured Joanna Lumley as Jessica Van Helsing. You may remember her from the British sitcom *Absolutely Fabulous,* better known as *Ab Fab*. She played Patsy, who was best buds with—"

"Mitch, you're getting your jabber on."

"Sorry. Cemeteries weird me out, too. Plus we seem to be out of sandwiches."

"I can't imagine how that happened."

"Hey, I know what . . ." He reached into his jacket pocket for his new cell. "I'll take your picture with my super-duper new Batphone. It has its own built-in flash."

"Maybe later."

"It can also tell us precisely where we are. . . ."

"Mitch, I know where we are."

"And answer any questions you might have about baseball,

agriculture, world religion, you name it. Ask it anything. Go ahead. You have no idea how amazing it is."

"Kind of do, wow man. I'm the one who's been begging you to upgrade to a smart phone, remember? You'd still be clinging for dear life to your vintage Agent Fox Mulder clamshell if you hadn't dropped it in the bathtub. Does this mean you've finally been won over?"

"Is it that obvious?"

"Only to me." She heard a night creature skitter in the woods a few feet away.

Mitch heard it, too. "Um, I forget, how long do we have to stay here?"

"Until they come."

"You think they will?"

"I know they will. My troop commander schooled me about this when I first took the job." The leafy New England village of Dorset, jewel of Connecticut's gold coast, came equipped with all sorts of peculiar quirks. Though none quite so peculiar as this one. "They've been pulling stuff since long before you and I were born—ever since Geoffrey Gant took his own life way back in 1938." Gant had been one of the leading lights of Dorset's artist colony, right up there with George Bruestle. He was renowned for his landscape paintings, many of which depicted the countryside near his farm up in the hills on Eight Mile River Road, where the painter had lived with his wife and two sons.

"Aurora Bing owned White Gate Farm right across the road from him. She was a widow in her late forties, and still a very beautiful woman. The two of them fell madly in love, but when Gant refused to leave his wife for her she broke it off. He couldn't deal with it and hanged himself right there in his studio. His sons blamed Aurora. On the first anniversary of his death 'someone' burned her barn to the ground. Gant's sons were questioned but released. She rebuilt it. On the second anniversary 'someone' set fire to her house. Again, Gant's sons were questioned but released. Again she rebuilt. After that the Gants marked the anniversary of his death by throwing farm-fresh eggs at Aurora if she dared to set foot outside of her house. The Gants are a stubborn bunch. Not even Aurora's own death has stopped them. Year after year, generation after generation, Geoffrey Gant's male heirs have marked the anniversary of his suicide by desecrating her tomb. I'm told that what they used to do was fairly harmless."

"Fairly harmless as in. . . ?"

"They'd pee on it, one by one." She glanced over at him in the foggy darkness. "Why do guys do that?"

"It's considered the ultimate show of disrespect."

"Why?"

"Dunno. Just is."

"There are times when I don't understand your gender."

"We're complex," Mitch acknowledged. "But we're not deep."

"No one got super upset about it until last year, when they decided to up their game by spray-painting the word *whore* all over Aurora's tomb. It was hateful, plus it took a lot of hard work to clean off."

"Did they get busted for it?"

"Geoffrey Gant's grandson, Sherm, and Sherm's son, Leland, were questioned but released. No proof that they did it. But it was them. And they'll show up here tonight and do it again. Or try. Sherm is not a very nice man."

Sherm Gant, popularly known as the mayor of Pitcairn Avenue, was a major player in the Dorset business community. And one of those crusty small-town New England types who, once you got to know them better, turned out to be just plain nasty to the bone. Sherm was an unpleasant bully with a drinking problem. Condescending, too. Someone who felt he was just a tiny bit superior to everyone else because his grandfather had been a famous artist and because he, Sherm, had inherited a substantial amount of real estate. Geoffrey Gant's paintings had fetched quite a bit of money after he died. Money which Sherm's father had used to buy up dozens of summer rental cottages in the 1950s, as well as most of the commercial properties on Pitcairn Avenue. Sherm came into all of it when his father died, and he had proven himself to be a thoroughly inept landlord. He'd lost many of the cottages to the bank in recent years, but still had a stranglehold on the summer businesses on Pitcairn Avenue. He collected rentals from the folks who ran the ice cream parlor and kiddie arcade and so on. And he owned and personally operated The Pit, the rock 'em, sock 'em beach bar that was not exactly a source of pride among Dorset's moneyed blue bloods. Nor was Pitcairn Avenue itself, which they considered to be a low-class, honky-tonk destination for low-class, honky-tonk summer people. In fact, they preferred to think of Pitcairn Avenue as belonging to the less affluent neighboring town of South Dorset, though it did not. Des had the arrest records to prove it.

"Sherm also has a personal grudge against Hubie Swope," Des pointed out. "Which means you've got bad blood on two counts." Hubie Swope, Aurora Bing's sole grandchild, was the town of Dorset's stickler of a building inspector. Last summer, two weeks before Labor Day weekend, Hubie had shut down The Pit for numerous building code violations. Sherm had been infuriated. Still was, because Hubie was refusing to let him reopen for the upcoming season unless Sherm undertook enough upgrades to pass a rigorous inspection. "Trust me, Sherm will be showing up here any minute now, spray paint in hand," Des said, shivering from the damp cold. "And he'll drag his son Leland along. I just hope they get here before we freeze to death."

"Want some more coffee?"

"No, I'm good. Thanks for doing this with me. By now you must be incredibly sorry you said yes."

"Not a chance. I'm sharing a blanket with the woman of my dreams in a spooky old New England cemetery. It's delightfully foggy out. The marsh is giving off the ripe aroma of rotten eggs and dirty sweat socks. This is my idea of a good time."

Des reached over and touched his face, smiling. After her bitter breakup with her cheating dog of a husband, Brandon, she'd been positive that she would never, ever let another man into her life. And then Mitch came along. They made no sense together. None. She was a woman of color, a West Point graduate and Gulf War veteran who'd risen fast to become a lieutenant catching homicides for the Major Crime Squad—until she'd tangled with the wrong people and ended up back in uniform. Mitch was a Jewish film critic from New York City who'd spent most of his life sitting in dark rooms staring at flickering images on a wall. And yet they'd fallen madly in love with each other from the moment they'd met. Still, they were taking it careful and slow. Des needed time alone to deal with what she'd experienced on the job. She did that at an easel in her cottage overlooking Uncas Lake, where she drew heart-wrenching portraits of the many—too many—murder victims she'd encountered, deconstructing the horror line by line, shadow by shadow. And Mitch still wasn't totally over losing his beloved wife, Maisie, to ovarian cancer at the age of thirty. Many nights, he sat up all night watching movies from yesteryear in his two-hundred-year-old cottage out on Big Sister Island. Old movies weren't just Mitch's life's work. They sustained him. When she'd met him, Mitch had been chief film critic of the most prestigious daily newspaper in New York City. After the paper got taken over by a media conglomerate, he'd joined his editor's start-up e-zine as an essayist. He also wrote quirky film encyclopedias that were very popular.

He reached over and took her hand. "But listen, if you're feeling guilty about dragging me out in the fog like this . . ."

"No way, doughboy. Not going to happen."

"How do you even know what I'm going to say?"

"Because I know you. And we're not getting freaky on this blanket in the middle of Duck River Cemetery."

"Are you trying to tell me you've never fantasized about having sex in a cemetery after dark?"

"Never."

"Not once?"

"I believe that's the working definition of the word *never*. I'm on duty, remember? I'm *not* dropping trou here in front of all of these dead people."

"You can keep your pants on if you'd . . . Okay, ow, that hurt."

"Why don't you school me about Aurora? She's in your wheelhouse, isn't she?"

"Sure is. Not that you hear her name much anymore. But the lady in that tomb with a view over there was a huge star in her day—her day being shortly after the turn of the last century, when Aurora Bing was considered to be *the* most beautiful woman to ever set foot on a Broadway stage. She played Portia in a landmark 1908 production of *The Merchant of Venice* that was staged by the great impresario Henry Harris, who died four years later on the *Titanic*. Went on to star in a string of Broadway hits before Adolph Zukor signed her to a three-year film contract for five thousand dollars a week, which was a lot of money in 1915."

"It's still a lot of money."

"Those were the early days of silent pictures. They were still making most of them in New York. For a brief while, Aurora was as big a film star as Mary Pickford. But when the industry moved cross-country to Hollywood, her film career fizzled out. She didn't like it out there. They barely had paved roads. Aurora was used to the life of a Broadway diva. So she returned to the stage and married a zillionaire financier named Maynard Swope."

"Who bought her White Gate Farm," Des said, nodding. "Aurora gave birth to a bouncing baby boy and the family spent their summers here happily ever after until Swope lost his shirt in the crash of '29 and took a flying leap off a tall building. Aurora had some money of her own that his creditors couldn't get their hands on. And she had the farm, which Swope had given to her outright. So she raised her son here and went on to have a wild love affair with Geoffrey Gant."

"Which, I believe, is where we came in," Mitch said.

"Have you ever seen any of her movies?"

"No one has. They're gone. Most of those early silents are. The nitrate film stock turned to dust. Would you believe that the great Will Rogers made a whopping eleven feature films that no longer even—" Mitch broke off. "Did you just hear that?"

"Hear what?"

"Footsteps."

Des heard them now, too, crunching on the cemetery's gravel drive. People had to walk their way in after dark. The front gate was locked to cars. Her Crown Vic and Mitch's truck were hidden around the corner on Buttonball Road. Now she saw a flashlight beam coming closer to them. And heard voices. One raised, the other quieter.

"Stay out of this, okay?" she whispered to Mitch as she climbed to her feet, Maglite in hand.

"No prob," he whispered in response.

She pointed the Maglite's beam at Sherm and Leland Gant. They blinked at her, startled. Sherm was clutching an aerosol paint can in his right hand and reeling more than a bit. Des could smell his whiskey breath from several feet away. He was in his mid-fifties, bald, jowly, and rosy-cheeked. Des had always thought he resembled a malevolent cherub, though a cherub he was not. He was a big, flabby guy. One of those men who looked as if he had a pillow stuffed down the front of his pants.

Leland, who was twenty-three, looked totally miserable as he stood there next to him. Leland didn't resemble his father at all. He was slightly built, with neatly trimmed blond hair and a narrow face. He didn't behave like his father, either. Sherm loved to rankle people. Leland didn't. He was a nice guy. "Hiya, Trooper Mitry," he said, ducking his head in shame. "How's it going?"

"You tell me, Leland. What are you fellows doing here?"

"You know what we're doing here," Sherm blustered at her. "And you're not stopping us, see? This is about family."

"Just head on home before there's any trouble," Des told them.

"Who's going to make us?" Sherm demanded. "You and your boyfriend Blubberstein over there?"

"That's *Mister* Blubberstein, you boozed-up cretin," Mitch shot back.

"What'd you just call me?"

"Mitch, you're not helping right now."

"He's the one who started it."

"Okay, now you're really not helping."

"We're not looking for any trouble," Sherm said, swaying as he stood there. "Just got to do our duty and then we'll be gone."

"Sherm, I need you to hand over that can of spray paint, then turn around and go back the way you came. If you don't I'll have to arrest you both for criminal trespassing. You don't want Leland to have an arrest record, do you?"

"Come on, Dad, let's go home," Leland said.

Sherm shook his head. "Not until we take care of that whore."

Leland snatched the paint can from his father's hand and gave it to Des. "Not tonight, Dad."

"What the hell. . . ?" Sherm was outraged.

"Thanks, Leland," Des said. "You've got good sense."

"No balls is more like it," Sherm snarled at him. "You let people push you around."

"Whatever," Leland said wearily. "Come on, let's go."

Sherm stayed right where he was. "This isn't over," he warned Des. "We'll be back. And tell that whore's grandson, Hubie, to stay away from me or he'll get what's coming to him."

"Which is what, exactly?"

"He calls me up this morning and says he's coming by to *inspect* The Pit tomorrow, like he's the landlord and I'm the tenant. It's *my* place!"

"He's the building inspector, Sherm. He's just doing his job."

"Sure, take his side," Sherm grumbled at her sourly.

"Go home," Des told them once again.

Leland put a hand on his father's back and started to steer him away.

Sherm was having none of it. "Let go of me!" he hollered, flailing his big arms.

One of those big arms smacked Leland in the chest and sent him backpedaling into Mitch, who lost his footing on the loose gravel, tumbled over, and whacked the back of his head against a grave-stone. Hard.

Mitch lay there on the ground and didn't move.

Des rushed over to him, aiming her flashlight into his eyes. "Are you okay?" His eyes were open but he didn't respond. "Mitch. . . ?"

"Yeah. . . ?" he said slowly, blinking at her. "What is it?"

"Are you okay?"

"I'm fine, why?"

"Don't move." She turned to the Gants and said, "Leland, get your father out of here before I lose my temper, hear me? Beat it!"

Leland started his way back toward the front gate. Grudgingly, Sherm joined him.

Des reached for her cell and called Madge and Mary Jewett, the no-nonsense sisters who ran Dorset's volunteer ambulance service. They lived two minutes away. Madge assured her they'd be there in a flash. Then Des crouched next to Mitch, who'd been very obedient. He hadn't moved. "Talk to me, wow man. How are you?"

"Still fine. Why are you making such a fuss?"

"Oh, I don't know. Maybe because you've had two concussions in the past year and you just got your bell rung again. I should never have let you come with me."

"It's just a minor bump on the head. Not to worry."

"Yes to worry. I put you in harm's way. I'm not going to let that happen again."

"Don't be silly." He reached over and took her hand. "I'm fine. Honest."

"The Jewett sisters will be the judge of that." She heard the ambulance pull up at the front gate, followed by their hard-charging footsteps on the gravel drive.

"What happened?" Madge demanded when they arrived, puffing.

"Sherm Gant is what happened," Des replied.

"I can't stand that man, especially when he's been drinking." Mary knelt next to Mitch. "Had he. . . ?"

"Most definitely. There was a slight scuffle. Mitch conked his head on that gravestone. He insists he's okay but I thought you'd better have a look."

Mary fingered the back of Mitch's head as he lay there. "He's not bleeding. Skin's not broken." She shined a pen-sized light into his eyes. "His pupils are normal and responsive. How's your stomach, Mitch?"

"I don't think I could sit through an entire film directed by Mr. Judd Apatow, if that's what you're asking. Is that what you're—?"

"Does your head ache? Are you dizzy?"

"Nope and nope."

"I want you to count backward from one hundred in increments of, say, seventeen."

"Can we pick a different category? I'm terrible with numbers."

Des said, "Mitch, what was the name of Sturges's last film?"

"Preston or John?"

"There's a John?"

"Most def. He directed *The Magnificent Seven* and *The Great Escape,* not to mention *Bad Day at Black Rock,* featuring the delectable Miss Anne Francis, who was one of my first boyhood crushes."

"And his last film was. . . ?"

"*Marooned* with Gregory Peck. Utter dreck."

"He's fine," Des assured the Jewett sisters.

"Sherm gets nasty when he drinks." Madge helped Mitch up to a sitting position. "Always looking to pick a fight with somebody. That man's had a chip on his shoulder ever since his wife, Tess, took off for Hawaii a dozen years ago and never looked back. Leland's grown up to be a fine young man. His aunt, Mary Ellen, made sure

of that. I don't know where he, or Dorset, would be without her."
Sherm's younger sister, Mary Ellen Tatum, was Dorset's town nurse.
"Mitch, are you okay to drive home?"

"Sure thing."

"No way," Des said. "Not going to happen."

"Des, I'm perfectly fine," he insisted. "You're overreacting."

"So I'm overreacting. I'll drive you home before I head over to
the barracks. I have a mountain of paperwork waiting for me there."

"What about my truck?"

"I can drive it home for you," Madge offered. "My sister will follow me in the EMS van and pick me up."

"Well, okay . . ." Mitch doted on his bulbous, kidney-colored
1956 Studebaker pickup. "It pulls a little to the left, and the steering wheel shakes."

"Not to worry. I've been driving old trucks my whole life."

"Speaking of Mary Ellen," Des said. "Maybe she ought to look
in on Mitch in the morning. Just to play it safe."

"Not a bad idea," Madge agreed. "I'll call her."

CHAPTER 2

MITCH WAS SOUND ASLEEP when a certain someone leapt onto the bed, streaked across him, and sprinted down the steep, narrow stairs from the sleeping loft to the living room. This certain someone raced around and around down there, yowled, then dashed back upstairs and sprang directly onto Mitch's chest, which he proceeded to knead with his front paws as he purred and purred.

The Dude was up.

Mitch opened his eyes. His alarm clock said it was 6:15 A.M. Not that he needed an alarm clock. Not since the Dude had taken up temporary residence. Des, a rescuer of feral strays, had found him living behind the little country market near Uncas Lake back when he was a few weeks old. After the vet had determined that the little guy was healthy, she'd persuaded Mitch to foster parent him until she could find him a permanent home. He was now about ten months old and seemed to be equal parts Maine Coon, snow leopard, and Huntz Hall. Mostly, he was all energy. Especially compared to Clemmie, Mitch's inert house cat, who was still sound asleep on Mitch's legs. The Dude had two gears—awake and asleep. Now that he'd made sure Mitch was awake, too, he let out another yowl, dashed back downstairs, and started batting his rubber mousey toy around. Or at least Mitch hoped it was his rubber mousey toy.

Yawning hugely, Mitch climbed out from under Clemmie and fingered the bump on the back of his head. A bit tender, but not too bad. Coffee. He needed coffee. He put on a pair of sweatpants and his New York Giants hoodie and made his way downstairs, where the Dude was now batting around his empty kibble bowl. Breakfast. He needed breakfast. Mitch gave him some kibble, put water on to boil, and built a fire in the big stone fireplace. Mitch's chestnut post-and-beam caretaker's cottage was basically one big room that had bay windows with views of the Sound in three different directions. Some of his furniture, like the overstuffed love seat and non-matching easy chairs, he'd found in a neighbor's barn. The rest he'd assembled from items he'd recovered from the town dump. For a desk he'd set an old mahogany door atop a pair of sawhorses. For a coffee table he had an ancient rowboat with an old storm window over it. Books and DVDs were stacked everywhere. Clutter was a permanent feature of his life. So was his sky-blue Fender Stratocaster and monster stack—a pair of Fender twin reverb amps, piled one atop the other, with a wah-wah pedal and an Ibanez Tube Screamer. Mitch could make amazing sounds come out of that Stratocaster. Not everyone called it music, but he did.

Last night's fog had blown away. It was clear and blustery. The high was supposed to approach fifty, though it was always at least five degrees cooler out on Big Sister Island, the forty acres of wooded Yankee paradise that Mitch was lucky enough to call home. There were five precious old Peck houses on the island, a decommissioned lighthouse that was the second tallest in New England, and a dock, tennis court, and strip of beach. Most of the island's houses were vacant except for a few weeks every summer. The only other year-round resident was Bitsy Peck, Mitch's cheery fifty-something garden guru. Bitsy had lived alone in her ginormous natural-shingled bungalow ever since her husband, Redfield, had been sent to jail due to a slight case of murder.

As the water came to a boil, Mitch heard Quirt bang his hard little head against the front door. Mitch opened it and let in his lean, mean outdoor hunter. The Dude scampered right on over to him, anxious to play. Quirt let out a hiss just to remind the upstart that he hadn't been formally accepted as a roommate. Then Quirt strutted into the kitchen to eat his breakfast, the Dude following him like a rambunctious kid brother. Mitch got the coffee started, extra strong.

He'd just taken his first grateful gulp of it when he got buzzed. He grabbed his binoculars from their hook by the door and peered across the rickety quarter-mile wooden causeway that connected Big Sister to the Peck's Point Nature Preserve. Waiting there at the barricade was Mary Ellen Tatum, Dorset's town nurse. He pushed the button to raise the barricade and she eased her way across in her battered Honda Civic.

Mary Ellen was one of those tireless, indispensable people who made Dorset the kindly place that it was. She saw to the needs of its residents day and night. Even made house calls to help bedridden oldsters with their medications, bandages, and various and sundry other things that Mitch never, ever wanted to know about. He intended to age gracefully and in full control of all of his sphincters.

He opened the door to greet Mary Ellen as she got out of the Honda wearing a brightly patterned nurse's smock and white pants. "Morning, Mitch," she exclaimed cheerfully. "The Jewett girls asked me to look in on you. How's your head today?"

"Just fine, Mary Ellen."

"Any double vision?"

"None."

"Good. I'm just going to check you over real quick." She came striding in the door with her bag as Quirt darted back outside. Mary Ellen was in her late forties, tall and big-boned like her older brother, Sherm. Although flabby she was not. Strapping was more like it. She had a shock of wiry copper-colored hair and a smattering of freckles on her cheeks, and always seemed to have an air of tolerant bemusement about her, which was something Mitch supposed was a must if you had to deal with as many cranky old hens and roosters as she did on a daily basis. Mitch was acquainted with her because one of the oldsters she frequently looked in on was Sheila Enman, the salty ninety-four-year-old retired schoolteacher for whom Mitch marketed. Back when he'd been a full-time resident of New York City, Mitch seldom did anything besides go to movies and write about them. But his life had changed when he took to calling Dorset home. When you live in a small town you help your neighbors.

Mary Ellen had a seat before the fire and warmed her hands. The Dude promptly jumped into her lap. She smiled. "My goodness, who is this cute little fellow?"

"I've taken to calling him Jeff Lebowski, but he prefers the Dude, his Dudeness, Duder . . . or El Duderino, if you're not into the whole brevity thing." Mary Ellen arched an eyebrow at Mitch curiously. Not a Coen brothers fan, apparently. "He's in need of a permanent home. Would you like to adopt him?"

"I wish I could, but Ward's allergic to cats."

Right away, the Dude sprang from her lap and darted upstairs to the sleeping loft.

"Come over here," Mary Ellen commanded Mitch. "I want to have a look at your bean."

"Is it going to hurt?"

"Will you stop being such a man and get over here?"

He bent down so she could probe the bruise on the back of his head with her fingers. "Looks okay to me." She took a small flashlight from her bag and shined it into his eyes. "I was wondering something, Mitch. Can you name all seven Dracula movies that Christopher Lee made for Hammer Films?"

"Have you by any chance been interfacing with our resident trooper?"

"Well, can you?"

"Here goes: *The Horror of Dracula, Dracula: Prince of Darkness, Dracula Has Risen from the Grave, Taste the Blood of Dracula, The Scars of Dracula, Dracula A.D. 1972,* and, lastly, *The Satanic Rites of Dracula,* which incidentally featured Joanna Lumley as Jessica Van Helsing. You may remember her from the British sitcom *Absolutely Fabulous,* better known as *Ab Fab.* She played Patsy, who was best buds with—"

"Most impressive, Mitch. It must be very odd living inside of your brain."

"Well, it's not for everyone but I enjoy it."

"You don't seem to be suffering any ill effects from your tussle with Sherm last night. I'm awfully sorry about that. Sherm's my big brother, and I love him, but he can be a real pain in the butt."

"The coffee's still hot. Would you like some?"

"Sounds good. Black, please."

He fetched her a mug, topped off his own, and sat down on the love seat.

Mary Ellen took a sip, gripping the mug in both hands. "Sherm's a bitter, angry mess," she said. "Always lashing out at other people when he should be looking in the mirror. Pitcairn Avenue's gotten terribly run-down, especially The Pit, and it's his own darned fault." She took another sip of her coffee, gazing into the fire. "Sherm wasn't always this way. But he never bounced back after Tess took off for Hilo. Just started sitting in that little cottage of his every night drinking. He brought that on himself, you know. Her leaving." Mary Ellen shot an uncertain glance at Mitch. "I don't mean he smacked Tess around or anything, but he took her for granted and made her real unhappy. Tess never complained. She kept her feelings to herself—until one day she just upped and left. I've never blamed her for that, though I do think poorly of her for leaving Leland behind. She abandoned that boy when he was eleven years old. That's an awful thing to do to a child. Leland never hears from her. I don't, either, and I was her best friend. She associates us with Sherm, I guess. She wants to forget him."

"Last night, he sure made it sound like he wants to smack Hubie Swope around."

"Which is totally unfair. It's not Hubie's fault that Sherm's so cheap and lazy. Four of those storefronts on Pitcairn Avenue have been sitting vacant for two years now because they're in such sorry shape nobody will rent them anymore. Personally, I didn't blame Hubie one bit for shutting down The Pit. If you're serving food you can't cut corners the way Sherm does. I wouldn't eat a potato chip in that place. We're talking health code violations, Mitch. Hubie *had* to shut it down. And it'll stay shut down until Sherm takes proper care of things. I know Hubie gives him a hard time. He gives everyone a hard time, even the fancy-pants builders like Gaylord Holland. That's what he's paid to do. Hubie's our neighbor. Ward and I live four doors away." Mary Ellen's husband, Ward, was a biology teacher at the high school. "Whenever Ward needs help digging a posthole or whatever, Hubie's right there to give him a hand. He's very generous with his time. He's our volunteer fire marshal, you know. But he's lonely. The poor man lost his wife, Joanie, to leukemia two years ago."

"Did they have any kids?"

"No, they married late. She'd been married once before, and Hubie was a lifelong bachelor. Joanie was so frail toward the end. I looked in on her every morning and evening for, gosh, must have been close to a year. It was so painful to watch her waste away like she did."

Mitch knew all about such pain from watching Maisie die. It was still tucked inside of him. Never went away. Never. He got up and put another log on the fire.

"I'd sit with Hubie for a few minutes every evening and we'd talk," Mary Ellen recalled. "He had no one else to talk to. No close friends. No family. He's a decent guy. He'd make a real good husband for someone, but he hasn't shown the slightest interest in taking up with another woman. And he hasn't lacked for opportunity, let me tell you. That man was subjected to a full-court press Casserole Courtship."

Mitch frowned at her. "A full-court press what?"

"Casserole Courtship. It's a time-honored Dorset mating ritual when a gentleman like Hubie loses his wife to an illness or accident."

"I swear, I learn something new about this place every day. How does it work?"

"It's pretty simple. After a suitable period of mourning, certain unattached ladies who are interested in a certain widowed gentleman will bring him an offering in the form of a casserole. They make sure to—"

"What kind of a casserole?"

"Does that matter?"

"Oh, it most certainly does."

"They might bring him, say, mac-and-cheese with shrimp. Or lasagne. Or maybe bratwurst, sauerkraut, and potatoes. Something that holds up well to being nuked in the . . ." Mary Ellen frowned. "What's that noise?"

"Just my stomach growling. Pay it no mind. You said they make sure to . . ."

"They stick a piece of masking tape on the bottom of the casserole dish with their name and phone number on it. That way he'll know who to return it to. If he compliments her profusely on her casserole, she offers to stop by with another one. If he's interested in pursuing a relationship, he asks her to stay and share it with him, and before long they're an item. Happens all of the time."

"But not in Hubie's case?"

"Not in Hubie's case. He washed the casserole dishes and returned them, period. And there were a couple of ladies who were *very* disappointed."

"Really? Like who?"

"Like Nancy Franklin."

"Our head librarian?"

"Nancy has always been interested in Hubie. And she's all alone in that big Victorian of hers on Dorset Street." Mary Ellen peered at him. "You look surprised."

"I am. We're pretty good friends, and Nancy's never so much as mentioned Hubie." In fact, Mitch reflected, Nancy had never mentioned any man being in her life. She was rather private that way. "Who else?"

"Inez Neto. No surprise there. She's been looking to latch on to someone dependable like Hubie since forever." Inez was a well-endowed blonde in her late thirties who worked as a cashier at the Big Y. "That woman flirts with every unattached man who sets foot in the market." Mary Ellen crinkled her nose disapprovingly. "And we all know that she does more than just flirt. Inez had that cheesehead son of hers, Petey, back when she was sixteen. Not exactly suitable wife material for a man whose grandmother was a great star like Aurora Bing. Not that you'd know that by Hubie. He puts on no airs at all."

"Did his family come into a lot of money when Aurora died?"

"Not a cent. She was land poor. Hubie's dad, Angus, had to sell off White Gate Farm just to settle her debts. Angus was a carpenter and contractor. He taught Hubie the trade. Hubie built quite a few homes around here, but he didn't care for the uncertainty. When old Joe Hart retired he jumped at the chance to be building inspector."

"How serious is this feud between your two families?"

Mary Ellen let out a hoot. "It's not. It's nothing more than an excuse for Sherm to get drunk and act like a big, dumb jerk. Back when we were kids our dad regarded it as a solemn family obligation. But dad was a solemn, responsible man. Sherm isn't," she said, sighing regretfully. "And he has real issues when it comes to Leland. Bullies him constantly. Leland hates working at The Pit. He wants to become a physical therapist. Someone who helps returning veterans. But he's so intimidated by Sherm that he hasn't got the nerve to speak up. Leland needs to break free and he can't and that pains me to see. I have strong feelings for him. Ward and I lost our own little boy, Wyatt, to a congenital heart defect when he was only three. I never got a chance to see Wyatt grow up. But I've been here for Leland. He's got a good head on his shoulders. I'll admit he was girl crazy back when he was seventeen, eighteen years old. There wasn't a cute young thing within a fifty-mile radius of Dorset who that boy didn't chase after. But now he's engaged to Brianna. She teaches fourth grade at Center School. Ward says Brianna's the most promising teacher they have. She goes the extra mile, same as Ward. My husband tutors kids in the study room at the library two evenings a week for free."

"Is his name really Ward?"

"Of course it is. Why do you. . . ?"

"Because I've never heard of anyone named Ward who wasn't, you know, Ward Bond. Unless you count Ward Cleaver, the father on *Leave It to Beaver*. Except, well, he wasn't a real person. Unless, that is, you consider TV sitcom characters real people."

She studied Mitch closely. "Are you sure you're feeling okay?"

"Tip top. This is how I roll. Ask the resident trooper if you don't believe me." The Dude came sprinting back down the stairs and proceeded to roll around on his back with a wadded-up piece of copier paper, attacking it with intense fervor. Mitch watched him, greatly amused, before he turned back to Mary Ellen and said, "Do you think Leland will work up the nerve to break free from Sherm?"

"I hope so. I want him to be happy. Just between us, it won't pain me one bit if Hubie tells Sherm that he can't reopen The Pit this summer. If that happens Sherm will lose the place to the bank for sure. Leland will be free to do what he wants."

"What'll happen to Sherm?"

"He'll probably drink himself to death. And not one person in Dorset will care."

"Not even you?"

Mary Ellen's mouth tightened. "Don't get me wrong, Mitch. I'd shed a tear over him. He's my big brother, after all. But whatever happens to Sherm will be his own damned fault. And he can go ahead and die for all I care."

CHAPTER 3

THE WORKDAY STARTED EARLY in Dorset, as it did in most small New England villages. Town Hall opened at 8:00 A.M. sharp. Hubie Swope could be found every morning at 7:30 on the same stool at McGee's diner on Old Shore Road before he headed to his office. If a local contractor was on his way to a job site and needed to talk to Hubie about something he was sure to find him there.

"Good morning, Hubie," Des said, tipping her big Smokey hat at him.

"And to you, Trooper Mitry," he responded with guarded cordiality. They were professional acquaintances, nothing more. "Would you like a cup of coffee?"

"I would, thanks."

She slid onto the stool next to his. Sandy, the frizzy-haired waitress, brought Hubie his scrambled eggs, sausage links, and rye toast, topped off his coffee, and filled a cup for Des, who sipped it while she watched Hubie methodically cut each of his sausage links into identical, bite-sized pieces, one by one by one. Only when he'd completed the job to his satisfaction did he begin to eat. Hubie was a quiet and careful man, a dour man. Des couldn't recall ever seeing a smile on his face. He was sturdily built but stood no more than five feet six, which made him a good deal shorter than most of the men whose work he passed judgment on. But contractors who tried to get chesty with Dorset's little building inspector were out of luck. He couldn't be bullied. In fact, the man who'd remodeled Des's

31

house had called Hubie a "petty tyrant." But Des understood where Hubie was coming from. Dorset treasured its quaint, small-town character. It took a stickler like Hubie to make sure that it didn't lose it. He was in his mid-fifties. Had a short thatch of white hair and alert blue eyes. He wore a tan L.L. Bean chamois shirt, olive-colored work pants, and work boots. On his belt was an all-purpose Leatherman knife.

"I was able to intercept Sherm and Leland last night before they had a chance to deface your grandmother's grave again," Des informed him.

"Thank goodness for that." Hubie forked some eggs onto a slice of toast, placed a piece of sausage on top, and tucked it carefully into his mouth, munching on it. "That obscene display last year was very hurtful."

"But Sherm made a specific threat in regards to you, Hubie."

"What sort of a threat?"

"Do you have an appointment with him today to inspect The Pit?"

He nodded. "Later this morning. Why, what did he. . . ?"

"He said that if you don't back off you're going to get what's coming to you."

Hubie forked some more eggs onto his toast, placing another piece of sausage on top. "I've known Sherm Gant since we were little boys," he told her as he ate. "He's a big fat windbag, nothing more. I have a job to do and I intend to do it. I gave him a detailed list of upgrades he needs to make. And I've warned him repeatedly—if he doesn't follow through on them then I won't let him reopen."

"I understand," said Des, who wouldn't mind it one bit if The Pit never reopened. She'd spent way too much of her time there last summer breaking up booze-fueled brawls. But if The Pit stayed shuttered another beer joint would open up in no time to take its place. There would always be a place like The Pit, just as there would always be sunburned kids smoking joints on the beach after dark. That's what summer meant when you lived in a shore-line town.

"It's a simple matter," he said. "Either Sherm has done the work or he hasn't."

"What sort of upgrades are we talking about, may I ask?"

Hubie reached for his briefcase on the floor next to him, opened it on the counter, and consulted his inspection report. "Just for starters, his six-burner electric range has inadequate venting for a commercial kitchen. The state code requires an exhaust fan that moves at least five hundred cubic feet of air per minute. I'd prefer a thousand. His barely moves a fraction of that. He relies on outdoor ventilation, which is plentiful on warm, sunny days when his slid-ing glass doors are open. But what about on cold, rainy days when the doors are shut? That won't do. Not at all. There are no safety railings on those wooden steps that lead from the sliding glass doors down to his patio. This is a serious, serious issue, especially for an establishment that serves liquor. Sherm is just plain lucky nobody's fallen and broken an arm or a leg. They could have sued him for negligence and bankrupted him. His septic system is woefully in-adequate, partly because he doesn't properly dispose of the grease from his fryers. Twice last summer he had to resort to Porta-Potties. That won't do. Not at all." Hubie continued to eat his breakfast as he glanced through the report. "I also spot checked his refrigera-tors and found that one of them was keeping the food at forty-eight degrees, which is three degrees warmer than the state health code requires. If I were a petty, vindictive person, the sort of person who was looking to get even with a certain someone for urinating on his grandmother's final resting place and spray-painting a vile obscenity on it, I could have brought the Connecticut Department of Environmental Health and Safety down on Sherm. But I didn't do that. I've kept it local. In fact, I've bent over backward to accommodate Sherm, not that he'd ever thank me."

"He seemed pretty riled up last night, Hubie. I'd be happy to accompany you today if you'd like."

"Not a chance," he responded abruptly. "I'm a public official. I do my job without fear and I for darned sure do it without a chaperone."

"I'm just trying to head off a situation before it turns ugly. That's my job."

"And I thank you for your consideration, Trooper Mitry. But Sherm's a perfectly reasonable man in the sober light of day."

"Fair enough," Des said, drinking down the last of her coffee.

That was when the door to McGee's diner swung open and a booming voice hollered, "Damn it, Hubie, this has gone far enough!"

She turned around. Everyone in the place turned around.

Gaylord Holland stood there with a sheaf of papers clutched in one hand, glaring angrily at Dorset's building inspector. Gaylord was a tall, athletically built man in his late forties who was blessed with chiseled good looks and a whole lot of wavy blond hair. Gaylord was Dorset's top restorer and builder of high-end homes. In fact, he was so high-end that he called himself a housewright, which wasn't something that Des could ever imagine doing with a straight face. But Gaylord had no problem pulling it off. He carried himself with an air of great self-confidence, not to mention deep-pocketed privilege—although the deep pockets were not his own. His wife, Loretta, was a Beckwith. A few years back he'd undertaken a major renovation of the three-hundred-year-old Beckwith family mansion up on Elmer's Ferry Road that Loretta shared with her then-husband, John Friday. By the time the job was completed Loretta's marriage to John was over and Gaylord had moved in. Gaylord was a man who was accustomed to getting what he wanted, Des suspected. He wore a Barbour waxed field jacket over a navy blue turtleneck sweater, gray corduroy pants, and work boots.

"Des, I'm glad you're here," he said, striding across the diner toward them. "This matter concerns you. Crime in Dorset is about to skyrocket. Shall I tell you why? Because half of the skilled workmen in town will be unemployed because of this man."

"Gaylord, you're talking like a crazy person," Hubie said as he polished off his breakfast.

"Am I? Maybe that's because you're *driving* me crazy, Hubie. This notification is completely unacceptable," he blustered, waving the papers in the little man's face. "I've done *everything* you've requested. I've jumped through hoop after hoop after hoop. The Executive Council of the Historic District has said yes. The Planning Commission, Zoning Commission, and Wetlands Commission have all said yes, too. And yet *you* are still blocking me!"

For months Gaylord Holland had been trying to get final approval to build two very expensive new homes on two very tiny slivers of land facing the Lieutenant River at the end of Maple Lane, smack dab in the middle of the Historic District.

"I have concerns, Gaylord," Hubie stated.

"So do I!" Gaylord shot back, as the other folks in McGee's hunched over their breakfasts, listening to each and every word. "I'm concerned that dozens of local tradesmen won't be able to make their mortgage payments this summer. They're counting on this job. They're counting on *me*. I've acted in good faith, Hubie. Bent over backward to address your concerns. Why do you keep fighting me?"

"Because you're planning to build on the edge of wetlands, that's why. I'm concerned about your septic systems."

"The Wetlands Commission gave me their okay."

"Their okay is conditional," Hubie pointed out. "They approved the project if it meets with my approval. And it doesn't. Both building sites have flunked multiple deep-hole perc tests." Deep-hole percolation tests were made to determine if the soil could absorb the amount of liquid that would be flowing into it. "Those sites can't handle septic systems, Gaylord."

"By yesterday's standards," Gaylord argued. "We have new technology now. I've brought in the top geotechnical engineer in the state. He's able to de-water the leaching area by installing trenches a safe distance away and pumping it to them through subsurface drain pipes."

Hubie studied Gaylord, his eyes squinting half-shut. "And what happens if there's a power outage? Our power grid in this state is held together with dental floss. Every time we're hit by a storm we go dark for hours, sometimes days. What happens to your subsurface drainage then? Where does the outflow go?"

Gaylord shook his wavy blond head at him. "Hubie, these new houses will be smart, just like your phone and TV are. If the power stays off long enough to trip the septic overflow alarm, then gas-powered generators will kick on automatically. I've detailed all of this in the paperwork that I filed with your office. You've read every word I've sent you. I know you have. Why won't you accept that it's valid?"

"Because I don't accept it," Hubie responded. "You can pump away the outflow to your heart's content but it still has to end up somewhere. My concern is that somewhere will be in the Lieutenant River. We have osprey nests there, egrets, great blue herons.

I don't want to see their native habitat jeopardized because you insist upon building two houses where they don't belong."

"I love those birds," Gaylord insisted. "So do the people who've bought these homes. Hell, man, it's the birds that are drawing them there. Do you honestly think I'd do anything to pollute the river?"

"Not intentionally. But you're in the business of building houses and I'm in the business of making sure those houses don't contaminate our natural resources. That's why I can't issue you a building permit."

Gaylord stood there furiously, his jaw muscles clenching and unclenching. "Hubie, I won't take no for an answer on this. I'm going over your head."

"You're welcome to try, but you won't get anywhere. The only person in Dorset who's empowered to issue building permits is the building inspector. And you're not getting those permits. Not as long as I'm the building inspector."

"We'll see about that!" Gaylord fumed. "We'll just see!" Then he stormed out of the diner, slamming the door behind him.

Everyone in McGee's sat there in wide-eyed silence. Des had no doubt that word of this little scene would be all over Dorset within the hour.

Hubie calmly finished his coffee. It didn't seem to bother him that he'd made Gaylord Holland angry. Didn't seem to delight him, either. The little man was unfazed.

"It's not easy being Mr. No, is it?"

"Gaylord's wrong. What's more, he knows he's wrong. Not that he'd ever admit it." He glanced at her curiously. "Our jobs aren't that different, are they?"

Des shoved her heavy horn-rimmed glasses up her nose. "The

resident trooper's generally not the most popular person in town, if that's what you mean."

"Right now I'd say you're the second most unpopular person in town."

"Who's the most unpopular?"

"That's easy," Hubie Swope replied. "I am."

CHAPTER 4

IT DIDN'T MATTER THAT the calendar said it was almost May.

Mitch still had to wear Capilene thermal layers under his hoodie and sweatpants when he went for his morning run on the island's beach. It was thirty-nine degrees out there. The wind was gusting. It felt like the middle of March as he jogged his way past the lighthouse, huffing and puffing, his mind on what he was going to write about today. That conversation with Des about Aurora Bing had gotten him thinking about just how many forgotten stars there were. Not just silent stars whose films were lost, but big names from the glorious 1930s whose films were still very much around. Because for every Humphrey Bogart and Bette Davis—icons who remained household names seventy years later—there were performers who'd once been just as big as them who were now practically unknown. Take Warren William, who'd starred in a string of blockbuster hits like *The Gold Diggers of 1933, Cleopatra, Imitation of Life,* and *Lady for a Day.* Yet hardly anyone could pick Warren William out of a police lineup now, just as hardly anyone remembered that it was Kay Francis who'd been queen of the Warner Brothers lot until Bette Davis snatched her crown away.

Mitch huffed and puffed as he plowed his way along, sorting out his thoughts. He was also wondering if it was time to plant his spring lettuce. Bitsy Peck, his garden guru, would know. He kept an eye out for her as he jogged past her three-story natural-shingled bungalow with its wraparound terrace, multiple turrets, and sleeping porches. Bitsy was almost always out working in her vast, terraced garden where she grew hundreds of species of flowers, herbs, and vegetables. She was a round, snub-nosed woman who'd had her share of troubles—not only her husband, Redfield, but her daughter, Becca, who was a recovering heroin addict. Yet Bitsy was a remarkably upbeat person. Also a fount of wisdom when it came to anything having to do with Dorset. She was a Peck. It was the Pecks who'd first settled Dorset back in the 1600s.

And, indeed, there she was in her vegetable garden, planting some of her greenhouse-raised seedlings. "Morning, Bitsy!" he called out to her.

She didn't respond. Just continued her planting, clad in a mud-splattered barn coat, denim overalls, and garden clogs. But there was something decidedly odd about her body language. Her shoulders kept rising and falling convulsively as if she were having some form of seizure. Concerned, he raced his way up the path to her garden and discovered that his cheery neighbor was bawling her head off.

"Why, Bitsy, what's wrong?"

"N-Nothing . . ."

"Is it Becca? Did she have a relapse?"

"N-No . . ." Bitsy groped for a Kleenex in the pocket of her coat and swiped at her eyes and nose. "It's nothing like that. I don't want to talk about it. Please just . . . leave me alone, will you?"

"I'm your friend. If you're upset I want to help. Talk to me, will you?"

Bitsy knelt there in stubborn silence, her eyes red and swollen.

He glanced at his watch. "I have to go make my deliveries, but I'm not leaving until you tell me what this is about."

"Mitch, you have six elderly shut-ins who are counting on you for a hot meal. Just go, will you? I'm fine."

"You're not fine. Take a ride with me. We can talk in my truck."

"Don't be silly."

"I'm not being silly," he said, holding his hand out to her. "I insist."

She let him help her to her feet and walked back to his cottage with him, her eyes cast despondently down at the ground. He went inside for his keys and his wallet. Then they climbed into his high-riding Studey half-ton pickup and eased over the wooden causeway and down the dirt road that snaked its way through the Peck's Point Nature Preserve. When they reached Old Shore Road Mitch coaxed the old truck up onto the pavement and started toward the village, feeling the steering wheel begin to shake and pull to the left as he picked up speed. He wondered if it was the tie rods. Probably ought to get them checked.

Bitsy rode beside him in silence, gazing forlornly out her window, before she finally said, "You may have noticed that I have someone in my life now."

What he'd noticed was that lately she'd been going out every Saturday night and not coming home until Sunday morning. When there's only one other resident on an island you pick up on such things. "So you've been seeing someone?"

"I'm in love, Mitch."

"That's wonderful, Bitsy."

"No, it's not. It's awful . . ." She stifled a sob. "I—I never, ever thought I'd have a man in my life again. I'd gotten used to being alone. I'm a fifty-five-year-old post-menopausal woman and, God knows, I'm no swimsuit model."

"Nonsense. You're very attractive."

"Mitch, if you're going to sit there and fling poo at me I swear I will jump right out of this truck. I'm being serious here. Men don't look at me *that* way anymore. Like they're wondering what I look like naked, I mean." She glanced over at him. "Do you know what I've missed more than anything else? Being wanted. That's how he makes me feel. When we're together I feel like I matter to someone."

"So you've been spending the night at his place?"

"No, we stay in a suite at the Mohegan Sun casino. We order caviar and champagne from room service, take bubble baths together. It's like a schoolgirl fantasy."

"And who, may I ask, is this lucky schoolboy?"

Bitsy shook her head. "I'm not going to tell you."

"Why not? Wait, is he married?"

She twitched her snub nose at him. "I'm not saying another word about him. So don't ask me."

Mitch steered the truck toward the village, dying with curiosity. *Who is Bitsy's boyfriend?* "Can I at least ask you how long it's been going on?"

"A couple of months, although he's someone who I've known for quite a while. He called me up to ask for my advice about a tree he was thinking about planting. We ended up having a drink together. . . . He loves me, Mitch. He's told me so. Many, many times. He's very affectionate. And we laugh a lot, sometimes for no reason at all."

"So why the tears? What's gone wrong?"

"Lately, he's . . . let's just say I've become aware that I'm not the only woman in his life."

"What has he done to make you think that?"

"Little things. Like he'll start to tell me a story and suddenly stop and say, 'Did I already tell you this?' Or he'll call me a pet name that he's never called me before. Or . . . I don't know, I just get the feeling that sometimes he can't remember which one of us he's with. Maybe it's all my imagination. Maybe I'm being silly and stupid and—and . . ." She sighed mournfully. "Mitch, how do I know if he's being faithful to me?"

"It's very simple. You ask him."

"Oh, I couldn't do that. I don't want to be *that* woman."

"What woman?"

"The possessive, clinging vine who makes him crazy."

"So instead you're making yourself crazy."

"What if I were to ask him, say, 'Where do you see our relationship going?'"

"God, no. That's the second worst thing a woman can say to a man."

"What's the worst thing?"

"The worst? 'That's okay, darling. Size doesn't really matter.'"

"Mitch, he doesn't like to be seen in public with me."

"The Mohegan Sun casino isn't exactly low profile."

"We take separate cars there and never go inside together. He checks in while I wait in the parking lot. Then he calls me and gives me the room number. He always pays. He insists on that. And we always leave separately. He insists on that, too."

"So the two of you are never seen together. . . ." Mitch considered this as he drove them toward the steepled white Congregational Church that was the Historic District's anchor, its trademark, its Eiffel Tower. "He sure sounds married to me. Is he married?"

"Please don't ask me anything more about him. Just be my friend, all right?"

"Sure, Bitsy. Whatever you say."

She mustered a faint smile. "Thank you. And thank you for letting me vent. I'm a total basket case. I really don't know what I'm going to do."

"Not to worry. We'll figure it out." He pulled into the church's gravel driveway and parked around in back behind the Fellowship

Center. "I'll just be a minute," he said as he got out, wondering, wondering.

Who is Bitsy's boyfriend?

The Fellowship Center, which had been added on to the church in the 1970s, functioned as Dorset's community center. Senior citizens gravitated there every morning to play cards. Support groups such as Alcoholics Anonymous met there in the evenings. Blood drives were held there. And it was the headquarters for Meals on Wheels, which was run by Loretta Beckwith Holland. Loretta was a blue-blooded go-getter who also headed up the Youth Services Bureau, which found part-time jobs for local teenagers.

Mitch went inside through the kitchen door and got in line behind the other drivers to collect his thermal carriers, his nostrils greatly intrigued by the scent that was wafting from them. Yesterday's hot lunch had been Salisbury steak and mashed potatoes. And he was pretty sure he recognized what today's was.

Loretta was handing off the thermal carriers and checking the names from the list on her clipboard. Loretta was in her late forties, slim, lithe, and extremely attractive. She had long, shiny black hair streaked with silver, great cheekbones, bright blue eyes, and a toothy, radiant smile. She was dressed in a sleek, raspberry-colored hooded sweater that looked like cashmere—probably because it was—and a pair of Ralph Lauren skinny jeans. Not many women her age could wear skinny jeans, but Loretta happened to possess a taut, nicely shaped little butt. Mitch knew this because he'd spent a lot of hours gazing at it. He and Loretta took the same heated vinyāsa yoga class twice a week at the Dorset Fitness Center. His mat was usually behind Loretta's because she was a highly accomplished front-row yogini and Mitch was a gasping water buffalo who hid in the back row hoping that their teacher, Amber, wouldn't holler at him. Loretta also used the fitness center's weight machines several times a week, biked, ran, kept to a vegan diet, and spent a lot of time at spas. Or so it seemed. She was always perfectly manicured and pedicured. Her smooth face positively glowed.

She smiled at Mitch warmly when he arrived at the head of the line. "Why, it's the great Mitch Berger. I still can't believe that a man of your stature shows up here to deliver hot lunches."

"My peeps count on me." He sniffed at the air. "Fish sticks and tater tots, right?"

"Do your peeps know that the free lunches you bring them aren't free? That you pay three dollars for each and every one of them out of your own pocket?"

"Loretta, that little detail is strictly between us. They wouldn't accept the meals if they knew that."

"I swear, sometimes I think you're just like a character from one of those old movies you're always writing about. Will I see you at yoga today?"

"You bet."

"Can you spare me a few minutes after class? There's something I'd like to speak to you about."

"If it's the secret to my one-legged crow pose that you're after, I don't know how I do it. I just do it, except for when I don't and hit the floor with my face."

"It's not yoga related. It's a sort of project. Shall we discuss it over a smoothie?"

"It's a date," Mitch said, grabbing his thermal carriers by their handles.

Loretta gasped. "Did you just say *date*? You shouldn't talk that way. You're an attractive young man. I'm an impressionable older woman. I'm likely to swoon."

"I'll try to remember that." Mitch lugged his carriers out to his truck and piled them on the floor next to Bitsy's feet. Then he got in, started up the engine, and eased his way out of the parking lot. Bitsy seemed much more composed now, though she did have a damp tissue clutched in her hand. "If I didn't know better I'd swear that Loretta just went Mrs. Robinson on me," he said to her.

"Mrs. Robinson as in. . . ?"

"She was flirting with me."

Bitsy narrowed her gaze at him. "Are you interested in her?"

"I'm in love with Des, remember?"

"That's not what I asked you."

"Why, does Loretta have a reputation?"

"For what?"

"Hello, what were we just talking about?"

"She doesn't fool around, if that's what you mean. Loretta didn't take up with Gaylord Holland until her marriage to John Friday failed. She's a class act—same as I used to be before I started sneaking off to the Mohegan Sun like a tramp."

"You told me you were in love."

"Maybe I've just been fooling myself," she said glumly. "Maybe I'm nothing more than a sad, pathetic idiot."

"Bitsy, I don't believe that for one second. And neither do you," Mitch said as he drove along, all the while wondering, wondering.

Who is Bitsy's boyfriend?

Chapter 5

Des was doing a routine sweep of the Big Branch Road shopping district when the call came in from the 911 dispatcher. A man who resided at 19 Appleby Lane wished to speak to her on the phone about a "personal matter." Des pulled into the Citizens Bank parking lot and called him.

An elderly man with a raspy voice answered on the first ring. Elderly men always answer on the first ring.

"This is Resident Trooper Mitry. How may I help you?"

"A young fellow just rang my doorbell and I didn't like the look of him."

"Why was that, sir?"

"Well, I'll tell you. When I answered the door he asked me if I needed any tree work done. Only, he wasn't looking up at any of my trees. He was looking in the front windows at my living room. Pale little fellow with soft white hands. I know what a workingman's hands look like. This kid was no workingman. Looked more like a barfly to me. When I asked him for a business card he got real shifty eyed and said he didn't have one, then got in his car and drove off."

"Would you happen to remember what kind of. . . ?"

"A bright blue Ford Fiesta. Itty-bitty thing. I've got the license plate number right here." He read it to her. She jotted it down. "He headed up the lane maybe three, four minutes ago and I haven't seen him come back down yet." Appleby was a dead-end road. "Don't mean to bother you, Trooper, but I thought I ought to call."

"No bother at all," Des assured him. "This is what I'm here for."

Appleby Lane was in the middle of the Historic District off of Dorset Street, right next to the library. As Des steered her Crown Vic there, she ran the Ford Fiesta's plate on her computer. It belonged to a Darla Romine, age twenty-one, who lived at 1709 Kelton Avenue, Apartment 1C, in Cardiff, which was Dorset's landlocked, less affluent neighbor to the north. She ran Darla and turned up one arrest for drunk and disorderly and one for drug possession. Both charges against her were eventually dropped.

She found the Fiesta pulled onto the shoulder up near the top of Appleby, a narrow twisting lane that was a mix of old farmhouses and new McMansions. The kid wasn't in it. He was knocking on somebody else's front door. Des idled two houses away, watching him. When nobody answered he stood there looking around rather aimlessly for a moment before he started back to the car, his shoulders hunched inside of the navy blue pea coat that he had on. It looked a couple of sizes too large for him, as if he'd borrowed it from his big brother. He got back in the Fiesta and started it up.

Des moved on in, flashing her lights at him. Then she got out, squared her big hat on her head, and approached him.

He was in his early twenties, scrawny and most definitely not someone who worked outdoors. He was pale and sickly looking, with dark circles under his eyes. Had a wispy goatee, stringy hair, and a runny nose that looked as if it had been squashed in a couple of fights. Skeejie. He looked skeejie. Also familiar.

"Sir, how are you today?" she asked, tipping her hat.

"Okay, I guess," he answered in a quavery voice.

"What's your name?"

"Petey Neto."

"Mr. Neto, may I see your license and registration, please?"

"Why, what did I do?"

"Mr. Neto, I simply asked to see your license and registration. May I, please?"

"It's my girlfriend's car. We live together." He pulled a messy heap of papers from the glove compartment and started sorting through them, his hands trembling.

"That's it right there," Des informed him. "Want to hand it to me?"

He handed it to her.

"And now your driver's license, please."

He pulled a worn black leather wallet from the back pocket of his jeans, found his license, and held it out to her.

His full name was Peter Michael Neto. He was twenty-two years old. The address on his license was in South Dorset, not Cardiff. "You said that you and Darla live together?"

"Yeah, for now. Kind of."

Des studied him as he sat there looking guilty and miserable. "I know you from somewhere, don't I?"

"I used to stock shelves at the Big Y. My mom's a cashier there. But I got into, like, this argument with the manager and he bounced me a couple of months ago."

"I've seen you somewhere else."

"At The Pit, maybe. I work the fryer there during the season, tend some bar. You showed up a few times last summer to break up fights."

"Sure, that must be it. What are you doing with yourself these days?"

"Not a whole lot," Petey replied glumly. "I'm looking for any kind of work I can get until The Pit reopens. Thought I'd knock

49

on some doors, see if maybe somebody needed help with their trees or brush or whatever."

"Are you having any luck?"

"No, ma'am."

"Excuse me a sec, will you?" She went back to her cruiser and ran him. Peter Michael Neto had no record. No outstanding warrants. He was clean.

He was nervously smoking a cigarette when she gave him back his license and Darla's registration.

"Mr. Neto, the reason why I stopped you is that you've scared some people on the lane, okay? You're not driving a truck that's full of landscaping equipment. You don't have a business card. Do the math, okay?"

"What, they think I'm going to rob 'em or something?"

"Or something. If I were you I'd run off a batch of flyers and put them in people's mailboxes. If they've got work for you they can call you."

"Are you telling me to move along?"

"I can't order you to. You aren't breaking any laws. Let's just say you'd be doing me a personal favor. And maybe I can do you a favor in return some time, okay?"

Petey took a drag on his cigarette, shaking his head. "I should have just stayed home. When I try to do *anything* I get in trouble. But Darla said she'd throw me out if I didn't go looking."

"Well, you went looking. Have a nice day."

He started up the Fiesta, turned it around, and drove off down Appleby Lane, taking it good and slow.

Des was getting back in her Crown Vic when she got another 911 call. A woman walking on Sound View Beach had just reported seeing three men out on the patio of The Pit throwing punches at one other.

She floored it down Old Shore Road with her lights flashing and made a right just past the Citgo mini-mart onto Pitcairn Avenue, speeding her way past the ramshackle storefronts that were still boarded up for the winter. Dorset's summer fun headquarters had the giddy joyfullness of an abandoned ghost town in the off-season.

The wind had picked up. Sand was blowing across the parking lot adjacent to The Pit, which was nothing more than a wood-framed beach bungalow with sliding glass doors and brewery signs in every window. There was a shuttered take-out window. There was an enclosed patio facing the beach that had an outdoor bar with a thatched roof.

Des saw no one out on the patio, though she did see three vehicles in the parking lot—a Toyota pickup, a Subaru Forester, and Hubie Swope's town-issued Ford Explorer. She parked there and got out.

A hand-lettered sign on the front door read: WE'LL SEE YOU AGAIN MEMORIAL DAY WEEKEND! HAVE A GREAT WINTER! Inside, there were two, three, four empty Budweiser pitchers made of thick glass on the bar next to the empty cash register, which had been left wide open for all to see. The wooden picnic tables and benches that spent the summer out on the patio were piled inside to keep them out of the harsh winter weather.

Hubie Swope sat on a stool at the bar holding a bloody bar towel to his nose. Sherm Gant was slumped against a picnic table sporting a fresh bruise under his left eye. Leland Gant was standing over by the sliding glass doors flexing a sore right hand. His chambray work shirt was torn.

"What are *you* doing here?" Sherm demanded, glowering at Des.

"Do any of you require medical attention?"

"I'm fine," Hubie said, dabbing at his nose.

"So am I," Sherm said.

"How about you, Leland? Does that hand need to be looked at?"

Leland flexed it again before he said, "No, it's okay."

"Hubie, do you wish to press assault charges?"

"Why are you automatically assuming *he's* the victim here?" Sherm wanted to know. "How do you know *he* didn't start it?"

"That's a fair question, Sherm. How about because last night you threatened him with bodily harm right to my face? How about because I know that he was making an official site visit here today to determine whether you would or wouldn't be allowed to reopen for the summer?"

Sherm had no response. Just slumped there in angry silence.

"It was a disagreement, Trooper Mitry," Hubie said quietly. "Men have disagreements. It got a little physical, but I have no interest in pressing charges."

Sherm looked at him in surprise. "Go ahead and tell her I assaulted you, Hubie. This is your big chance. You can ruin me. It's what you've always wanted."

"No, it isn't, you big dope," Hubie said. "I'm trying to help you. You have no hand railings on those steps out there. Don't you realize what'll happen to you if somebody falls and gets hurt?"

"He's got a point, Dad," Leland said.

"You shut your mouth," Sherm growled at him. "And don't ever take another man's side in front me."

"I'm j-just trying to be reasonable," Leland sputtered, reddening.

"*Reasonable?*" Sherm let out a mocking laugh. "You're *soft*. Ask anyone who worked here last summer. Ask the fry cooks who didn't ring up half the orders from the take-out window whenever you were on shift. They kept an idiot jar under the counter. Called it their 'Leland Jar.' Pocketed fifty, sixty bucks apiece every night before I got wise to them. You can't be soft in this business. I need you to be tough. I need you to grow the hell up. You're going to be in charge one of these days, you know."

Leland's stood there in tight-lipped, frustrated silence before he turned to Des and said, "Am I done here?"

"You're free to go."

He stormed out the door and got in the Forester and drove off.

"I don't understand that boy anymore," Sherm said, shaking his head.

Des tipped her hat back on her head and said, "Sherm, I want to see you and Hubie shake hands. Shake or I'm running you both in. I mean it."

Grudgingly, they complied.

"Okay, that's a start. Now how do we go about resolving your differences?"

"That's entirely up to Sherm," Hubie stated flatly.

"Sherm, do you intend to make the improvements that Hubie has requested?"

"They're not requests. They're mandatory," Hubie said sternly. "*If* he wants to be open for business Memorial Day weekend."

"I'll do what I can," Sherm grumbled. "But you've got to be reasonable, Hubie. This stuff costs a lot of money. And I just plain haven't got it."

"I'll be back here in two weeks," Hubie informed him. "If you haven't made the improvements you won't be opening for the season, which will give me no pleasure whatsoever. Folks look forward to coming here every summer. I don't want to take that away from them. But if you're not in compliance you leave me with no choice." Dorset's little building inspector deposited the bloody towel on the bar, squared his shoulders, and marched out the door.

Des watched him through the window as he got in his Explorer and sat there for a moment, staring out at the choppy waters of the Sound. Then he started up the engine and drove off.

Sherm gazed around at his walls, which were adorned with brightly colored bikini tops and bras—the trophies of many wild summer nights. "Those sour-faced Historic District snobs will love it if Hubie shuts me down," he said bitterly. "They think I don't belong here. But Dorset belongs to me just as much as it does them, you know."

"I do know that, Sherm."

"I'm an asset to this community. I contribute to the tax base. I'm a member of the Lions Club and Chamber of Commerce. I provide jobs."

"That reminds me, does the name Petey Neto ring a bell?"

"Yeah, that loser worked here last summer. Why?"

"Will you be taking him on again this summer?"

"Not a chance."

"He's under the impression that he still works here."

"Then he must be smoking something funny, because I fired his ass. It was Petey who was keeping the Leland Jar. He stole from me. No way I'm taking him back. And don't tell me I should because I won't."

"Whatever you say. It's your business."

"Damned straight," Sherm said defiantly. "My dad opened this place in 1972, and I intend to keep it open. I've *got* to. I just don't know where I'm going to get the damned money. I'm only open five months out of the year, and my overhead's a killer. I've got to pay workman's comp, flood, fire, theft, third-party liability. . . . If I was smart I'd go out of business. I'd come out way ahead." He fingered his tender eye, which was starting to swell shut. "Hubie wants me to pump out the septic system more often. Fine, I can do that. And the safety railings I can install myself. And maybe I can swing a new refrigerator. But those commercial-grade exhaust fans cost a fortune. Plus they need their own circuit breaker, which means a couple of licensed electricians camped out here for who knows how many hours. I'd borrow the money if I could, except I've maxed out my line of credit at the bank. And my other places on the avenue need work, too. The roofs on two of them are totally shot." He glanced up at the ceiling. "The roof's bad here, too, but that's the least of my worries right now."

"So what are you going to do, Sherm?"

Sherm Gant slumped there in gloomy silence for a long moment before he said, "I don't know, Trooper Mitry. I really don't."

CHAPTER 6

Who is Bitsy's boyfriend?

Mitch kept wondering about it as he sat before his computer tapping out his essay on forgotten Hollywood stars, which was entitled *Where Have You Gone, Warren William?* The guy had to be married, right? Otherwise Bitsy would have no reason for keeping his name a secret. Except how could a married guy manage to spend every Saturday night with her at the Mohegan Sun? Was he separated from his wife? Or, wait, what if Bitsy was ashamed about being involved with him because he wasn't in her blue-blooded league? Maybe he was a lowly Swamp Yankee carpenter, like that lean, tanned fellow who worked around the island every summer, usually with his shirt off. But somebody like that couldn't afford to stay over at the Mohegan Sun every Saturday night, could he? And he always paid the tab, Bitsy said. Insisted upon it.

Then again, maybe he was unattached, socially acceptable, and she was simply being cautious about outing him in case things didn't work out. Which was totally understandable—especially if, as she suspected, he was boinking another woman. Because in Dorset, once word got around about two people being an item there was no going back. Bitsy and her mystery beau could call it quits tomorrow and five years from now the village hens would still be gossiping about who broke whose heart.

Who is Bitsy's boyfriend?

Mitch kept thinking about it as he worked away at his computer, the Sir Douglas Quintet's forever fresh *Mendocino* blasting from his stereo, Clemmie dozing in her easy chair, the Dude burrowing underneath the love seat for his nerf ball, snuffling and yowling.

Mitch was someone who wrote quickly but edited slowly. After he'd printed out his first draft he worked over it carefully, pen in hand, polishing, whittling, choosing each word with exacting precision. When he was satisfied he input his edits, read the piece over one more time, and then sent it off to his editor, Lacy.

By then it was time to head over to the Dorset Fitness Center on the second floor of The Works for his heated vinyāsa class, which was comprised of Mitch and eight other legally responsible adults who chose to flow from one sun salutation to the next in a yoga studio that had been warmed to ninety-five degrees, fogging up the studio's windows that looked out over the Connecticut River. Amber, a Zen-y Cossack, urged them on. As Mitch transitioned from one pose to the next, the sweat streaming from every pore of his body, his misty-eyed gaze fell upon Loretta Beckwith Holland and her tight little tush on the mat in front of his. Loretta didn't teeter, didn't tire, didn't even sweat. Mitch hated her.

Somehow, he survived all of the way to *savasana*—the oh-so-aptly-named corpse pose—and assumed the position of a limp, damp, dead person on his mat, wondering what Loretta wanted to talk to him about. He hoped she wasn't trying to recruit him to serve on a town commission. Mitch was intensely allergic to any group activity that took place around a conference table. Not the kind of allergy that makes you sneeze. The kind where you start yawning and can't stop.

After they'd chanted "Om" he wobbled off to take a shower and drink an entire liter of water. When he emerged in his complimentary *Sharknado 2* hoodie and blue jeans, Loretta was waiting for him by the club's front door, looking as energized and alive as Mitch didn't feel. Also super chic in her tight black Lululemon après yoga jacket and pants.

"Wasn't that wonderful?" she exclaimed. "I feel ten years younger."

"And I feel ten years older. Are you okay with being seen in public with a bona fide Dorset geezer?"

Loretta let out a cascade of laughter. "Mitch, you're a riot. Let's go get those smoothies."

They strolled out into the European-style food hall that anchored The Works, an abandoned red-brick piano works that had been transformed into high-end shops and office spaces. The food hall was very popular. There were stalls where meat, fish, cheese, and locally grown produce were sold. There was a coffee bar, juice bar, bakery, deli. People gathered day and night at the cluster of bright green Parisian park-style tables to munch and sip and gab.

Loretta walked with an air of easy self-confidence that Mitch had always admired when he observed it in other people. He'd never possessed it himself, being a shlub. "I'm buying," she informed him. "Why don't you grab us a table?"

He found them one and settled onto a wrought-iron chair, feeling as if every muscle in his body had just been transformed into overcooked fettucine.

Loretta joined him a moment later, clutching two tall cups of bright green extruded liquid. She handed him one as she sat.

Mitch examined the cup's contents warily. "Exactly what's in this?"

"Kale, spinach, wheatgrass, mango, avocado, and coconut water. It's good for you. Try it."

Mitch, who wasn't crazy about drinking anything green, took a cautious sip.

Loretta eyed him over the rim of her cup, amused. "Taste okay?"

"I'm guardedly optimistic."

"That was a great class today. Amber always pushes me past my limit."

"I didn't think you had a limit. You have an incredible amount of energy."

"I'm lucky that way. But so are you. My goodness, you write all of those wonderful articles and books. You garden, practice yoga, help so many elderly people in town. *And* you keep our resident trooper happy. A successful relationship takes a lot of hard work. Believe me, I know." She sipped her smoothie. "Actually, that's what I was hoping to talk to you about, if you don't mind a genuinely clumsy segue. You know my husband, Gaylord, don't you?"

"I met him at a gallery opening once."

"And do you know what our thing is?"

"There's a thing?"

"A most definite thing," she said, waving to a pair of smartly dressed members of her social set who'd settled four tables away. Well out of earshot. "I've known Gaylord since I was six. I was a skinny, awkward girl with buckteeth and bony knees. Gaylord was handsome and popular and good at sports. Every girl in Dorset had a crush on him. I sure did. After high school he went off to Bowdoin and I never saw him again—until he moved back to town four years ago. I was married to John Friday at the time. We ran into Gaylord at a cocktail party. I thought he was still handsome and quite charming. My mother had recently passed away and John and I had taken over her sprawling antique of a house, which needed a lot of work. As it happened, Gaylord told us he'd become a housewright."

"Did he say that with a straight face?"

"Sorry?"

"Never mind. You had an old house that needed work . . ."

"Naturally, I thought he might be interested in having a look at it. Although he did keep staring at me with the oddest expression on his face. Finally, I said, 'You don't remember me, do you?' And he said, 'You couldn't be more wrong, Loretta. I was madly in love with you when we were little kids. I even carved our initials in a beech tree way back in the third grade.' I didn't believe him, of course. And dared him to show it to me. So the very next day he marched me into the Nehantic State Forest and found the tree— 'our tree,' he called it—and there were our initials carved inside of a heart and aged by time. I was so touched that, well, we ended up making love right there in the woods on his coat. *The* best sex I'd ever had in my life. I knew right then and there that my marriage to John Friday was over." She took a sip of her smoothie. "I'm not shocking you, am I?"

"Not at all," said Mitch, who'd learned that when Dorset's upper-crust ladies decided to talk to him, friend to friend, they *talked.*

"I stayed married to John while Gaylord was renovating our house. But as soon as Gaylord completed the project I informed John that he would have to move out because Gaylord was moving in."

"You said he came back here four years ago. Where was he living before that?"

"In Larchmont, New York. He moved there after Bowdoin with a friend whose dad was a builder. Gaylord went to work for him and learned the trade. When he had enough money set aside he bought an old house and renovated it. Married a local girl from a wealthy family and he was on his way. Except the marriage didn't last. A friend of mine who lives in Larchmont told me that Gaylord developed quite a reputation there for breaking up marriages.

Practically every time he renovated a high-end home he'd steal his high-end client's wife. When I confronted Gaylord about it he admitted it freely. And do you know what he said to me?"

Mitch took another cautious sip of his smoothie, hoping that it would start to taste like something other than liquefied lawn cuttings. "I can't imagine."

"He said he'd been searching his entire adult life for that little girl whose initials he'd carved in that beech tree. And now that he'd found me again his days of searching were over. I believed him, Mitch. And we've been incredibly happy together. Or so I believed. It turns out I'm a terrible judge of character. I was wrong, you see. I'm not Gaylord's ultimate destination. Someone else is. You've heard about those two houses he's so very, very anxious to build on the Lieutenant River, haven't you?"

Mitch nodded. "Sure."

"One of them is for his current flame, who's living in Greenwich right now. She's thirty-two, a former Dior model, and loaded. Her ex-husband's a New York City real estate tycoon. I'd been . . ." Loretta bit down on her lower lip, her bright blue eyes shining at him. "I'd been hearing whispers about her for weeks before I confronted him. Gaylord admitted that it was true. He hasn't asked me for a divorce, and I don't believe he will. I happen to be quite wealthy myself. I'm also extremely valuable to him socially. So what we have now is an open marriage. We're free to see other people if we wish. I've been seeing someone for several weeks, as it happens. A local man. I'm planning to end it, though. I have a certain reputation to protect, and we're all so cheek by jowl here in Dorset that I . . ." She frowned at him. "Did I say something wrong?"

"No, no. Something about that image just made me shudder is all. My bad." Mitch wondered who her boyfriend might be. He was picturing a younger man, fortyish, with muscles. Someone who she'd met at the Fitness Center. The lady exercised her body relentlessly. She wasn't about to give it to someone who was fat, bald, and sixty.

"You still spend time in New York City, don't you?"

Mitch nodded. "I have a place on the Upper West Side."

"What I wanted to ask you is . . ." Loretta hesitated, coloring slightly. "Oh, dear, this is turning out to be more difficult than I thought."

"What is? Wait, you're not asking *me* out, are you?"

"Is that what you think I'm doing?" Loretta let out another cascade of laughter. She was amused. Highly amused. "Mitch, you're so sweet. I'd go out with you in a heartbeat if I weren't nearly old enough to be your mother. Besides, you don't do that sort of thing, do you?"

"I'm in a committed relationship, if that's what you're wondering."

"You'll forgive me, but it's been my experience that most men who say they're in a committed relationship really aren't. Not if they're offered a chance to un-commit."

"I'm not most men."

"I know you're not. That's why I felt I could have this conversation with you. Okay, here it is—I was wondering if you might have a male friend in the city who I could go out with. Someone interesting like, say, an author."

"I thought you just said you wanted to go out with someone interesting."

"I'd like to meet someone who has a sense of humor. He doesn't have to be great looking but he does have to be reasonably fit. And tall would be nice. Self-assured, upbeat. The gloomy, neurotic type has never appealed to me."

"That's too bad. I happen to know a lot of gloomy, neurotic types."

Loretta tilted her head at him. "You're teasing me now, aren't you?"

"Little bit."

"I'd like to go to the theater, have dinner, have *fun*. And, yes, that would involve spending the night together there. So I'd prefer someone who's single."

"How would you explain spending the night in New York City to Gaylord?"

"I don't have to. We have an open marriage, remember? But I'd be discreet. I've been thinking about getting certified to teach yoga. I can tell him I'm taking teacher training classes at a studio there an evening or two a week."

"That doesn't sound like discreet to me. That sounds like lying."

"Does it matter?"

"I guess not." Mitch drank some more of his smoothie, gazing down into the cup with dismay. It didn't appear as if he'd drained so much as a drop. If anything, his garden-fresh beverage seemed to be growing. *Alive*. It was *alive*. "So you want me to fix you up with somebody."

"What do you say, Mitch?" Loretta flashed her big, bright smile at him. "Do you know someone?"

"Well, do you?" Des asked him.

"Offhand, no. My editor probably knows someone. And she loves to fix people up. But I feel funny about this whole thing."

"Funny ha-ha or funny weird?"

"Weird. Definitely weird."

It was just past six o'clock. Outside Mitch's cottage the wind was howling and the waves were crashing against the rocks. Inside, a big fire was crackling in the fireplace and *The Road to Escondido,* a laid-back Eric Clapton–J. J. Cale collaboration, was playing on the stereo. Des had gotten out of her uniform and into the four-ply dove-gray cashmere robe that he'd bought her in Paris. They were snuggled before the fire on the love seat, sipping Chianti.

"Would you like to know why I put up with you, thin person?"

Des gazed at him with her almond-shaped pale green eyes. "Do tell."

"Because you don't mind drinking red wine even though we're having fish for dinner."

"It's a red wine kind of an evening."

"That it is." He petted the Dude, who was dozing peacefully between them on the love seat. Clemmie was curled up on her easy chair, purring. Quirt was curled up on his easy chair, purring. "I feel like we've wandered into our own private version of a Norman Rockwell painting."

Des leaned over and kissed him softly on the mouth. "Life is good."

"You know what? I should take a selfie of this moment with my new super-duper Batphone."

"Mitch, if you take a selfie of this moment I can promise you that it will no longer be Rockwellesque."

"Why not?"

"Because you'll be searching around on the rug for your teeth."

"So is that a no vote on the selfie?"

"What kind of fish did you get us?"

"Fresh gray sole from Point Judith. I thought I'd bread it and pan fry it."

"Let me guess, Meals on Wheels served fish sticks today."

He drew back from her, startled. "How on earth did you know that?"

"I'm a trained detective, remember? And you do have the most suggestible stomach I've ever encountered. Are we having tater tots, too?"

"Des, you know I don't go in for that kind of fake, processed non-food anymore. I'm all about eating healthy now, thanks to you. We're having brown rice and locally grown organic asparagus, okay?"

"More than okay." She kissed him again, running her fingers through his unruly mop of hair. "How does your head feel?"

"Totally fine. You weren't serious last night, were you?"

"About what?"

"Some foolishness to do with me staying out of the fray from now on."

"I was totally serious. I don't want to lose you."

"But we're a team. You need me."

"I'll just have to muddle along without you somehow."

"Does this mean that you don't want me to share the rest of the incredibly juicy gossip I heard today?"

"Not exactly." She nudged him with her shoulder. "Dish."

"Bitsy Peck is having a wild, top-secret love affair."

Des's eyes widened. "No way."

"Yes way. She hasn't been coming home Saturday nights for a while. I just figured she was keeping one of her doddering aunts company. She has a dozen of them. But it turns out that she's been getting naked in a suite at the Mohegan Sun with a certain man. Bitsy won't tell me who he is, but she was sobbing her head off over him this morning. She thinks he's dogging her."

"Poor Bitsy." Des sipped her wine, staring into the fire. "The ladies sure unloaded on you today, didn't they?"

"Yes, they did. How did I suddenly end up playing the role of trusted confidant?"

"Sometimes women need a man's advice about things. And they know you won't go blabbing to other people."

"I'm blabbing to you."

"That's to be expected. But they know that it'll stay between us. We don't spread gossip. If we did they'd be aware of it." She shoved her heavy horn-rimmed glasses up her nose. "Exactly what did Loretta tell you about Gaylord?"

"That he had a rep as a serial home wrecker back in Larchmont, and it sounds as if he hasn't changed his wicked, wicked ways since he returned home to Dorset. He did break up Loretta's marriage to John Friday, after all. Want to know how he won her over? By telling her he'd carved their initials in a beech tree in the Nehantic State Forest back when he was in the third grade."

"And she *bought* that line of bull?"

"He showed her the tree. Their initials were carved there just like he said. She was so moved that she got freaky with him right there on the spot. Best sex she's ever had."

"How much do you want to bet he carved their initials in that tree an hour before he showed them to her."

"She said they looked like they'd been there for a long time."

"Trust me, the man knows a thing or two about how to age fresh-cut wood. He's a housewright, remember?"

"How could I forget? It's the only job title I've ever heard that's even more annoying than entrepreneur. Oh, and Gaylord's current girlfriend? One of those houses that he wants to build on the Lieutenant River is for her."

Des nodded her head. "That would explain why he's leaning so hard on Hubie to approve the project. It's not his workmen's mortgage payments he's thinking about. It's his slice on the side." She sat there in thoughtful silence, her eyes narrowing. "I can't say that

I like Hubie, because he's not exactly warm and fuzzy, but he sure does stand his ground. I offered to escort him to The Pit this morning, seeing as how Sherm did threaten him last night. He turned me down cold. Ended up costing him a bloody nose."

"Sherm punched him?"

"And Hubie punched him right back. Leland got into it, too. He seemed super upset."

"That's because Leland doesn't want to have anything to do with the place. He'd like to become a physical therapist. Help returning veterans."

"How do you know that?"

"I started my day out with Mary Ellen, remember? She thinks he's a good kid, but she sure doesn't have anything nice to say about big brother Sherm. She thinks Sherm's a bully and a drunk and just an all-around rotten businessman."

"She's not the only person in Dorset who feels that way."

A hickory log burned through and broke in half, crashing to the hearth floor in a shower of sparks that sent Quirt darting for the front door. Clemmie opened one eye but didn't budge. The Dude didn't even open one eye. Just went right on snoozing.

"He feels safe here," Des observed. "Look how nice and calm he is."

"I wish he was this nice and calm at five o'clock in the morning." Mitch got up to put another log on the fire and let Quirt out. "But I know what you mean. El Duderino does seem awfully at home here."

"Are you trying to tell me something?"

"Why, no. I just . . ." He settled back down on the love seat, the Dude dozing there between them. "If it turns out that you can't find a good home for him, well, Clemmie's gotten kind of attached to the little guy."

"Oh, Clemmie has, has she?"

"And Quirt's starting to tolerate his presence, too."

Des showed him her smile, the one that did strange, warm things to the lower half of his body. "You want to keep him, don't you?"

"I didn't say that. But I don't hate having him around. Do you think I'm turning into a bizarre, pathetic cat person?"

"I think you're a big softie. And he's all yours if you want him."

"I'll give it some thought."

"You do that, wow man."

"Want me to start dinner?"

"Feel free to start something," she said, snuggling closer. "But here's a hint—it's not food that I'm thinking about right now."

"Are you getting frisky with me, Master Sergeant?"

"Trying to."

"Sorry, you had your chance last night in the cemetery. I was in the mood then. I'm not in the mood now."

She buried her nose in his neck and kissed him in that spot behind his ear that never failed to make him quiver all over. "Are you absolutely sure. . . ?"

"Okay, I *may* be in a position to reevaluate the situation." He kissed her gently. Then not so gently. And then he ran his hand inside her robe, his fingers probing for whatever points of interest they might find in there.

She untied the robe and shrugged out of it. He put his arms around her and held her tight, reminding himself just how lucky he was to be with this incredible woman in this incredible place at this moment. That was when he saw it out of his bay windows— a bright orange glow in the eastern sky.

He pulled back from her, staring at it. "What do you suppose that is?"

Now he heard sirens off in the distance. One, two, three of them.

And now her cell started ringing on the coffee table. Des took the call and listened before she said, "I'll be right there." Rang off and darted into the bathroom, where her uniform was hanging on the back of the door. "It's The Pit," she called out to him.

"What about The Pit?"

She came out of the bathroom buttoning her uniform shirt. "It's on fire."

CHAPTER 7

SOMEONE WHO'D STOPPED FOR a carton of milk at the Citgo mini-mart phoned it in.

By the time Dorset's forty-man volunteer fire department arrived, backed up by volunteer fire companies from South Dorset, Cardiff, and Hubbard's Point, the fire had already engulfed The Pit. They needed water tankers since there were no hydrants on Pitcairn Avenue. And they needed every high-beam headlight and searchlight on every truck because there were no streetlights. Specially trained RITs—two-man Rapid Intervention Teams—stood by with oxygen, ready to assist any firefighters who got trapped or overcome. The Jewett sisters stood by in case anyone required emergency medical attention.

Des was the first state trooper to arrive, followed a minute later by two more from the Troop F barracks in Westbrook. The TV crews from Connecticut's four local news stations showed up soon after that. They loved, loved fires.

The wood-framed building was pretty much gone by the time she got there, the flames fanned by the gusty winds that were blowing off of the Sound. Part of the wall where the kitchen had been remained standing, but the rest of the place was nothing more than a smoldering heap. Des could feel the residual heat on her face as the firefighters continued to douse the wreckage just to make absolutely sure it was out. They were also hosing down the neighboring wooden buildings, which were susceptible to being ignited by flying embers.

Ed Hurst, Dorset's fire chief, was there in full gear. His Dodge Ram was parked in front of the boarded-up ice cream parlor next to Hubie Swope's Ford Explorer. Hubie would be there in his capacity as fire marshal. Des spotted Gaylord Holland, who was Dorset's assistant fire chief. Men such as Gaylord, who knew construction from top to bottom, were extremely valuable to a volunteer fire department.

"We've got it contained, Trooper Mitry," declared Ed, who was a plumbing contractor. "Damned place went up faster than any building I've ever seen."

Des said, "Sherm had all of the picnic tables from the patio piled inside, as I'm sure Hubie's already told you. They made for an excellent source of fuel."

"That they did," he acknowledged. "Doesn't explain what started it, though. Have you seen Hubie?"

"No, I haven't. I just got here, Ed."

"If you spot him tell him I'm looking for him, will you?"

Des found Sherm Gant slumped against his pickup over by the tattoo parlor, utterly devastated, his left eye swollen nearly shut from that altercation with Hubie earlier in the day. "We were holding our monthly Lions Club meeting at the Clam House when Gaylord g-got the call," he told Des, his voice choking with emotion. "I—I followed him here. Can't believe it's gone."

"I'm sorry, Sherm," she said, as Leland came running down Pitcairn Avenue toward them.

"They wouldn't let me through, Dad. I had to leave my car back at the Citgo." Leland paused to catch his breath, gawking at the remains of The Pit in disbelief. "My God, there's nothing left. . . ."

"Nothing," Sherm said glumly. "I called you three times. Where were you?"

"At Center School. I was helping Brianna set up chairs for parent-teacher night. Had my phone on mute."

Mary Ellen Tatum showed up now, along with her husband, Ward, who was tall, thin, and gray bearded. Mary Ellen hugged her nephew and then her brother, distraught. "We were sitting down to dinner when you called," she told Sherm, her voice trembling. "Ward had just walked in the door from the library."

"I was tutoring the Miller boy," Ward said. "He's bright but he just doesn't 'get' mitosis."

"What on earth happened?" Mary Ellen wondered plaintively.

"Kids," said Sherm, puffing out his cheeks. "Must have been."

Des studied him curiously. "Kids?"

"They break in every once in a while looking for booze. Like I'd be to stupid enough to leave any lying around."

"Could be they were partying," Leland said. "That's been going on since back when I was in high school. They know that nobody's down here so they break in and smoke joints and fart around. Maybe things got out of control."

"Maybe," Des said. "Sherm, did you keep anything flammable in there?"

"I'm not stupid," he growled. "I strip the place from top to bottom before I shut it down. Will you be able to tell if somebody broke in?"

"I doubt it. That wreckage looks pretty far gone to me."

"I never bothered to install a security system. I figured, why bother? There's nothing to take. I always left the cash register wide open. Empty pitchers on the bar, which is the universal language for 'I got no beer.' And now . . ." Sherm sighed. "Now I got nothing."

The firefighters from the neighboring towns were securing their gear and preparing to pull out. Dorset's firefighters were beginning to perform their overhaul, proceeding into the wet, charred remains of The Pit and pulling the wooden debris apart, piece by piece, to make absolutely certain that the fire was out. They were slogging their way toward the center of the wreckage, working carefully and quietly, when one of them—Tommy Burns, a young guy who repaired furnaces for Ballek Oil—suddenly called out for Chief Hurst in a loud, strained voice.

Ed went over to him and the two of them stood there together, gazing down into the rubble, until Tommy abruptly staggered from the wreckage and threw up.

Ed looked around for Des and motioned to her. She stepped her way through the water-soaked rubble. Didn't have to go very far before her nostrils picked up the scent, her stomach tightening instantly. She knew exactly what she was smelling—once you've smelled it you never forget it. Des hadn't eaten grilled steak for many years. Mitch was aware that she didn't, but he didn't know why. Des didn't think he could deal with why. He'd led a sheltered life.

Ed stepped back as she drew nearer, his face drawn tight in the searchlights' beams, eyes locked on what lay there on the puddled wooden floor.

It was an adult male. He was on his back in the classic pugilist pose—fists drawn up close to his chest, knees bent. He was too charred to be in any way recognizable. His face and hair were gone. His upward-facing clothing was burned to a crisp.

"Hubie Swope...!" Ed called out in a husky voice, waving his gloved hands in the air for attention. They were heavy, structural firefighter gloves with gauntlet cuffs. "Fire Marshal Swope, can you come over here, please?"

Des glanced around but she didn't see Hubie making his way toward them. Just the other men standing there in wide-eyed silence. Many of them were young like Tommy. Hadn't seen a dead body before. Des only wished she could say the same. She would need crime-scene photos of this. Would need to draw it.

Now Ed hollered, "Assistant Chief Holland. . . ! Gaylord?"

"I'll look for him, Ed!" Gaylord went heading off to check out the adjacent buildings.

Ed swallowed, breathing in and out. "I don't have to tell you it's been seven different kinds of hectic here, Trooper Mitry. But I haven't laid eyes on Hubie since I got here. Nobody has."

"Did you try calling him on his cell phone?"

"A bunch of times. Went straight to voice mail."

"Ed, are you trying to tell me that's Hubie we're looking at?"

"I'm telling you it's got to be. His car was here when I got here, okay? But he wasn't. He must have run inside the building to take a look and got hit by a falling beam. Poor Hubie. I've known him since we were in Cub Scouts together."

"Slow down, Ed. We don't know that's him. Could be a homeless person who broke in and started the fire."

"Hey, Ed?" Gaylord Holland called out. "I can't find him, sorry!"

Ed stuck his jaw out at her. "It's him, I tell you. That's Hubie."

Des took her Maglite off of her belt and flicked it on, crouching on the wet floor for a closer look. Right away she didn't like what she saw—a burn trail that led from the body directly across the floor to the middle of the room where the picnic tables had been stacked. The kind of burn trail that was made by a petroleum distillate accelerant.

"Ed, are you seeing what I'm seeing?"

"Sure am. This means I'll have to call Fire and Explosions." The Fire and Explosions Investigation Unit was the State Police's arson squad. "But right now I'm in charge of this scene and I want to know if that's my fire marshal lying there."

"That's not for us to determine. You know that, Ed. If we touch the body we might compromise critical physical evidence. The ME won't like it."

"I don't give a goddamn. Firefighters are brothers. We don't leave a brother lying there like a—a stray dog. We treat him with respect. Here's what I'm thinking," he said to her. "We had a house fire years ago at old Dick Nen's place. Faulty space heater. We found Dick on his back just like this, charred to a crisp. But the clothing on his backside was still okay. And his wallet was right there in the back pocket of his trousers."

Des stood there and listened. He wasn't telling her anything she didn't already know.

Ed stared down at the body. "I intend to roll him over and check his wallet. Are you going to fight me on this?"

"I'm not in a position to. Right now this is a fire scene, not a crime scene. Whatever you say goes. But let me do it, okay?" Des slipped on the latex gloves that she always carried in the back pocket of her uniform trousers and squatted there beside the body, her stomach tightening once again from the powerful smell. Gently, she turned the body over onto its side. "Ed, can you hold him steady for me? Hold him at his shoulder and his hip, please."

Ed did as she asked. Des shined her Maglite on the victim's backside. His clothing was wet but in fair condition. He wore a tan-colored shirt. Hubie Swope had been wearing a tan chamois shirt that day. A Leatherman pocketknife lay on the floor next to the victim's hip. Hubie had been carrying a Leatherman on his belt. The victim's belt had burned up, was gone.

"Hubie always carried a Leatherman," Ed pointed out in a husky voice.

"I'm aware of that." She was also aware that blood was pooled on the floor under the victim's head where it had flowed from a scalp wound on the back of his head. Make that multiple scalp wounds. And multiple skull fractures. He hadn't been felled by any falling beam. He'd suffered repeated blows from a blunt object. Des tried to remember what had been on the bar when she was here earlier in the day. All she could think of were those empty beer pitchers. She reached gingerly into the soggy back pocket of the victim's trousers—olive-colored work pants just like Hubie had been wearing—dug out his damp wallet, and opened it. Inside, she found Hubie Swope's driver's license. She showed it to Ed in the light of the torch. "Seen enough?"

Ed nodded grimly. "It's him, all right."

"Appears to be, but it won't be a positive ID until the ME matches his dental records. Any idea who Hubie's dentist was?"

"Bob Sorin here in town, same as me."

Des carefully tucked the wallet back inside of the pants pocket. "Okay, let's try to ease him down just the way we found him."

When they'd done that they stood back up, gazing down at him.

"You'll call the ME?" Ed asked her.

Des nodded. "And the Major Crime Squad. We've got what appears to be arson here. We've also got an accompanying death. They'll have to determine whether it was a natural death, an accidental death, or none of the above."

"Meaning what?"

"Meaning this man was struck several times on the back of his head."

"Are you telling me Hubie was *murdered*?"

"We won't know that until an autopsy is performed. For now, please keep your men away from the body."

Des made her way from the smoldering wreckage toward the parking lot, breathing the clean sea air deeply in and out. Reached for her cell and phoned it in to her troop commander in Westbrook.

Called Mitch, too, to tell him she wouldn't be back for dinner, which was just as well because she couldn't imagine eating anything ever again. Then she went over to the ice cream parlor to have a look at Hubie Swope's Ford Explorer. She could see his cell phone and laptop right there on the front passenger seat, but the vehicle was locked. She pressed her hand against the hood. Cold. She went around to the rear end of the vehicle and felt the tailpipe. Also cold. Then she pressed her hand against the hood of Chief Hurst's Ram. It was warm. So was the tailpipe. Translation: Dorset's fire marshal hadn't arrived with the other men in response to the fire. His Explorer had been parked there for quite some time.

Now just exactly what in the hell did that mean?

The Fire and Explosions Unit arrived first—a lead investigator and a detective in a Crown Vic followed by three cube vans full of techies in windbreakers who'd brought their own lights and generators and a supply of clean paint cans in which to store any evidence that they happened to find.

By now Dorset's volunteer firefighters had all taken off except for Chief Ed Hurst, who'd stayed put. So had Sherm and Leland Gant and Mary Ellen and Ward Tatum. Mercifully, the local TV news crews had left, although not until Ed Hurst had agreed to take questions about the extent of the fire's damage and Des had confirmed, in her very best Don Cornelius police-speak baritone, that they'd discovered the remains of an unidentified male victim. She'd declined to elaborate and instructed them to contact the public information officer in Meriden if they had any further questions. In a hoarse, emotional voice, Sherm had vowed to rebuild The Pit just as soon as humanly possible.

The lead arson investigator was someone who Des didn't know.

Lieutenant Jack Latham was in his forties, balding and paunchy. Latham's suit was loose and baggy. Latham's skin was loose and baggy. Everything about Latham seemed loose and baggy. His gangly young detective, Steve Zimmer, had on trail hikers and white socks with his dark blue suit, and wore his black hair in a tennis ball buzz cut. Zimmer's see-through scalp was a pale white, which wasn't Des's idea of a happening look.

"Do you have a firebug around these parts, Master Sergeant?" Latham asked after they'd introduced themselves.

"If we do this is his first go."

"Any idea who our victim is?"

"Pretty darned good idea," Ed Hurst spoke up, his voice cracking. "Hubie Swope, the town's building inspector. Also our fire marshal."

"Let's have a look, Chief," Latham said gently.

They stepped carefully into the water-soaked wreckage, staying several feet away from the charred body.

Latham shined his flashlight on the burn pattern on the floor. "Looks like it was squirted, wouldn't you say, Zim?"

"I would, sir," the young detective agreed. "I'd guess charcoal lighter fluid in a squeeze bottle."

Latham looked at Des. "Did the owner keep any of that around?"

"He says not."

"Any idea where our point of origin is?"

"The charring gets more intense the closer you get to the victim. And there's a streamer leading directly from his body to the middle of the room, where there was a stack of weathered picnic tables. Excellent fuel source."

"Are you telling us that the victim is our point of origin?"

"Appears to be."

"You've got some serious game for a resident trooper," Latham observed. "I'm guessing I know why, too. You're the Deacon's daughter. Used to be a hotshot on Major Crimes. Tangled with the wrong people, didn't you?"

"Yes, I did."

"Well, stuff happens."

"Yes, it does."

"So I guess we're looking at parallel investigations," he concluded, scratching his head. "No prob. We'll get along just fine."

"Absolutely," said Des, whose experience had been that the men and women on Fire and Explosions had to be good at getting along just fine because their job required them to work alongside of local police and fire officials without ruffling too many feathers. So they tended to be accommodating sorts as opposed to the turfy and/ or chippy variety. Besides, Fire and Explosions wasn't exactly the fast track, not like the high-profile Organized Crime and Drug Task Forces, which were stuffed full of climbers from the Waterbury Mafia, the Brass City-based clan of Italian-Americans who ran the Connecticut State Police.

Latham's techies had their generators up and running now. Their portable lights illuminated the burnt wreckage of The Pit so brightly that Des had to squint.

"Tell 'em what we need, Zim," he said to his young detective.

"You got it, boss." Zimmer went off to brief the techies.

"First thing in the morning we'll have Waldo Pepper nose around," Latham told Des. "He's our pup. If your perp left so much as the slightest trace of petroleum distillate on his shoes Waldo will follow his tracks out to the parking lot and halfway to Willimantic if he has to. Trust me, his nose knows. Me, I'm old school. I like to hit the ground running so I know right away if we got lucky."

"Lucky as in. . . ?"

"Sometimes we find the remains of the plastic squeeze bottle.

Perp just leaves it behind instead of trying to dispose of it elsewhere. Sometimes we find evidence of an ignition device. You wouldn't believe how many times I've encountered trace evidence of a lit cigarette inside of a matchbook. It's as low-tech as they come, but it'll still buy a perp ten minutes to get far, far away before the place goes up." He paused, tugging at an ear thoughtfully. "Once the ME removes the body we'll take a Sawzall to a section of the floor underneath the victim. If a flammable liquid seeped down between the floorboards into the subflooring our lab people will find it. When they isolate the highest concentration we'll know for sure where our point of origin is."

"Is that you in there, Jocko?" a booming male voice called to them from outside of the wreckage.

"Hang on a sec, Chuckster! We're coming out!" Latham called back. "That's my old partner, Chuck Ranberg," he said to Des. "We went through the academy together." To Ed Hurst he said, "Chief, thanks for your cooperation. You can take off now."

"I'm not going anywhere," Ed snapped. "Not until they've seen to Hubie."

"That's fine, Ed," Des assured him. "Whatever you want to do."

"Chuck's with Middlebury Mutual now," Latham explained as the two of them stepped out of there.

"Insurance investigator?"

"That's right. But Chuck's good people and he's useful. Gets to ask our suspects all sorts of personal questions that we can't. And he shares what he finds out."

Chuck Ranberg was waiting for them by one of the cube vans with a big smile on his face. If he and Latham had gone through the academy together then that meant they were about the same age, but Ranberg looked ten years younger than his ex-partner. He was trim and fit. Had thick, glossy black hair and nice, white teeth and that four-day-stubble thing going on. He wore a good leather jacket, Armani maybe, and gray flannel slacks.

"I was wondering if you'd catch this," Latham said, grinning as they shook hands. "This is Master Sergeant Des Mitry. She's resident trooper here."

"Glad to know you," Ranberg said, showing her his teeth.

"Okay, fork 'em over," Latham ordered him.

"Fork what over, Jocko?"

"You know what."

"Well, now that you mention it . . ." Ranberg pulled his cell out of his jacket pocket, called up a photo, and held it out for them to see. A baby picture. Two babies, actually.

"Twin girls, can you believe it?" Latham said to Des. "Good thing they take after their mother. I can't imagine what a beautiful young woman like Karen sees in a disreputable old scoundrel like you. She does know that you've got a son who's a year older than she is, right?"

Ranberg beamed at him. "What can I say? I'm a lucky man."

And another double dipper, Des reflected. Very, very common among sworn personnel of the male species. They joined the State Police when they were young, married their high school sweetheart, and started a family right away. By the time they reached their mid-forties they'd put in their twenty years, the kids were out of the house, and they were ready to divorce the high school sweetheart and start over again with a second wife, family, job, and pension plan.

"Middlebury holds the policy on The Pit and several other commercial properties along this avenue," he informed them. "Sherman Gant is our policyholder. You got anything for me, Jocko?"

Latham nodded. "Immediate suspicion of arson and a crispy

critter who's been tentatively ID'd as Hubie Swope, Dorset's building inspector."

"Whoa. That means Gant's staring at a sixty-day freeze right from the get-go. You don't have any reason to suspect him, do you?"

"I just got here." Latham looked at Des. "Do we, Master Sergeant?"

"You'll hear about this soon enough," Des said, "so you may as well hear it from me. Sherm and Hubie had a physical altercation earlier today. Hubie was threatening to shut down The Pit for the season if Sherm didn't make good on a number of building code violations. Sherm said he couldn't afford to."

"He also couldn't afford *not* to," Ranberg pointed out. "The policy he's been carrying on The Pit cost him an arm and a leg. We're talking about a wood-framed structure smack dab on the beach that was serving food and alcohol. And the alcohol constituted more than fifty percent of his business. That's a slam dunk for sky-high premiums. It's not as if he's been carrying a sweetheart policy, either. It's for replacement costs only."

"Replacement costs would translate to how much?" Des asked him.

"Ballpark? I'd say $150,000, maybe $200,000."

"Hell, you can't build a one-car garage in Dorset for that kind of money."

"The Pit wasn't much more than that," he pointed out a bit defensively. "So Gant's your prime suspect, am I right?"

"That'll be up to the Major Crime Squad to determine."

"I'll take that as a yes."

"Take it however you want," Des said, raising her chin at him.

"Where do I find him?"

"Big fellow over there by that pickup."

Ranberg showed her his teeth again. "Master Sergeant, I'm looking forward to working with you. Now if you'll excuse me, I have to go represent the interests of Middlebury Mutual. Later, Jocko." He went off to talk to Sherm.

"Chuck's okay," Latham said. "You don't have to worry about him."

"Trust me, I'm not."

The Major Crime Squad's cube vans began to arrive now. One, two, three sets of crime-scene techies followed by one of those new silver turbo-charged Taurus cruisers that were slowly replacing the venerable Crown Vics that Ford stopped making in 2011. Out stepped two people who Des knew very well.

The lead investigator was Des's protégée and friend Yolanda Snipes, a fierce half-black, half-Cuban rottweiler with jugs who'd played point guard for Vivian Stringer at Rutgers before she joined the state police. Yolie was street tough and wicked smart. Most men on the job, and off, were terrified of her. Her pint-sized, big-haired sergeant was Toni Tedone. Toni was one of the Waterbury Mafia Tedones. And she was a first-of, as in the first Tedone who'd been handed a choice slot on the Major Crime Squad who wasn't a he. Toni wore a dark blue blazer over a silk blouse, slacks, and pumps. Yolie, who was big into pumping heavy iron, wore a snug-fitting V-neck sweater, slacks, and boots.

"How do you like the new ride?" Des asked, admiring its lines.

"Damned thing's a rocket," Yolie replied. "Except the trunk's too damned small. You can only stuff one bad boy in there at a time." Her battle-scarred face broke into a grin. "How are you, Miss Thing?"

"Just fine."

"And how's your Jewish teddy bear?"

"My Jewish teddy bear's fine, too. How are you, Yolie?"

"Me? I'm going on fourteen hours straight since I strapped on my piece this morning and I'm standing here at a fire scene in the cold instead of relaxing on my sofa with a glass of cognac and some handsome man massaging my feet. Check that, he don't even have to be handsome."

"Are you seeing anyone?"

"Went out with a guy on the New Haven P.D. a couple of times last month, but he turned out to be a little boy. I want me a man. Whatever happened to men, anyhow? Are they all in Witness Protection out in Pocatello?"

"You could move to Pocatello and find out."

"I ain't moving to Pocatello."

"Good, I'd miss you," Des said. "And how's life treating you, Toni?"

"Life is awesome," exclaimed Toni, who was still sporting the huge diamond promise ring on her ring finger that her lover, a tall, blonde district prosecutor named Vicki Dmytryk, had given to her.

"So what have you got for us?" Yolie asked.

"Arson with an accompanying death. The victim's burned beyond recognition, but he appears to be Hubie Swope, Dorset's building inspector."

"And we know this how?"

"Hubie was also the fire marshal. Chief Hurst insisted that we try to confirm his identity, so we turned him on his side and checked his wallet."

"We'll keep that little nugget to ourselves," Yolie said. "What the ME doesn't know won't piss him off."

"Oh, he'll know."

"Any chance that the fire marshal was killed in the line of duty?"

"That's a no. He has several blunt-force trauma wounds on the back of his skull, and I found blood pooled underneath his head. You may want to look for shards of broken glass near the body. When I was here earlier today there were four beer pitchers on the bar made out of thick glass. Killer might have used one as a weapon. I didn't see any sign of them when I was in there just now. Didn't expect to in all of that wreckage. But if the techies can find any shards in the debris they might turn up traces of blood or fingerprints."

Yolie shot a glance over at Toni.

"On it, Loo." Off she went, her little legs pumping.

"I take it she and Vicki are still an item," Des said.

"You take it right. They're moving in together next week."

"Does her family know yet?"

"Not even. They're still trying to fix her up with guys. I keep telling her she's got to say something. I mean, it's liable to come up if somebody drops by." Yolie's eyes flicked over to the illuminated remains of The Pit. "Why's that fireman still hanging around?"

"That's Chief Hurst. He's watching over his friend until the ME arrives."

"Sure, okay." She continued to glance around. "And who's that guy with the pearly white teeth styling in Armani leather?"

"Insurance investigator named Ranberg. His company holds the policy. He'll show you his baby pictures if you're nice to him."

"What if I'm not nice to him?"

"He used to be partners with Latham, who caught it for Fire and Explosions. Latham's around here somewhere. The big fellow who Ranberg's talking to is Sherm Gant, the owner of this smoldering pile of rubble. Sherm had a physical altercation here earlier today with Hubie Swope. Sherm's son, Leland, was in the middle of it, too. He's the smaller one with blond hair standing next to Sherm. Hubie was insisting that Sherm make several upgrades before he'd let him reopen for the season. Sherm was accusing

Hubie of trying to put him out of business. It also so happens that the Swopes and the Gants share a long, ugly family history."

"Ugly as in. . . ?"

"Sherm and Leland attempted to desecrate Hubie's grandmother's tomb last evening by spray painting the word *whore* all over it and then peeing on it. I managed to head them off."

Yolie's eyes widened. "Now why would they want to do that?"

"Because their grandfather killed himself over her. Every year on the anniversary of his death they pay a visit to her tomb. It's a family ritual."

"I swear, this is the strangest damned town in Connecticut."

"Not just Connecticut."

"So we're liking Sherm Gant for this?"

"You'll want to take a good, hard look at him, no question. He claims he was attending the monthly meeting of the Lions Club at the Clam House when the fire broke out. Told me he first got word about it from Gaylord Holland, our assistant fire chief, who was at the meeting, too. Gaylord had issues of his own with Hubie. Yelled his head off at him this morning at McGee's diner for refusing to green light a project of his. The man's a housewright."

Yolie looked at her blankly. "Sorry, he's a what?"

"Housewright. It's like a contractor, except more pretentious. You'll want to take a look at him, too. He has motive, not to mention possible knowledge."

"Possible knowledge of. . . ?"

"A low-tech ignition device. These volunteer firefighters are well trained. Gaylord could have rigged up something slow-burning to buy himself enough time so he'd be safely tucked away at the Clam House when the call came down."

"Any chance that Sherm and Gaylord might have pulled it together?"

"I'd say everything's on the table right now."

"How about the son, Leland? Where was he?"

"His girlfriend teaches at Center School. He says he was there with her setting up chairs for parent-teacher night. I was here when he arrived. He didn't look as if he'd just been in an altercation, and he didn't smell of accelerant. Neither did Sherm, for that matter."

"What about the housewright?"

"I didn't get a whiff of Gaylord, and he'll reek of smoke now. Sorry."

"Don't be sorry. You're doing half my job for me. And I'll be sure to get you some crime-scene photos of the victim because I can tell by the look on your face that you're going to need them." Yolie reflected on it for a moment. "Could Sherm have hired someone to torch the place for him?"

"Like I said, everything's on the table. I do know that Hubie was extremely conscientious. Could be he stopped by here before dark for another look. Could be he accidentally stumbled upon Sherm's hired torch and a fight ensued. That plays. It would also explain why the tailpipe on Hubie's Explorer was cold. He got here well before the fire started. An hour, maybe two. His cell and laptop are on the front seat, by the way. And the vehicle's locked."

"And we can't go near it until the ME signs off," Yolie grumbled as Toni rejoined them. "Sergeant, we'll need a trooper to keep guard over Swope's vehicle until we have our search warrants. Somebody will have to babysit the man's house tonight, too."

Toni nodded her big head of hair. "Right, Loo."

Yolie studied Des intently. "You got anything else for us?"

"Well, there's always the 'Hello, Dummy' thing."

"What's the 'Hello, Dummy' thing?" Toni asked.

"Check out that Citgo mini-mart on the corner," Yolie explained. "See if some dummy stopped in there shortly before the fire to, hello, buy lighter fluid. And while you're at it check their Dumpster for, hello, an empty bottle of lighter fluid, complete with fingerprints. Also any discarded articles of clothing that might be reeking of it. There any other Dumpsters near here, Miss Thing?"

"There's a pizza place a half-mile east of here on Old Shore Road that stays open all year. Not much else is open until Memorial Day. The Dorset Motor Lodge is being remodeled. There's a Dumpster there. And the businesses here on Pitcairn Avenue all have trash barrels. They should be empty but . . ."

"Hello, you never know," Yolie said, nodding.

Toni said, "On it." And went darting off again.

"What's *his* deal?" Yolie asked. Jack Latham was making his way toward them from the charred wreckage. "Am I going to have a problem?"

"I don't think so. He seems okay."

"How about his partner?"

"Just a kid."

Latham approached Yolie with his hand stuck out. "Jack Latham, Lieutenant Snipes," he said as they shook. "I've heard nothing but good things about you. You ask anybody about me and they'll all tell you the same thing—I'm not into turf battles. We're all on the same team. Whatever our people find out you'll be the first to know. You have my word on that."

"Well, hell, if you're going to be all cooperative and professional then I'll have to be cooperative and professional right back at you," Yolie responded as another vehicle started its way down Pitcairn Avenue toward them. "Ah, good, here come the happy, smiling people."

It was the ME's van. His people had to come all the way down from Farmington. And they'd have to shlep the body all the way back there for the autopsy once they were done photographing it.

"I have a feeling that we're going to be around here for a while, Master Sergeant," Latham said. "What can we do about a field command center?"

"I believe I can fix you up in our auxiliary conference room in Town Hall."

Yolie let out a groan. "Is that the one smells like mothballs and Bengay?"

"You haven't been inside our Town Hall lately," Des said to her. "Our new first selectwoman has worked wonders. That musty old carpeting's gone. The floors have been refinished. The wiring's new, lighting's new. The whole vibe around there's as cutting edge as Dorset can get. I promise you, Yolie, you close your eyes and breathe deep, you're going to swear it's 1979."

CHAPTER 8

THE WHOLE BREADING OF fish fillets thing had gotten a lot more complicated ever since the Dude and his busy little nose had moved in. Still, Mitch had devised a canny system, if he did say so himself. He placed the three flat bowls containing flour, egg wash, and breadcrumbs on the counter while his cast-iron Lodge skillet heated. Then, when the skillet was starting to smoke, he dredged the gray sole in flour, removed the Dude from the counter and placed him on the floor, dunked the floured sole in the egg, removed the Dude from the counter and placed him on the floor, coated the battered filet in bread crumbs, removed the Dude from the counter and placed him on the floor, and then into the skillet went the fish. It was simple, efficient, and the results were quite superb—as long as you didn't mind the occasional cat hair in your crisp, golden-brown crust.

He was dining solo. Des had caught herself a nasty one. The Pit had been torched. Someone had been found dead in the rubble, and she was 99 percent certain that it was Hubie Swope.

Mitch would not want to be in Sherm Gant's shoes right now.

He scooped his perfectly cooked golden-brown fish onto his plate, helped himself to heaping portions of brown rice and blanched asparagus, topped off his wineglass. and settled on his love seat to dine while he continued watching *The Mind Reader,* a blistering 1933 Roy Del Ruth drama about a con-man clairvoyant played by a wondrously slimy Warren William. The forgotten star was so terrific in it that Mitch was genuinely surprised that *The Mind Reader* wasn't more widely known. For sheer unmitigated nastiness it ranked right up there with *Nightmare Alley,* Edmund Goulding's 1947 cult classic starring Tyrone Power.

Mitch had just started to eat when his super-duper new Batphone rang. He glanced at its screen. It was Des's father, Buck Mitry, aka the Deacon, the steely six-feet-four-inch deputy superintendent of the Connecticut State Police. The Deacon was *the* most intimidating man Mitch had ever met, though they seemed to get along reasonably okay. He was satisfied that Mitch was good for Des despite the obvious differences in their background and pigment. But why was the Deacon phoning him? He never did. Ever.

Mitch paused the movie and took the call. "Good evening, sir. Des isn't here, I'm afraid. She's out on a case."

"I know that, son. . . ." he responded, sounding highly ill at ease.

Mitch was immediately seized by terror. When the worst kind of disaster you can possibly imagine has struck once you never, ever stop expecting it to strike again. With Maisie it had been cancer. With Des and her job it was . . . God knows what it could be. He gulped, his heart racing. "Is Des okay?"

"Why, yes, she's fine. Just spoke with her from the crime scene. That's why I'm calling. I was hoping to catch you alone."

"Why is that?" Mitch yanked his dinner plate full of crisp, golden-brown fish away from the Dude. "Is everything okay with you? How's your heart? Do you have to undergo another procedure?"

"Not a chance. My cardiologist says I'm doing great. Relax, son. I'm not the bearer of bad news. I simply wanted to speak with you, okay?"

Mitch couldn't imagine what his ladylove's scary father wanted. The Deacon and her mother, Zelma, had divorced three years ago. Zelma had taken up with her high school sweetheart back home in Georgia. The Deacon had taken up with no one. He was a self-contained loner. "Sure, okay. What can I do for you?"

"You can let me buy you lunch tomorrow. There's something I'd like to discuss with you." The Deacon cleared his throat. "And I'd appreciate it if Desiree didn't know about this."

"I'm not very good at keeping secrets from her."

"Believe me, no one is."

"Why don't you want her to know?"

"We'll go into that tomorrow. I can come to you. Where shall we. . . ?"

"The Mucky Duck, right next to the marina. It's Dorset's designated man cave. Women never go near it, so she won't hear about it on the gossip mill."

"Sounds perfect, son. I'll see you there at noon," the Deacon said before he rang off.

Mitch went back to work on his dinner, wondering what on earth the man wanted to discuss with him that he didn't want Des to know about. He couldn't imagine. He was reaching for the remote to restart his movie when he heard Bitsy's minivan come *chunkety-chunk-chunk* home over the old wooden causeway. She pulled up in the gravel driveway outside of Mitch's cottage, got out, and tapped on his door.

"Come on in, Bitsy!"

She came on in, toting a canvas shopping bag and acting a whole lot perkier than she had that morning. "Good evening, young sir. It's your friendly neighborhood delivery girl. I come bearing a tub of Sheila's tapioca."

"Excellent," Mitch said happily as she set a Tupperware tub on the coffee table. Sheila Enman made him her world-class tapioca as payment for the errands he ran for her. "How is the old dear?"

"Sneaky. We played gin rummy after dinner and I swear she

cheats." Bitsy frowned at the Dude, who was inspecting the tapioca tub with his nose. "Mitch, why is young Mr. Jeff Lebowski covered in flour and bread crumbs?"

"I made fried fish for dinner and he helped."

Bitsy started to pursue the matter further, then decided to let it go. She gazed out of his bay window in the direction of Pitcairn Avenue, which was so lit up by police lights that it resembled an old-time movie premiere at Grauman's Chinese Theater. "I heard on the radio that they had a fire down there."

Mitch nodded. "The Pit burned down. Arson, they think. And they found a body in the rubble."

"Someone died in the fire?"

"Not exactly. Des thinks the person was murdered and then the killer torched The Pit to try to cover it up."

"Do they know who. . . ?"

"Hubie Swope."

Bitsy's face turned white, then her eyes rolled back and her knees buckled.

Mitch rushed to her and caught her before she hit the floor, steering her like a limp doll into an easy chair. He fetched a bottle of ammonia from under the kitchen sink, opened it, and waved it under her nose until she reacted by pulling away. "Bitsy, are you okay?" he asked as he continued to administer first aid.

"I'm . . . fine," she answered weakly. "Why are you rubbing my wrists?"

"I saw Lew Ayres do it in a *Dr. Kildare* movie once."

"Are they . . . They're sure it's Hubie?"

"The medical examiner will have to confirm it from his dental records. But the victim was carrying Hubie's wallet and wearing what Hubie had on today. Plus Hubie's car's there and he's not. He's not out walking on the beach. He's not home. It's Hubie. " Mitch took her pudgy hand and squeezed it. "I'm going to take a wild guess here. Was he the man you were involved with?"

Bitsy lowered her eyes, nodding. "He asked me to keep it quiet. Didn't want people whispering about us. He hated that about Dorset. The whispering."

Mitch sat back down on the love seat, reaching for his wineglass. "From what I knew of him he hardly seemed like a man who'd be drawn to the Mohegan Sun every Saturday night."

"That's because you didn't know the real Hubie. No one did. Everyone thought he was a humorless drip. He wasn't. He was charming and funny and a wonderful dancer. We'd drink champagne in our suite and dance the waltz, giddy with laughter. Hubie always made me laugh. And he was so romantic. That man called me every single morning just to tell me how much he adored me."

"And yet you thought he was seeing another woman."

"I'm positive he was. And not just because of the reasons I gave you this morning. I'd also . . . I started finding fingernail scratches on his back." Bitsy held up her gardener's hands with their short nails. "He didn't get those from me."

"Do you know who the other woman is?"

"I don't want to know. Besides, what difference does it make now? He's gone," she said forlornly. "I loved him and he's gone."

"Bitsy, where have you been this evening?"

"At Sheila's, I just told you."

"Did you go anywhere else?"

"No. Why are you. . . ?" She looked at him in dismay. "Am I going to need an *alibi*?"

"I do think you're going to get swept up in this. You were romantically involved with him. Your phone number will be on his cell log. If you exchanged e-mails they'll be on his computer."

"Somebody's going to read our e-mails?" Bitsy reddened. "Those weren't meant for other people to see. They're private."

"Not anymore they're not. I'm sorry. What time did you arrive at Sheila's?"

"Five o'clock. She likes to eat early."

"What did she make for dinner?"

"Do you really think the police will care about that?"

"They may not, but I'm dying to know."

"Crab cakes and cole slaw."

"Sheila makes crab cakes? How did I not know that?" He studied Bitsy across the coffee table. "Does she know about you and Hubie?"

Bitsy shook her head. "I respected Hubie's wishes. I didn't tell a soul. For darned sure not Sheila. Her kitchen table is the birthplace of half of the gossip in town. No one knew about us, Mitch. Not a living soul. Not unless . . ."

"Not unless what?"

Bitsy gazed out of Mitch's bay window in the direction of the police lights on Pitcairn Avenue. "Not unless Hubie told someone."

What on earth does he want to talk to me about?

Mitch wracked his brain for an answer as he washed his dinner dishes. Clearly, it had something to do with Des. Otherwise the Deacon wouldn't have asked Mitch to keep quiet about it. But what *about* Des? Had she pissed somebody off at the crime scene tonight? Somebody from, say, the Major Crime Squad? Was that it? She'd certainly made her share of enemies in the Waterbury Mafia when the Deacon had gone in for quadruple bypass surgery a few months back. They'd tried to oust him. Played dirty. Des played dirty right back to save his job, and they didn't like that. For that matter, quite a few of Dorset's WASP elite didn't like her, either. Not her color, gender, or directness, which they regarded as a lack of proper respect. Had she worn out her welcome in Dorset? Was that it? Was she being transferred somewhere else?

What on earth does he want to talk to me about?

Mitch was attempting to de-flour the Dude with a brush when he heard Des's cruiser return over the causeway. It was late, nearly eleven, and he hadn't known whether he'd see her again tonight. But he was glad she'd decided to come back, even if she did look exhausted and shaken when she walked through his door, stinking of smoke, charred wood, and something else he couldn't quite identify and didn't want to.

She barely murmured hello. Just headed straight for his shower, peeling off everything she was wearing along the way.

He brought her a glass of Chianti and some fresh-cut orange peel while she was toweling off. The orange peel was for getting rid of the lingering smell of nasty in her nostrils. It was a trick that she'd taught him the first day they met.

"Thanks, baby," she said, rubbing the peel with her fingertips and then sniffing them. She got into her robe and dug a clean pair of his white sweat socks out of the wardrobe cupboard, then settled on the love seat in front of the fire and sipped her wine while the Dude proceeded to roll around on the floor with one of her black merino wool socks, shredding it with his razor-sharp teeth. "Why does he always destroy *my* socks?"

"He likes you. He's always liked you. Are you hungry? I've got a fresh tub of Sheila's tapioca."

"You know I hate tapioca. It looks like eyeballs floating in custard."

"But you missed dinner. You should eat something."

"Forget it. I have zero appetite."

"I cooked up all of the fish. There's plenty left. I could pop it in the microwave for you."

"Mitch, you don't own a microwave."

"You see? This is what makes you such a great detective. Nothing gets by you. Did everything go okay out there tonight?"

She gazed into the fire. "Define okay."

"Did anybody give you trouble?"

"Why are you asking me that?"

"I'm taking an interest in your work. It's just like when you ask me what a gaffer does."

She looked at him curiously. "You're acting really odd. What's going on?"

"Nothing. Not a thing." God, she really was a great detective. Either that or a demon. "How about I heat up some of that chili we made the other night?"

"Baby, I'm not hungry, okay?"

"Not okay. I won't let you come to bed and have fabulous sex with me until you eat something. That's the reality you're facing. Now what can I get you? Just name it and it's yours."

"You don't have any Cocoa Puffs, do you?"

He let out a huge laugh. "That's hilarious. You know perfectly well that my Cocoa Puffs days are behind me. I don't eat that crap anymore."

"Too bad. If you had any Cocoa Puffs in the house I'd have a bowl."

Mitch peered at her. "Are you actually serious about this?"

"I am. For some reason I have a bizarre craving for them."

"And nothing else will do? That's the only thing you'll eat?"

"What I'm saying."

"Well, in that case, I *may* have a really, really ancient box under the kitchen sink. Behind the laundry detergent."

Des raised an eyebrow at him. "Uh-huh. And what's it doing there?"

"It's totemic."

"Sorry, it's what?"

"A symbol of my junk food past. Assuming, that is, you consider Cocoa Puffs to be junk food. Or food at all."

"Would that symbol be too stale to eat?"

Mitch let out another laugh. "You are so naïve. Cocoa Puffs don't go stale. There's nothing in them that *can* go stale. One heaping bowl of Cocoa Puffs coming right up," he said, starting toward the kitchen. "Do you want half of a banana with those?"

"No, that would ruin the purity of the experience."

He dug the cereal out of the cupboard and filled a bowl. Added milk, grabbed a spoon, and brought it to her.

She promptly dug in, shoveling down spoonful after spoonful. "Yum, I'm feeling better already."

"That's because of all of the vitamins they're fortified with," he said, watching her in amazement.

"And the sugar."

"Also the many essential minerals."

"And the sugar."

"Des, I have to ask—are you sure you haven't been replaced by your evil identical twin? Because I've seen this movie and it never, ever works. As soon as we go upstairs and start having fabulous sex I'll know you're not the real you."

"You sound pretty confident about that."

"Are you doubting my keen powers of perception?"

"No, I meant the part about the fabulous sex." She reached for his hand and brushed it with her lips, holding it against her smooth cheek. "I had a crispy critter tonight. It does strange things to my appetite, okay?"

"That's why you don't eat grilled steak, isn't it?"

"Can we not talk about this anymore?"

"Deal." He put another log on the fire and sat down next to her on the love seat. The Dude immediately climbed between them with his new merino wool sock toy. Clemmie decided that the little interloper was getting too much attention and jumped into Mitch's lap, pad-padding his thighs with her front paws before she curled up there, purring. "Are you still sure that the victim is Hubie Swope?"

"It's Hubie," she said, nodding. "Unless he's just staged the most elaborate disappearance I've ever seen. And I can't imagine why he would."

"That's because you didn't know the quote-unquote real Hubie."

"There was a quote-unquote real Hubie?"

"There was indeed. He was warm, funny, romantic, and quite some dancer, too, I've been led to believe."

"Led to believe by. . . ?" She blinked at him. "Don't tell me Hubie was the man who Bitsy was getting busy with at the Mohegan Sun."

"They'd drink champagne and dance the waltz together in their luxury suite high atop beautiful Uncasville, Connecticut. And don't bother trying to erase that image from your mind. It can't be done. He was also two-timing her, let's not forget. Bitsy told me he had fingernail scratches on his back that he didn't get from her. The man was carrying on two secret affairs at once, which takes some pretty serious chops around here. Hell, it's front-page news in Dorset if you get a plantar wart." Mitch stroked Clemmie, gazing into the fire. "We do have a talent pool to draw from. Should Hubie's love life become an element in his murder investigation, I mean."

"I'm not telling you for a fact that it won't," Des said, finishing off her Cocoa Puffs. "But the signs aren't pointing that way."

"Are they pointing Sherm's way?"

Des nodded. "He's the most obvious person of interest. Sherm had motive. Sherm had the most to gain. The opportunity part's still a bit iffy. It seems he was attending his monthly Lions Club meeting at the Clam House when the fire broke out. So was Gaylord Holland, as it happens. Sherm could have hired someone to torch the place for him. Happens all of the time. There's also Leland to consider. As a possible accomplice, I mean."

"Or Leland could have been acting on his own. He wanted out of the family business. There's no better way to get out than by burning it to the ground."

"True that, but he was helping Brianna set up chairs for parent-teacher night at Center School. Or so he claims. Showed up while I was at the scene. So did Mary Ellen and Ward, who'd just been sitting down to dinner."

"What were they having?"

"That didn't come up."

"You see? This is why you need me involved. You never ask the right questions. Was Hubie still alive when the fire started?"

"We won't know that until the autopsy is completed. Why?"

"Because it still doesn't add up."

"What doesn't?"

"On the one hand you're dealing with someone who was really pissed off at Hubie. He got whacked hard over the back of his head several times, right?"

"Right . . ."

"But on the other hand you're dealing with someone who was calculating enough to bring a bottle of lighter fluid along. Unless the lighter fluid was already there. Was it?"

"Sherm said there's no way he'd leave a flammable liquid lying around. But just because he said it doesn't make it so."

"Nope, I'm afraid I don't buy your scenario. I don't believe Sherm did it. Or Leland. Or Gaylord Holland, for that matter. In fact, I don't believe a man did it at all. What you've got here is a classic crime of passion."

"Slow down, doughboy. This is real life, not a Barbara Stanwyck movie."

"I understand. But you need to understand that Hubie Swope was a man who inspired passion in women. Bitsy was gaga over the guy. And so was someone else. I say he was murdered by an angry lover who torched The Pit to try and cover up her crime."

Des looked at him doubtfully. "Are you suspecting Bitsy?"

"No, I'm not. She fainted dead away when I gave her the news. Plus Sheila can vouch for her whereabouts at the time of the fire. And Bitsy didn't smell of smoke or accelerant when she showed up here, tapioca in hand. But, like I said, you do have a talent pool to draw from. After Hubie's wife, Joanie, died there were at least two women in Dorset who had their eye on him, according to Mary Ellen. Have you ever heard of Casserole Courtships?"

"Can't say that I have."

"After observing an appropriate period of mourning, a woman who's interested in a widower such as Hubie displays her interest by bringing him a casserole dish. If Hubie had been interested in one of these casserole courters, a dinner date and possible romance would have ensued. But neither of them had any luck—that we know of, I should say."

"So who were they?"

"One was Nancy Franklin, our head librarian. Mary Ellen told me Nancy's always had a thing for Hubie. She's an attractive woman of sixty, has that huge Victorian mansion on Dorset Street, and no man in her life. Or at least she's never mentioned one to me, and we chat all of the time."

"Okay, who else?"

"Inez Neto, the cashier at the Big Y. She's in her late thirties and somewhat sexy in a Sheree North kind of way."

"Sheree *who*?"

"Sheree North. She was an extremely zoftig B-movie actress in the fifties who specialized in playing blowzy blonde strippers and gangster molls who tended to be employed as strippers. I was madly in love with her when I was twelve."

"Was she before or after Arlene Francis?"

"Not *Arlene* Francis, *Anne* Francis. I was a red-blooded American boy, not a perv. Inez has a son named Petey. She was only sixteen when she had him."

Des sat up a bit straighter. "Petey Neto. . . ?"

"Do you know him?"

"He was poking around on Appleby Lane today looking for odd jobs, or so he claimed. Told me he expected to go back to work at The Pit once Memorial Day rolled around. But Sherm told me he fired him for stealing last summer and wouldn't take him back in a million years. So Petey's mother, Inez, and Hubie Swope may have been an item?"

"May have been."

They fell into silence. The fire crackled. The cats purred. Mitch didn't know what Des was thinking about now, but he sure knew what he was.

He put his arm around her and kissed her on the cheek. "It's late. You must be awfully tired."

"After all of that sugar I just mainlined?" She gazed at him through her eyelashes. "I'll be wide awake for hours."

"Good, so will I. Let's go up to bed."

CHAPTER 9

THE DORSET STREET HISTORIC District, with its stately old maples and picture-postcard Colonial mansions, was as serene and lovely as ever that morning. But the mood inside of Town Hall was somber. Voices were hushed. And the door to Hubie Swope's office was conspicuously closed when Des arrived.

Mary Ellen Tatum's office, which was directly across the hall from hers, was open. Dorset's town nurse was bustling around in her flowered smock and white trousers preparing to receive her "boyfriends." She had several diabetics, elderly single men all, who were too squeamish to administer their own insulin injections. They stopped by first thing every morning for Mary Ellen's help. Also to get frisky with her. It got them out of the house.

"Good morning," Des said from the lady's open doorway.

"Good morning, Des." Mary Ellen mustered a faint smile. "I don't know about you but I'm finding it really painful to look at Hubie's closed door. That poor little man had so much sadness with Joanie, and then he was all alone, and now this. It's just awful. Have your people figured out who did it?"

"Not yet."

"How is Mitch feeling today?"

"Oh, he's fine. How about Sherm?"

Mary Ellen sat down behind her desk, sighing. "I've never seen him so distraught. He was *crying* last night over that crummy old bar. Can you imagine?"

"It's been in your family for a long time."

"He's vowing to rebuild. Assuming, that is, the insurance people come through."

"And if they don't?"

"He'll sell his other properties on Pitcairn Avenue if he has to. Whatever it takes to raise the money. He's absolutely determined." Mary Ellen reached for her coffee mug and took a sip. "A state trooper was parked outside of Hubie's house when Ward and I got home last night. And one was still parked there this morning."

"We don't have a warrant yet to enter his house. They're just keeping an eye on it. Strictly routine."

"Sure, I understand. I used to have their spare key when I was taking care of Joanie, but I gave it back to Hubie after she passed. I believe his next-door neighbors, Tommy and Shannon Burns, have it now. Shannon ought to be home. She just had a baby."

"Thanks, that's good to know." Des spotted Glynis Fairchild-Forniaux, Dorset's first selectwoman, striding energetically down the corridor. She excused herself and caught up with her.

Glynis, a fluffy blonde juggernaut in a pants suit and pearls, was fuming. "Des, this is just plain horrible. I keep getting phone calls from the media, one after another, and all they want to know is whether I'm glad The Pit is gone. What a dreadful thing to ask me! The place was a dump, but it was *our* dump. We're a community. They want me to say that I'm hoping it never gets rebuilt."

"Are you hoping that?"

"Speaking as a private citizen and mother, nothing would make me happier. Speaking as first selectwoman, I'm looking forward to drinking a celebratory glass of beer there the day it reopens. Des, can I do anything to help with the investigation?"

"You can, as a matter of fact. Could you make the auxiliary conference room available to our investigators as a temporary field office?"

Glynis wrinkled her nose at Des. "Will they be all sooty?"

"No, I wouldn't think so."

"Then by all means. Town Hall is at your service." Glynis gazed at Hubie's closed door. "He won't be an easy man to replace."

"What will you do for now?"

"Old Joe Hart called me at seven o'clock this morning to say he'd be happy to come back for a few weeks. It was Joe who hired Hubie way back when. He's seventy-eight years old now but still plenty sharp, and he's got nothing to do all day except drink coffee at Dagmar's bakery with his pals. Joe will hold down the fort until we can find someone. I'd been urging Hubie to break in an assistant, but he preferred to work alone. Hubie was a private man. I'm ashamed to say I didn't know him very well."

"Glynis, I don't think anyone did."

The morning air down at the beach was crisp and fresh—except for that lingering scent of charred wood where The Pit had once stood. The perimeter of the crime scene remained sealed, and the site was still crawling with techie teams. Waldo Pepper, a big German shepherd, was sniffing his way through the wreckage alongside of his two-legged partner, who had the arson dog on a leash.

Latham and Zimmer were sucking down tall cups of coffee from the Citgo mini-mart. Zimmer's see-through scalp was an even whiter shade of pale in the bright morning daylight. Latham looked bleary eyed and in need of a nap.

"Waldo has spoken," he informed Des. "The scent of accelerant is strongest right where the body was. Which confirms what we figured last night—the victim was our point of origin. But Waldo hasn't found an accelerant trail leading from the building out to the parking lot or anywhere else. The scent's confined to the wreckage. Our perp was plenty careful, I'm sorry to say."

"Any luck finding traces of an ignition device?"

Latham shook his head. "None."

"The auxiliary conference room at Town Hall is all yours. Make yourselves at home. If you need anything, just let me know."

"We appreciate the hospitality, Master Sergeant."

"Hey, you're in small-town New England. Hospitality is what we do."

Yolie was standing over by Hubie Swope's Explorer talking on her cell and looking plenty bleary eyed herself. She rang off when she spotted Des. "You just missed Sherm Gant. He showed up here looking like he spent the night inside of a whiskey bottle. He and the insurance guy with the teeth went off to have breakfast together."

"Did you get some sleep?"

"I intended to. Just never got around to it. I made Toni go home for a couple of hours. She's parked outside of a judge's office in New London now waiting for word from the ME." Yolie took a gulp from her own tall container of coffee. "We found no clothing in the Dumpster at the Citgo. No squeeze bottle of lighter fluid. Nobody bought lighter fluid there yesterday. No kids showed up there looking to party. The owner said it was a real, real quiet day. He does remember selling a carton of milk to a guy shortly before six P.M. That's the one who reported the fire. His name is . . ." She leafed through her notepad. "Hunt. Ronald Hunt. He handles summer rental properties. Was working late at his office on Old Shore Road. We can run a full background check on him if we decide we want to like him. Right now he's way down on the list. The pizza place was deserted. No customers. Hardly a thing in their Dumpster. How do these places stay in business?"

"A lot of them don't."

"We found nothing of interest in the Dumpster outside of the Dorset Inn or in the trash cans on this street." Yolie glanced over her shoulder at the beach. "The tide's going out. We'll comb the beach again to see if anything turns up. So far we haven't found diddly squat."

"Any luck finding those beer pitchers in the wreckage?"

"The techies turned up some shards of shattered glass not far from the body. They could be from one of those pitchers. If there are any traces of blood or prints on them they'll be seriously degraded, but the lab people might find something. Then again, our killer could have brought the weapon—a pry bar, length of pipe, whatever—and left the scene with it. In which case we're nowhere." Yolie's cell rang. She took the call and listened very intently for a long moment, her eyes narrowing, before she said, "Got it. Thanks." Rang off, speed-dialed a number, and barked, "We're good to go, Sergeant. The victim's dental records are a match. We need warrants to search Hubie Swope's house, car, and office. Also the contents of his laptop and cell. Get the same set of warrants for Sherm Gant. Leland Gant, too. Then hightail it back here and meet me at the victim's residence at twenty-seven Lavender Lane, okay? I'll be waiting there for you." Yolie rang off and gulped down more coffee. "Hubie Swope was still alive when this place was torched. The ME found traces of soot particles in his trachea and lungs. It was the fire that killed him. He suffered multiple skull fractures and subdermal hematomas. The blows were made by something heavy and blunt. Considerable force was applied. Whoever hit him was either strong or really, really pissed. Since we have no way of knowing whether our victim was standing, sitting, or falling when the blows were struck the ME has no way of determining his assailant's height. Wouldn't even take a guess as to whether he was right- or left-handed."

"Could he have been a she?"

"The findings don't rule out a woman." Yolie frowned at her. "*Was* there a woman in Hubie Swope's life?"

"Bitsy Peck."

"Wait, Mitch's neighbor? That round little lady who gardens?"

Des nodded. "She and Hubie spent every Saturday night together in a suite at the Mohegan Sun. And, hear this, Bitsy thought Hubie was dogging her with another woman."

"Who?"

"No idea."

Yolie mulled this over. "You're not selling me a scorned girlfriend theory, are you? Because I'm liking Sherm Gant all of the way."

"So am I."

"Good, because we're going to be working this together. And when I say 'we' I mean you and me. This investigation is already crowded enough. I don't want to have to call in the Computer Crimes Unit, too. That's too damned many cooks in the kitchen. I can't function that way. Can't *breathe*. Toni speaks fluent nerd. Knows how to use our program that deciphers passwords to banking and credit card records. She can access cell logs, e-mails, all of that. While she's busy doing her thing I want you by my side. You know these people. I don't. Do you mind being my partner for the day?"

"Not a bit. Let's ride. While we're on our way to Lavender Lane I'll school you on the ins and outs of Casserole Courtships."

"The ins and outs of *what*?"

· · ·

Lavender Lane was a narrow village lane off of Dorset Street that twisted around behind Duck River Cemetery before it ended at a pond that people ice-skated on in the winter when it got cold enough. Many of the houses were smallish ones from the early 1900s that had belonged to the village's shopkeepers and tradesmen. Even the newer houses were modest in size by current McMansion standards. It was a nice street where people who weren't rich could afford to live. The houses were well cared for and the schools, library, and Town Hall were all within walking distance.

Hubie Swope's place was a decidedly small natural-shingled cottage. As Des eased her cruiser to a stop out front she noticed that his lawn needed mowing and that the rhododendrons under his front windows were overgrown. The flower bed just inside of his white picket fence had more weeds in it than flowers.

Trooper Olsen from the Troop F barracks in Westbrook was parked in the driveway in his Crown Vic.

"Anyone stop by?" Yolie asked him after they'd gotten out.

"Just some lookie-loos," he answered.

Shannon Burns, Hubie's twenty-something next-door neighbor, came out onto her front porch with her baby cradled in her arms. Des moseyed over to say hello just as Toni pulled up in the turbo-charged Taurus, jumped out, and dashed toward Yolie, warrants in hand.

"Hi, Shannon," Des said, tipping her hat.

"Hiya, Trooper Des." Shannon wore an old flannel shirt with the sleeves rolled up and a pair of jeans. Her blonde hair was in a ponytail. She was a big girl with wide hips and red, knuckly hands. Her baby seemed very contented there in her strong arms. "Is everything okay with Hubie? I'm getting kind of concerned."

"I'm afraid not. Hubie's been confirmed as the victim of last night's fire."

Shannon's eyes widened. "No way! My Tommy was there last night. He said it was *awful*." Her husband was the young firefighter who'd found the body. And lost his dinner. "Hubie was such a nice man. You'd never have guessed that his grandmother was a famous film star. He was just a regular guy, you know? And he did amazing things in that wood shop in his basement. When I was pregnant with T.J. here—Tommy Junior—Hubie made me a rocking chair from scratch out of maple. It was so sweet and thoughtful."

"I'm told that you might have his spare key."

"Sure do. I'll fetch it for you."

Shannon went inside as a Major Crime Squad cube van pulled up outside of Hubie's place. A pair of techies got out.

Shannon returned and handed Des the key.

Des thanked her. "Did you see much of Hubie?"

Shannon lowered her eyes. "Not really. I took him some pot roast or whatever sometimes. He didn't do much cooking for himself."

"Did he go out much on weekends?"

Shannon's eyes continued to avoid Des's. "I don't really know. Sometimes, I guess."

Des smiled at her. "Okay, Shannon. Thanks again for the key."

Des put on a pair of latex gloves as she strode next door to Hubie's. She used the key to open his front door. The air inside smelled stale. She and Yolie stood in the living room gazing around while Toni went prowling in search of a home computer. It was a small, plainly furnished room. Tan sofa and armchair. Coffee table with nothing on it. There was a dining area on the way to the kitchen. On the dining table, in pieces, was a cuckoo clock that Hubie was either taking apart or putting back together. There were shutters over the windows. No paintings or photos on the walls. The walls were bare.

"I want this place scoured from top to bottom," Yolie told the techies. "The garage, too. Bag and tag any personal paperwork you find—his mail, bills, address book, memo pads, note pads, old income tax returns, everything."

Toni returned from her search of the house. "There's no computer here."

"He have a desktop in his office at Town Hall?" Yolie asked Des.

"I don't recall seeing one."

"Everything we want must be on his laptop. Okay, Sergeant, get to it."

"Right, Loo. I'll be at Town Hall if you need me."

"Here, wait . . ." Des pulled a key from her key ring and handed it to Toni. "Use my office. It'll be quieter in there."

"Thanks," she said as she scurried out the door.

The kitchen was spotless. The stove and sink were clean. The counters were clean. There wasn't much food in the refrigerator. He had no alcohol other than a dusty bottle of Kahlúa in the cupboard.

In the bathroom medicine chest they found a prescription bottle of Viagra. Evidently Hubie had needed some help getting on up with Bitsy and whomever Girlfriend No. 2 was. He was also taking a statin drug for his cholesterol. Both meds had been prescribed by Dr. Harold Ostrom, who practiced in Cardiff. There were a number of OTC remedies in there which indicated that Hubie suffered from constipation, heartburn, jock itch, toenail fungus, hemorrhoids, and problematic earwax buildup.

Des sure did hate looking in other people's medicine chests.

The house had two bedrooms. The bed in the master bedroom was made. There was a library book on the nightstand—one of those Aubrey-Maturin historical sea adventures by Patrick O'Brian. Hubie's clothes were neatly put away. No dirty laundry was strewn about. No nothing. The walls in there were bare, too. The man seemed to have an aversion to wall hangings. There was no bed in the spare bedroom. Just an exercise bike and a set of barbells.

Down in the cellar they found a serious workshop for serious woodworking. Hubie had a professional-grade lathe, circular saw, jigsaw, and drill press. His workbench was crowded with hand tools, jars of screws, and dozens of tins of stain and solvent. But there were cobwebs down there, and everything seemed to have a coating of dust on it. Over in one corner a freezer chest was humming away. Des went over and opened it. Inside, she found at least twenty foil-wrapped packages that were labeled BLUEFISH and dated August of last year. Half of the men in Dorset had stockpiles of foil-wrapped bluefish in their freezers, the reason being that bluefish was all they ever seemed to catch when they went fishing out on Long Island Sound and they seldom got around to eating any of it—possibly because it tasted remarkably like 10W-30 motor oil.

"I've got a new theory," Yolie informed Des as they started back up the narrow basement stairs. "I'm thinking the man squirted lighter fluid all over his own clothes and then set fire to himself. Because I sure would if I had to live in this place. I've been here five minutes and I'm already getting the jimjams."

"It's a little drab," Des conceded.

"Drab? This ain't no drab. This is the hellmouth." Yolie barged out the front door onto the porch and took several deep, grateful breaths of fresh air.

Chuck Ranberg was leaning against Trooper Olsen's cruiser wearing his nice Armani leather jacket and nice white smile. The man from Middlebury Mutual looked rested and refreshed. His red Chevy Impala was parked next to Des's cruiser. Sherm Gant was seated in the passenger seat, stone faced.

"What do you suppose *he* wants?" Yolie wondered.

"We're about to find out," Des said as he strolled toward them.

"It's a lovely day, isn't it, ladies?" he said brightly. "I don't know about you but this is my absolute favorite time of year, especially along the shoreline."

"What can we do for you, Mr. Ranberg?" Yolie asked, her jaw clenching.

"My policyholder, Mr. Gant, has volunteered some personal information to me. I've encouraged him to share it with you rather than wait until you find it out for yourselves, which you no doubt will."

"Uh-huh. What is it?"

"It seems that Mr. Gant made a three-thousand-dollar cash withdrawal from the bank yesterday morning, and he's worried about how it might look."

"You mean like, say, a down payment to whoever torched his place?"

"Well, yes."

"He's right to be worried," Des said. "Did he say why he withdrew it?"

"Well, no. As a matter of fact, he's gotten rather surly with me."

"Don't take that personally. Sherm's surly with everyone."

"What's your interest in this?" Yolie asked Ranberg.

"Jack Latham's the best partner I ever had. We're like brothers. I have a new employer now, but I haven't changed my stripes."

"*And* you want to get out of paying your policyholder, right?"

"I'm here doing my job," he responded calmly. "I found out something that I thought could prove helpful and I'm sharing it, okay?"

Yolie studied him in chilly silence before she said, "Okay, Mr. Ranberg."

He smiled at her. "Make it Chuck."

"Thanks for the share, Chuck. We'll have a conversation with

Mr. Gant about it. Why don't you call your brother, Jack Latham, and ask him to join us at Town Hall?"

"When?"

"Oh, I don't know, Chuck. How about right goddamned now?"

"Do I need a lawyer?"

"I can't answer that for you, Mr. Gant. Do you think you need a lawyer?"

"Am I under arrest?"

"You're free to leave anytime you want," said Yolie, who was seated across the table from him in the new-and-improved auxiliary conference room. Morning sunlight streamed through the windows, which no longer had heavy drapes over them. The polished wood floor gleamed. "We'd just like to ask you some questions."

"Sure, whatever," sighed Sherm, who looked as if he'd aged five years since last night. The mayor of Pitcairn Avenue was an ashen, devastated shell of his flabby self. His jowls were unshaven, his eyes bloodshot—the left one bruised purple and swollen mostly shut from that fight he'd had at The Pit with Hubie. Sherm wore a plaid flannel shirt that was fraying at the collar and a pair of khaki work pants. His big hands, which were folded on the table before him, trembled slightly. He'd asked for coffee. Des had brought him some in a Styrofoam cup. He took a sip, fumbling in his shirt pocket for a pack of Marlboros.

"There's no smoking in here," she told him.

"Why not? It's a public building."

"Which is why there's no smoking, Mr. Gant," Jack Latham said. "See that sign over the door?"

Sherm pocketed his smokes, grumbling to himself.

Des heard footsteps out in the hallway and Leland came rushing into the room, his brow furrowed with concern. "Dad, is everything okay? Mary Ellen called me. She said that they were . . . that you were . . ."

"He's fine, Leland," Des said. "We're just having a conversation."

"And don't you have somewhere else to be?" Sherm growled at him.

Leland's face fell. "Yeah, I guess maybe I'd better get back to work."

"You're welcome to stay," Des said.

"Join us," Yolie urged him. "Please."

Leland sat, glancing around uncertainly. Unlike his father, he was clean-shaven and neatly dressed. His right hand, the one he'd been flexing after the fight, didn't look to be swollen or discolored.

"Where you been?" Sherm asked him.

"I was looking at the ice cream parlor with Ned Rigby. He's going to call me with an estimate this afternoon."

"What for? We can't afford to paint that place."

"You promised the Tomassos we would when they signed the lease, remember?"

"I told them I'd pay for paint. I never said I'd pay for a painter—especially that bandit Ned Rigby. Show some damned sense for a change, will you? I'm getting awful tired of having to tell you *everything*."

Des watched Leland get redder and redder as he sat there in tight-lipped silence. She wondered whether he was the type to get an ulcer, snarl at his fiancée, or do something more extreme. Like, say, burn his father's pride and joy to the ground.

Yolie removed her suede jacket and draped it over the back of her chair. She wore a sleeveless knit top underneath it—the better to show off her hugely muscled arms, which were an extremely intimidating sight when she folded them on the table before her.

Her mammoth left bicep was inked with a tattoo of a heart and the initials *AC* inside of it. "Mr. Gant, I'm told that you were attending a Lions Club meeting at the Clam House last evening when the fire broke out."

"That's right," Sherm said, staring at Yolie's flexed pythons. "So was Gaylord. He got the call about it and told me. The two of us took off right away, but The Pit was already gone by the time we got there."

"How long did it take you to drive there?"

"Ten minutes, maybe."

"When was the last time you'd been down there?"

"Yesterday morning." Sherm shifted uncomfortably in his chair. "I met Hubie there to go over some things."

"And got into an altercation with him, I understand."

"It was nothing."

"That shiner you're wearing don't look like nothing."

"It's not easy to run a business here, especially when you're only open a few months out of the year. Hubie just wouldn't see my side of things. Not just me. Lots of men tangled with him. He was a full-time pain in the neck." Sherm ran a hand over his unshaven face. "But I had nothing personal against him."

"Really? I thought it *was* personal in your case. And fires are kind of your thing, too, I understand."

Sherm shifted around in his chair again. "Don't know what you mean."

"Torching property is a Gant family tradition going back to when Hubie Swope's grandmother, Aurora Bing, was still alive, isn't it? Her house, her barn . . ."

"You're talking about something my grandfather's cousins were accused of doing seventy-five goddamned years ago. And they were never charged because there was no proof. That stuff's ancient history."

"Is it?" Yolie glared across the table at him. "The night before last you attempted to deface her tomb and urinate on it."

"It wasn't personal," Sherm said stubbornly.

"Man whips out his johnson, it sure sounds personal to me."

"Look, this is Dorset. Family is important here. It's who you are. Hubie knew that. Didn't mean the two of us couldn't get along." Sherm stuck his chin out at Yolie before he added, "People who've been raised different might not understand."

She bristled. "You saying I'm a stray animal who got left at the pound or something?"

In fact, Yolie had no idea who her father was and could barely remember her dead crack whore of a mother. It was her Aunt Celia who'd raised her, hence the AC tattoo.

"No, I just mean . . ." Sherm reached for his coffee cup and took a sip, his hand shaking. "Family's everything here. That's why I've kept up The Pit, and why Leland will run it after I retire."

"Wake up, Mr. Gant!" Yolie roared at him. "The Pit's gone."

"We'll rebuild."

"Is that so?"

"Damned straight. My insurance company will come through."

Chuck Ranberg of Middlebury Mutual had nothing to say about that. Just sat there, the sunlight gleaming on his glossy black hair, his face a blank.

"According to Mr. Ranberg," Yolie said, "you withdrew three thousand dollars in cash from the bank yesterday."

Leland seemed genuinely startled to hear this, Des noticed. It came as news to him. Either that or he was one hell of an actor.

"Practically every cent I had," Sherm conceded grudgingly.

"Why did you withdraw it?"

"Because he wanted the money in cash. That's how he does business."

"*Who* are we talking about?"

"A guy I know."

"Does this guy happen to be a freelance torch artist?"

"No way. Not a chance. But . . . I was afraid you might get the wrong idea. That's why I wanted to, you know, come forward and explain."

"Explain away. We're all ears."

"Hubie had a problem with my stove's venting system, okay? That money was for the commercial-grade exhaust fan he wanted me to put in. See, I know a guy in Bridgeport who deals in restaurant supplies."

"He runs a supply house?"

"No, he's more of an independent operator."

"Meaning, what, his supplies fell off of the back of a truck?"

"I wouldn't know. I'm a small businessman. The guy who the politicians say they care about but don't. Nobody does. You folks don't. You're all sitting here looking down your noses at me while you collect your nice fat salaries and health benefits and pension plans. You have *no* idea what it's like to fend for yourself. So I cut a few corners sometimes. So what? You think the fat cats don't? Besides, I don't even know the guy that well. He's a friend of a friend."

"Does this friend of a friend have a name?"

Sherm hesitated. "I wouldn't want to get him into trouble."

"We can be very tactful. Besides, you're the one who's staring at trouble if you don't get out in front of this, believe me."

"It's Sid, okay? His name's Sid."

"What's his last name?"

"I don't know."

"You have a phone number for Mr. Sid I-Don't-Know?"

Sherm pulled his cell out of the back pocket of his pants, checked it, and gave her the number.

Yolie jotted it down. "When did your transaction with Sid take place?"

"It didn't. I was supposed to meet him at ten o'clock this morning at the I-95 rest stop in Milford. He was going to wait for me in the McDonald's there, and then we'd go out to the parking lot to take a look at what he had."

"Sounds like it *did* fall off the back of a truck," Latham cracked.

"But there was no point in going through with it," Sherm said. "What with the fire and all."

"And what happened to the money?" Yolie asked him.

"I still have it."

"Where?"

"Right here in my jacket pocket. Want to see it?"

"I can't speak for anyone else," Yolie said. "But I'd love to."

Sherm's denim jacket was draped over the back of his chair. He pulled a fat letter-sized envelope from an inside pocket and tossed it on the conference table.

Yolie removed the hundred-dollar bills that were stuffed inside, fanning them out. "How do we know this is the same money that you took out of the bank yesterday?"

"Because I don't *have* any other money," Sherm blustered at her. "I already told you that. Use your head. And stop talking to me like I'm some kind of a criminal, will you? I'm the victim here."

"Hubie Swope might disagree with you on that."

"Right, he's dead. And I'm sorry. But it's my business that burned to the ground. I got bills piling up everywhere. Tenants who want this. Tenants who want that. And now my biggest source of revenue is gone. How do I make it through the summer, huh? Tell me. I'd really like to know."

"You have my heartfelt sympathy, Mr. Gant," Chuck Ranberg said with well-lubricated reassurance. "And I want you to know that Middlebury Mutual won't let you down. You're dealing with a company that makes good on its promises. That's what we do, and we've been doing it for a hundred and fifty-seven years."

"What a boatload of crap," Sherm shot back at him. "You'll be looking to weasel your way out of paying me my money any way you can. That'll be your idea of a good day's work. Hell, they'll probably give you a bonus. I don't know how people like you can live with yourselves."

"We're not here to talk about me, Mr. Gant," Ranberg said, his voice hardening.

Sherm's bloodshot eyes flickered balefully around the table at them. "You've already made up your minds about me, haven't you? But I didn't kill Hubie. I didn't torch The Pit. I didn't do *any* of it. I'm an innocent man, you hear me? I'm innocent!"

Maple Lane was a teeny tiny road off of Dorset Street that dead-ended at the Lieutenant River after no more than a hundred yards. There were only four places on the lane. Rut Peck's old farmhouse sat on one corner directly across Dorset Street from the firehouse. The former grain and feed store, which was now law offices, sat on the other corner. Behind Rut's house, facing the river, was Nan Sidell's cottage, and across the lane from her place was Ray Smith's riverfront cottage. Both Nan and Ray vehemently opposed Gaylord Holland's plan to squeeze two new homes onto two narrow slivers of land between their houses and the river.

Des parked her cruiser at the river's edge next to Gaylord's Range

Rover. A pickup belonging to Sanitation Solutions, based in Farmington, was also parked there. She and Yolie got out. The Lieutenant River was incredibly tranquil on this bright, cool spring morning. The water lapped gently against its banks. Ospreys circled slowly above their platform nests out in the marsh. A great blue heron took flight low over the water, its huge wings making a creaking noise that sounded as if it belonged back in prehistoric times.

Toni was still closeted in Des's office at Town Hall scouring Hubie's laptop and phone. Latham had put Zimmer to work trying to track down Sherm Gant's alleged kitchen supply dealer, Sid, so as to find out if a) Sid actually existed and b) would corroborate Sherm's explanation for the three thousand dollars he'd withdrawn from the bank. Latham was conducting searches of Sherm's pickup and house for physical evidence linking him to the arson. Also Leland's car and the condo in Essex that Leland shared with Brianna.

A narrow footpath ran alongside the river, which was no more than two hundred feet across at this particular spot. There were no homes on the opposite side. Nothing but marsh. They found Gaylord standing on the mucky staked-out building site that he'd managed to shoehorn in between the edge of Nan Sidell's property and the waterline. An identical site was staked out between Ray Smith's place and the water. A white-haired man in overalls was tromping around in the muck with an engineer's transit. A kid with stakes and string lines was helping him. Gaylord was watching them work, his wavy blond hair rippling in the breeze, hands stuffed in the pockets of his Barbour field jacket. He looked as if he were posing for a cologne ad.

When he heard Des and Yolie squishing their way toward him, he turned and smiled at them. "You found me."

"Thanks for sparing us a few minutes."

"Not a problem, Trooper Mitry. Always happy to help out."

"This is Lieutenant Yolanda Snipes of the Major Crime Squad."

"Nice to meet you, Lieutenant," he said, his eyes treating Yolie to a highly appreciative undressing. Thorough, too. The man not only helped her off with her panties, he folded them neatly for her. "You have some questions for me?"

"Yes, I do," Yolie replied, her nostrils flaring. She had zero use for players, especially the married kind. "Although now that I'm standing here what I really want to know is how you can build two houses on *no* land."

"Technology, Lieutenant," Gaylord explained, thumbing his chiseled jaw. "Our water usage will be a fraction of that of older homes. Low in-flow means low out-flow. Sam Spielman here is the top man in the state at making sure we have adequate drainage. And he *is* sure. These houses will be fully computerized. The home-owners will be able to monitor and tweak each and every function of their physical plant either on-site or by phone app. And, just to be clear, these will *not* be gargantuan trophy mansions. We're talking eleven hundred square feet max—two bedrooms, one full bath, one half-bath. Natural cedar shingles over a classic exposed post-and-beam structure. The houses will look as if they've always been here."

"And yet Mr. Swope was fighting you, I understand," Yolie said.

"He was," Gaylord acknowledged, running a hand through his hair. "I simply couldn't convince him that I'd never, ever do anything to compromise the Lieutenant River. If I thought for one second that my project might contaminate these bird habitats I'd walk away. I love this river. I go kayaking in it all of the time. But Hubie refused to see things my way. He was a small-town guy. Not real comfortable with new technology. And, speaking candidly,

Hubie enjoyed sticking it to me. He'd resented me ever since we were kids."

Yolie frowned. "Why's that?"

"Because I was popular and Hubie was a pimply little twerp who had no friends. But for some strange reason I always had a soft spot for him. Dorset won't be the same without Hubie. He loved this town. He loved his job. And he was a very lucky guy."

"Lucky?" Des looked at him curiously. "How so?"

"He'd found his role in life. Not very many people can say that. Hubie couldn't make a decent living as a contractor. He was too persnickety. People didn't warm to him. But the job of building inspector fit him like a glove."

"What'll happen to this project now that he's gone?" Yolie asked.

"Old Joe Hart's going to come back on an interim basis. I just spoke to him on the phone a few minutes ago. Joe was always a reasonable guy. I believe he'll green-light it. In fact, I'm sure he will." Gaylord glanced at Yolie uneasily. "I know how this looks. . . ."

"Like you and your project are going to benefit from Hubie's death?"

"Well, yes, if you want to cast it in the harshest possible light. But I would have won Hubie over eventually."

"You sound pretty confident of that," Yolie said.

"I am. Confidence is a must in my business. If you exude self-doubt then people will never believe in you."

"And do they believe in you?"

"Absolutely. My buyers are as excited about this project as I am."

"Move back, Kenny. . . !" Over at the other building site the older man, Sam Spielman, was squinting through his transit and barking directions at his young helper. "Now left, Kenny. . . !"

"One of them's an elderly widow who has retired to Hobe Sound but wants to maintain a summer residence here. It'll be perfect for her. The other's a woman from Greenwich who recently went through a divorce."

"Is she the one who's your mistress?" Yolie asked.

Gaylord shot an angry look at Des. "Now, listen, I don't know who you've been talking to . . ."

"It's all over town, Gaylord."

"And it's nothing more than cheap, nasty gossip. The old biddies at the Coastal Cuts beauty salon make the stuff up. They love, and I mean *love,* to paint Loretta as a no-good tramp because she divorced John Friday and married me. We happen to be incredibly happy together, but they won't accept that. Take my word for it, there's nothing going on."

Gaylord Holland was a very convincing liar, Des reflected. Plausible, persuasive, and thoroughly believable—*if* you didn't happen to know that he was lying. It was Loretta herself who'd told Mitch about their open marriage. So why was he lying to them about it? Out of habit or because the truth somehow bumped up against their investigation?

"I'm told you were attending a Lions Club meeting last evening when you were summoned to the fire," Yolie said. "And Sherm Gant was at the meeting, too."

Gaylord nodded. "Quite a few local businesspeople belong. Men mostly, but we have some women now, too. We sponsor a free vision screening at the annual health fair, and award a college scholarship every year to one of our high school graduates. We also maintain a stretch of Old Shore Road. You'll see us out there every Saturday morning picking up the garbage that people throw out of their cars."

"What time did your Lions Club meeting start?"

"Six o'clock on the dot. We're very punctual."

"And what time did you arrive at the Clam House?"

"A few minutes after five."

"How about Mr. Gant?"

"The same. He walked into the bar right after I did."

"Why did you get there so early? If the meeting didn't start until six."

"A few of us like to catch up over a beer before it starts. We've gotten used to doing it ever since . . ." Gaylord trailed off, clearing his throat. "Let's just say our meetings aren't like they used to be."

Des peered at him. "You mean because it's not a boys' club anymore?"

"I'm not complaining," he said hastily. "I'm delighted that we have women in the Lions Club now. It's the right thing to do. But the meetings are a lot more formal now. We have to watch every word we say. So some of us like to have an informal little pre-meeting get-together."

"And do the women know about it?" Des asked.

"You'd have to ask them that," Gaylord answered, as Sam Spielman called out to him, gesturing that he needed him. "Anything else I can help you with?"

"We're good for now," Yolie said. "Thank you."

"Happy to help," Gaylord said, smiling at Yolie as he removed a business card from his wallet and handed it to her. "You can reach me at my cell number anytime, day or night. Please don't hesitate to call, okay?" He smiled at her again before he went striding off.

Yolie watched him go. "I feel like I need to take a shower now."

"Hot or cold?"

She let out a guffaw. "Give a girl some credit, will you?" They started their way back to Des's Crown Vic on the narrow, squishy footpath. "Sounds like he can account for his whereabouts a solid half hour before that fire started. His and Sherm's both."

"Sounds like."

"Are the two of them tight?"

"Not that I'm aware of. But they did share a strong common interest."

"Getting Hubie Swope out of their lives?"

"Indeed."

They were approaching her car when the turbo-charged Taurus pulled up behind it with a screech and Toni hopped out. "Glad I caught you, Loo," she exclaimed breathlessly, her eyes bright with excitement. "I just went through the victim's banking and credit card activity for the past three months, and we have to talk. I mean, we really, really have to talk."

"Slow it down, Sergeant," Yolie said. "Talk about what?"

Toni took in a deep gulp of air, steadying herself. "Our investigation, Loo. I think we may have this whole goddamned thing wrong."

CHAPTER 10

BY UNWRITTEN ACCORD, THE Mucky Duck, a dark, narrow pub adjacent to the Dorset Marina, was where the village's divorced men went to eat and drink. Most of them were middle-aged professional men. At noontime they grabbed lunch together at the bar and followed the stock market's ups and downs on CNBC. After work they drank martinis together and watched the business wrap-up on CNBC. They were in no hurry to go home. Had no homes to go to. Those belonged to their ex-wives now. So they sat at the Mucky Duck and they drank. There was a name in Dorset for these men. They were called Mucky Duckers.

There was a small dining room in back with maybe twenty tables. Even though Mitch showed up five minutes early, Buck Mitry was already sitting there at a table checking out the menu. You could never out-early the Deacon. Des's steely-eyed father wore his usual charcoal-gray suit and muted tie, and was drinking his usual cup of black coffee. He drank something like fifteen cups a day.

He stood to greet Mitch, all six feet four inches of him. When they shook hands, Mitch's disappeared. The Deacon had the biggest hands Mitch had ever seen. The man had played first base in the Cleveland Indians organization for two years before it became clear to him that he couldn't hit a curveball. So he'd come home to Connecticut, joined the State Police, and risen through the ranks to become Deputy Superintendent. He was, at age fifty-six, the highest-ranking black man in the history of the State

Police. A disciplined man. A tight-lipped man. A monumentally scary man.

"How are you, sir?" Mitch asked as he took a seat.

"Better than our New York Mets. I simply do not understand what they're planning to do for offensive production."

"Stay close to the phone. They may give you a call."

He took a sip of his coffee, smiling faintly. "How is Desiree?"

"She's great."

"Of course she is. That girl hasn't stopped smiling since she met you."

"That's very nice of you to say."

"Just speaking the truth, son. When she was married to that no-good cheat Brandon she weighed ninety pounds. Didn't eat, didn't sleep. And if you said so much as 'boo' to her she'd burst into tears. He had her so on edge it was criminal. There's nothing lower in my book than a man who treats a decent woman that way."

"Especially when that decent woman happens to be your only daughter."

"Don't know if I've ever said the words out loud but I'm extremely grateful that you came into her life. It means a lot to me that she's found a good man."

Mitch studied him with a mixture of curiosity and alarm. Because if there was one thing the Deacon wasn't it was sentimental. "Please don't take this the wrong way, but are you *sure* you don't have to go in for more bypass surgery?"

"Positive. My ticker's fine."

Their waitress moseyed over to them now.

"What's good here?" the Deacon asked Mitch.

"I'm partial to the clam chowder myself. It's Rhode Island style." Most seafood places in Southeastern Connecticut served Rhode

Island style, which was a broth-based chowder. "Shall we try two bowls of their finest?"

"Sounds good."

She went off to fill their order.

"By the way," the Deacon said. "On the off chance that Desiree, Yolanda Snipes, or Jack Latham should happen to stroll in and find us here together, we ran into each other strictly by accident."

"Got it. And you're in Dorset because. . . ?"

"An arson-homicide joint investigation often leads to a turf battle. I stopped by to make sure everyone plays nice."

"Makes perfect sense to me."

"Desiree won't buy it for one second, but that's my story. And you are *not* to repeat one single word of the conversation we're about to have, understood?"

"Yes, sir."

Their bowls of steaming chowder arrived along with a basket of bread.

The Deacon sampled his soup and gave it a nod of approval before he said, "Do you remember the evening when I met your parents?"

"How could I forget? It was epic."

That was the night they'd reenacted a postmodern version of *Guess Who's Coming to Dinner,* complete with strained dialogue and numerous awkward silences. That was when Mitch found out that Ruth and Chet Berger detested their well-earned retirement in Vero Beach, Florida, and wanted to move back to New York City and do something useful. His dad had taught high school math in Brooklyn for thirty-seven years. His mom had been a middle school librarian. They were living in Jackson Heights now, working as volunteer tutors every day and happy as can be. Actually, the two of them had gotten along fine with Des's father. Except for when Mitch's dad, a full-time practicing buttinsky, kept insisting that the Deacon needed to start dating again. Which, according to Des, he hadn't done since her mom left him. The man lived a stubbornly monastic existence in his home in Kensington.

The Deacon dunked a piece of bread in his chowder, chewing on it thoughtfully before he said, "Your dad mentioned a guidance counselor at Boys and Girls High whom he wanted me to meet. A good-looking widow of color named Marcia."

"My mom thinks he has a crush on her. And that's a pretty big deal, let me tell you, because the only other woman he's ever had eyes for is Sharon Gless. I swear, he's watched every episode of *Cagney and Lacey* at least ten times." Mitch helped himself to more bread. It was sourdough with a good crust. "He wanted you to come into the city so the four of you could double-date. You weren't wildly enthusiastic about the idea, as I recall."

"Well, it so happens that Chet talked me into it, Mitch."

"He can be plenty persuasive, can't he? That man must have convinced at least a thousand troubled kids to stay in school over the years. So when is this double date going to be?"

"It's been." The Deacon cleared his throat uncomfortably. "Marcia and I have been seeing each other for a while now. I go into the city regularly. We have lunch, take in a show, go for a stroll in Central Park."

"Well, hey, that's great."

The Deacon stared across the table at him in chilly silence.

"Allow me to rephrase that," Mitch said. "Is it great?"

"I truly don't know," he answered heavily. "That's what I'm attempting to ascertain."

Mitch worked on his soup in silence for a moment. He'd been dead wrong. His ladylove's fearsome father hadn't arranged this clandestine lunch date to talk about her. He wanted to talk about *him*. "Well, what's to ascertain? Do you like her?"

"Very much. In fact, I haven't had such strong feelings for a woman since I first met Zelma. Marcia is smart, funny, caring. She's her own person. And every time I look into her eyes I feel like a lovestruck teenaged boy again."

"Does she have children?"

"Two grown daughters. One is a speech therapist, the other a nurse. They're both very nice people. We went out for Sunday brunch together a few weeks ago."

"So Marcia has introduced you to her kids but you still haven't . . ."

"I haven't said a word to Desiree about her," the Deacon acknowledged.

"Why not?"

"Because it's a mighty big step. I want to be sure before I take it."

"That part sounds like baloney to me, no disrespect. When it comes to love you don't have to ask yourself whether you're sure or not. Either you know it or you don't. And it sounds to me like you do."

"You're right, I do." His brow furrowed. "Your parents haven't mentioned any of this to you?"

"Not one word. I don't know why."

"I asked them not to."

"Okay, now I know why. But I still don't understand why you haven't told Des."

"Because I'm not sure how she'll take to the idea."

"What idea?"

"Me being involved with someone other than her mother."

"Are you kidding me? She'll be ecstatic. She loves you. She wants you to be happy."

The Deacon's eyes searched Mitch's face carefully. "I'm glad to hear you say that, because I'd like her to meet Marcia. I really would. And I was hoping you'd allow me to bounce an idea off of you."

"Bounce away."

"I thought that Marcia might like to spend a weekend out here in Dorset. I could book her a room at the Frederick House, and the four of us could have dinner there together. How does that sound?"

"I'm good with her staying at the Frederick House, but not the part about us eating dinner there. The ambience is much too stuffy and formal for Des, who's going to be super tense. If I know her, and I do, she'll spend the entire evening in the ladies room throwing up. No, you're going to come out to the island for a relaxed, casual meal at my place. The two of them can go for a walk on the beach together. Trust me, it'll work out much, much better."

"That's a good, concrete suggestion." He produced a pen and small notepad from the chest pocket of his suit and jotted it down.

"Shall we choose a weekend?"

The Deacon started to respond, then stopped. Pocketed the notepad and pen and sat there in uneasy silence.

"Forgive me, sir, but what's the real problem here?"

"I haven't . . ." The Deacon took a deep breath, letting it out slowly. "What I mean is, there hasn't been anyone since Zelma left. And then there's also the issue of my bypass surgery, although my cardiologist has cleared me for . . ." His eyes latched on to Mitch's. "For *any* sort of activity that I wish to participate in."

Mitch sat there wondering just exactly how he'd become the Mary Worth of the Cialis set. First Bitsy, then Loretta, and now Des's father. It seemed like only yesterday when he'd been a highly respected film critic. Actually, it *was* only yesterday. He had some more chowder, weighing his next move carefully. He knew this wasn't easy for the Deacon. Buck Mitry was an emotionally walled-off man. A man who kept his feelings to himself. A man who was carrying a loaded semiautomatic weapon. "I take it that you and Marcia haven't. . . ?"

"We're seriously considering taking our relationship to the next level," he answered, gazing down into his coffee mug. "Marcia's ready to. More than ready to. She's told me so in no uncertain terms. That's one of the things I like best about her. She speaks her mind. I'm the one who's been reluctant, and I have no proper excuse. My heart's fine, like I told you, and there's still plenty of lead in the pencil, as the old saying goes. I'm just . . . I guess you could say I'm a bit rusty, and maybe more than a bit apprehensive. I don't want to disappoint her." He grimaced. "I apologize for dumping this in your lap. I almost called you this morning to cancel. But I don't know who else to talk to. You're someone I trust, and you're practically family."

"I am family. And I'm glad you called, because I know exactly what you're going through."

He looked at Mitch in surprise. "You do?"

"Hell, yes. After Maisie died I couldn't look at another woman without getting sad all over again. A year after she was gone I was supposed to be ready to get on with my life. She had friends who were ready and willing to help me do just exactly that. Bright, nice-looking women, too. But I wasn't interested in any of them. Believe me, it was a long, long while before I met someone who I felt that way about. The way you say you feel about Marcia."

"This would be Desiree?"

"Yes, it would. And I want to let you in on something, since we're being honest with each other here. There is no such thing as rusty. And no need to be apprehensive. When the right person comes along you don't have a thing to worry about. Believe me, it's an amazingly cathartic experience. In fact, I cried after the first time we made love."

The Deacon raised an eyebrow at him. "What did Desiree say?"

"She said, 'Are you going to do that every time?'"

"Yeah, that sounds like her." He signaled for the check. Mitch tried to grab it but he wouldn't let him. "Mitch, I'm glad we had this conversation."

"Same here. Shall we set the date for that dinner?"

"Let me think it over, okay?"

"Absolutely. Whenever you're ready. Have you seen my folks recently?"

"The four of us had dinner in Chinatown together just last weekend. Marcia's very fond of them. So am I."

"Where's my dad wearing his slacks these days?"

"On his legs. Where else would he be wearing them?"

"How high up, I mean. The last time I saw him they were starting to creep their way north of his chest. Any higher and they're going to run into his Adam's apple."

"I can't give you an informed answer, I'm afraid. It was a chilly evening and he was wearing a V-neck sweater. He said it was a Father's Day gift from you, as a matter of fact."

"Was it powder blue?"

"Yes, it was."

"I got that sweater for him at Brooks Brothers when I was twelve years old. I can't believe he still has it."

"Believe it, son. I have every present Desiree ever gave me, including a birdhouse that she made out of tongue depressors when she was in the second grade. Fathers are very sentimental. You'll be finding that out for yourself one of these days." The Deacon allowed himself a smile. "Or so I'm hoping."

Chapter 11

"Loo, our victim wasn't two-timing Bitsy Peck. He was *three*-timing her."

They were parked next to the Lieutenant River in the turbocharged Taurus, Toni behind the wheel, Yolie up front next to her, Des in back. Hubie Swope's laptop and cell were on the front seat in between Toni and Yolie.

"How do we know that, Sergeant?"

"Des told us he spent every Saturday night with Bitsy at the Mohegan Sun, which totally checks out. Hubie Swope ran up charges in the neighborhood of seven hundred dollars every Saturday night at the Sun. And every *Friday* night he ran up charges of roughly the same amount at the Foxwoods Resort Casino. That's Girlfriend Number Two, right? Well, get this, he spent an additional thousand every other Wednesday at Pure, a high-end spa retreat in North Fairburn. That's Girlfriend Number Three. That's also my idea of living large. According to my math, our victim was spending about seventy-five hundred a month on his ladies—which is a solid twenty-five hundred more than the monthly salary he was collecting as Dorset's building inspector."

"How did he manage that?" Des asked.

"He didn't. Over the past six months Hubie Swope had drained his Vanguard investment portfolio from a balance of a hundred and twenty thousand to, like, a dollar. As in one dollar. He'd maxed out his lines of credit on all three of his credit cards. He also took out a hundred-thousand-dollar home equity loan on his house and missed his last three payments. The man was going to lose his house at the rate he was going. He was out of control. Me, I'm amazed. I didn't know that guys his age could get it up that often."

"He had some little blue helpers in his medicine chest." Des stared out the window at the tranquil waters of the Lieutenant River. "But color me amazed, too. It's hard to keep one secret in this town. I wouldn't have thought it was even possible to keep three."

"If Hubie Swope was mixed up with that many women at once," Yolie said, "then we may be dealing with a pissed-off-husband scenario. Any idea who these other two women are, Sergeant?"

"More than an idea, Loo. He left a trail behind."

"E-mails?"

"He exchanged e-mails with Bitsy. Plenty steamy ones, too. But he didn't communicate with his other ladies that way."

"So, what, he texted them?"

"Talked to them on the phone. According to his cell log he placed calls to the same three numbers each and every morning. I'm talking constant contact."

"Bitsy told Mitch that Hubie used to call her every morning just to tell her how much he adored her," Des said.

"Well, he also used to call someone named Inez Neto."

Des let out a groan. "I swear, if this goes down in Dorset history as the Casserole Courtship Killing I'll never hear the end of it from Mitch. I told him last night it played Sherm Gant all of the way."

"Still does," Yolie said. "We're just gassing. What's Inez Neto's deal?"

"She's a cashier at the Big Y, late thirties, single, kind of hot if you like them on the blowzy side. Her cheesehead son, Petey, worked at The Pit last summer until Sherm caught him nicking money and fired him."

"Her kid has a grudge against Sherm? I'm liking the sound of this."

"Yesterday, I shooed Petey away from Appleby Lane, where he claimed to be looking for tree work, which he knows squat about. He told me his girlfriend was going to throw his butt out if he didn't start bringing in some money. We're just gassing here, but it seems to me that if Sherm was looking to hire a handy, inexpensive nobody to torch The Pit for him . . ."

"Mr. Petey Neto, cheesehead, fits the bill. We need to have us a talk with him, Sergeant. But first you need to tell us about Girl-Friend Number Three."

"Her name's Loretta Beckwith Holland, Loo."

Yolie's eyes widened. "Wife of Gaylord Holland, housewright?"

"Okay, this case has just officially taken a sharp right turn into way too weird," Des said, shaking her head.

"I hear you," Yolie said. "This gives Gaylord a motive times two. Hubie was hosing his real estate deal *and* his wife."

"And that's not even the weird part. Loretta is the wealthiest, classiest, and most beautiful woman in all of Dorset. And it so happens she had a very frank conversation about her love life yesterday with Mitch."

"Girl, how does that man always end up in the middle of our thing?"

"Loretta told him that she and Gaylord have an open marriage. She also told him she'd been seeing someone local but was planning to end it."

"Is that right? Well, *somebody* sure ended it."

Des fell silent for a moment, wondering why on earth Loretta would go playing in the dirt with Hubie. Was this about more than just humpage on the sly? "That high-end spa in North Fairburn where Hubie dropped a thou every other Wednesday," she said. "I'm guessing it was Loretta whom he met there. She's the spa type. Inez would be the one he took to Foxwoods."

"I want you to contact this Inez, Sergeant. Tell her we'd like to speak with her at Town Hall as soon as she punches out. And bring in that son of hers."

"Right, Loo. Any idea where he. . . ?"

"Petey lives in Cardiff with his girlfriend, Darla Romine," Des said. "I ran her yesterday. She has priors for possession and D and D. I'll shoot you her address as soon as I get back in my ride."

"Bring her in, too, Sergeant." Yolie opened the car door and got out. "Let's go, Miss Thing."

"Where to?"

"We are going to get up close and personal with a rich lady."

The fields and meadows in the rolling hills north of the village were a lush, vivid green. The fresh-tilled soil smelled rich and loamy. Cows grazed in the pastures. Horses frolicked. Roosters crowed. It was a lovely time of year to be in gentlemen's farm country with its old fieldstone walls, weathered red barns, and fine historic homes. Although Des had found that pretty much any time of year was a lovely time to be there.

"Hubie Swope was a quiet, steady little guy," Des said as she steered her Crown Vic up Route 156. "He cut his breakfast sausages into identical bite-sized pieces. He repaired cuckoo clocks. You saw his house."

"I saw it, and I still have the jimjams," Yolie said to her from across the seat. "You going somewhere with this?"

"I encountered Hubie just about every day at Town Hall. He was always polite and professional. Not once did I see him getting flirty with the ladies. He didn't kid around. Hell, he didn't even smile. I would never, ever have pegged him as a hound."

"I hear you. When I think *player* I picture someone who looks and acts the part, like Gaylord Holland. And yet it sure sounds as if the little man was solid gold with the ladies."

"That part I can believe. Babe magnets come in all shapes and sizes. I'm living proof of that. Believe me, when I first met Mitch he was not my idea of mattress worthy. But the more I got to know him the more I wanted to be around him. And before I knew it all I was thinking about day and night was *him*."

"Mitch doesn't have a brother, does he?"

"Afraid not. Although his dad's awful cute if you don't mind a man who's into high-riding pants. He's plenty peppy, too."

"Oh, yeah?"

"But so's his mom."

"That's the thing. They're never available. Somebody always grabs 'em."

Des slowed up and made a left onto Eight Mile River Road, easing her way past the old red mill house that was built right out over the river facing a twenty-foot waterfall. There were some flower beds next to the house that the indomitable Sheila Enman, age ninety-four, was tidying with a hand rake.

"May as well make a quick stop while we're here," Des said, pulling into the driveway.

Sheila, a retired schoolteacher, had lived in the red mill house her entire life. She was a feisty, opinionated, and cranky old Yankee. Refused to move into an assisted living facility. Refused to get a hip replacement. Just hobbled around with the aid of a walker. Mitch fetched her groceries and mail for her. Bitsy drove her to church every Sunday. Sheila was a big-boned old woman with snowy white hair and knobby arthritic hands. She was dressed in a plaid wool jacket, dark blue slacks, and orthopedic shoes.

"How are you doing, Sheila?" Des asked, tipping her big hat.

"I'm still here," she answered as she raked dead leaves from a flower bed, seated on a three-wheeled rolling garden stool. Her walker was positioned right next to her. "Let's just leave it at that, shall we? I cannot abide old people who are constantly complaining about bladder control and bunions."

"You remember Lieutenant Snipes, don't you?"

Sheila looked up at Yolie, her blue eyes squinting. "Why, yes, I do. I recall feeling absolutely certain I never, ever wanted to arm wrestle you. It's Yolanda, is it not?"

Yolie's face broke into a smile. "You've got quite some memory."

"Once you get past ninety a memory is pretty much *all* you've got."

"Sheila, I saw you out here as we were driving by. Just wanted to stop and tell you how much Mitch and I enjoyed the tapioca you gave to Bitsy for us last evening."

"You are a liar, Des Mitry." Sheila shook a crooked finger at her. "I know for a fact that you *detest* tapioca. What you want to know is whether Bitsy was really here with me when Hubie Swope got bumped off—seeing as how she was madly in love with him."

"So you knew about the two of them?"

"Of course," she sniffed.

"It was my understanding that Bitsy hadn't told a soul. Not even you."

"She didn't have to tell me. It was obvious. Bitsy has had that special glow for weeks. Mind you, I didn't know who the man was, until a few days ago when we got onto the subject of those awful houses that Lord Gaylord of Holland is trying to plop down on the Lieutenant River. When I applauded Hubie for standing up to that four-flusher Bitsy turned bright red—and just like that I knew her boyfriend was Hubie-Doobie-Do. That's what the kids used to call him way back when." Sheila's face darkened. "And that's not all I know. Hubie was breaking that woman's heart."

"How do you know that, ma'am?" Yolie asked.

"Her eyes were all swollen last evening, Yolanda. She'd been crying. She insisted that it was just her seasonal allergies acting up. Horsefeathers. It was Hubie. And now somebody has killed him. And in answer to the question that you didn't ask, yes, Bitsy *was* right here with me when The Pit went up in flames. We heard the fire trucks go by."

"That's good to know, Sheila," Des said. "Thank you."

"Think nothing of it." She went back to her hand raking.

"Do you need some help with these flower beds?"

"I do not," the old schoolteacher barked indignantly. "I've been tending my own garden since FDR was in the White House. Besides, you have a murder to investigate."

"Did you know Hubie's grandmother, Aurora Bing?"

"Of course. We all did. Aurora was a nasty, stuck-up b-i-t-c-h who never paid her bills. She stiffed every tradesman in town. And she drank, too. One winter night she missed that old stone bridge over there and plunged her Packard right into the river. My father had to dive into freezing cold water to save her. She'd have died if he hadn't. He almost froze himself. And she never even thanked him. No, not the great Aurora Bing." Sheila paused, gazing at the stone bridge. "She also had an open-drawers policy. Once she'd set her sights on a man she wouldn't rest until she'd bedded him, and to hell with the consequences. Geoffrey Gant was a gifted artist, kindly and sensitive. Aurora destroyed his marriage for no good reason other than that she could. Believe me, no one in Dorset shed a tear when that woman died. But let's not spoil a lovely morning by talking about Aurora. That would make her happy and I wouldn't want to give her the satisfaction." Sheila looked up at them, smiling faintly. "It was lovely to see you again, Yolanda. Stop by any time."

They strode back to the car. Des started it up and eased it across the stone bridge. It was a narrow bridge. And quite some plunge down to the river below. Twenty feet at least.

"So Bitsy's alibi checks," Yolie said. "Unless the old lady's lying for her."

"If she is we'll never crack her, believe me."

"Oh, I do."

After a couple of steep, climbing hairpin turns Eight Mile River Road descended into Dorset's choicest farm country. This was where Aurora Bing had lived on her sprawling two-hundred-acre spread, White Gate Farm, which was currently owned by a big-name New York City chef who grew organic produce there to supply his many successful restaurants. Directly across the road was the farm that had belonged to Geoffrey Gant. A local family bought it from Sherm's father many years back, although the Gants still owned the small, weathered cottage close to the road that had been Geoffrey Gant's studio. It was where the great artist had painted. It was where he'd hanged himself. These days, Sherm called it home.

That home was in the process of being searched by crime-scene techies from the Fire and Explosions Unit. Two cube vans were parked there along with a Crown Vic. Waldo Pepper was busy nosing his way around.

"Want to stop?" Des asked Yolie.

"Not really."

Des kept on driving. As Eight Mile River Road rolled its way west toward the Connecticut River it made several more hairpin twists and turns around massive outcroppings of mossy granite ledge before it reached Elmer's Ferry Road, which traversed a half-mile of low-lying marshland before it dead-ended at the river. Long ago, there'd been a ferry landing there. Now there was a granite barricade, and a spectacular view downriver to the light-house on Big Sister Island. On moonlit nights the local kids liked to get busy there.

Just before the granite barricade, on the right, was a steep gravel driveway. Des turned in. The driveway climbed through what must have been fifty acres of dense forest before it reached a clearing where there was a barn, greenhouse, and four-car garage. Then it climbed some more before it arrived at a magnificent cream-colored center-chimney Colonial mansion that overlooked the river and was surrounded by acres and acres of meadows and wildflowers. A vintage powder-blue MG ragtop was parked out front.

"Damn . . ." Yolie was gawking at the house, the view, it all. "The lady's living large."

The lady was waiting there for them with the front door open. "Nice to see you, Des," Loretta Beckwith Holland said, smiling serenely.

"And you, Loretta. This is Lieutenant Yolanda Snipes of the Major Crime Squad."

"Welcome to my home, Lieutenant. Won't you please come in?"

The floor of the entry hall was polished bamboo. An antique stone Buddha fountain burbled away there.

"Would you ladies mind taking off your shoes?"

"No problem," Yolie said. "Socks, too?"

"You may leave your socks on."

Loretta Beckwith Holland was barefoot herself. Her feet were long, slender, and elegantly pedicured. Her toenails were painted that shade of grape that was currently so popular, as were her fingernails, which she kept short. Loretta had smooth, lovely hands. The hands of a young woman. Her silver-streaked black hair was tied back in a ponytail. She wore a pair of snug-fitting charcoal-gray yoga pants and a pale gray yoga hoodie. She was a slim, remarkably fit woman considering that she was pushing fifty. She held herself very erect, her shoulders back, head high, stomach flat. She was also strikingly attractive, with big blue eyes and terrific cheekbones. Her smooth, unlined face glowed with rosy vigor. Des wondered if she'd had some work done on it or if her youthful beauty was simply the product of healthy living, high-end moisturizing, and good genes.

She smiled at them again after they'd removed their shoes. "Shall I lead the way?"

They started down the center hallway. Loretta's barefoot stride was soundless. The woman positively glided. Des felt like a thudding giraffe as she followed her. She could only imagine what Yolie felt like.

The décor was minimalist and vaguely Eastern. There was the occasional wall hanging or urn that looked as if it might have come from Thailand. There was no clutter. And no sounds. No dogs barking, no kids hollering, no TV blaring, no music playing. There was no bustle of life at all. It was utterly silent inside the big house. But for some reason it was not a tranquil silence. There was an edge of anxiety that Des could feel deep down inside of her bones.

Loretta's kitchen was the size of Des's entire house. It had a six-burner Viking range, an immense center island topped with granite, a deep double soapstone sink, and yards of counter space topped with more granite. The cupboards and drawers were made of cherry. A trestle table, also of cherry, was set before a bay window that enjoyed a panoramic view of the Connecticut River and the hills of Essex beyond.

Yolie let out a low, appreciative whistle as she looked around. "Have you lived here long, ma'am?"

"The house has been in my family for generations. We restored it from top to bottom a few years ago. This kitchen was never nice. It was dark and cramped and there was nowhere to sit. Gaylord took out two walls and now it's much, much homier."

"How much land do you have?"

"Either just under or just over three hundred acres, depending upon whom you talk to."

"Let me tell you—if this was my house I'd never, ever leave. I'd just sit here and look out at that river all day long."

"That's not me, Lieutenant," Loretta said politely. "I need to feel useful. That's why I'm at the Fellowship Center every morning and the Youth Services Bureau every afternoon. May I get you ladies something? Coconut water, green tea?"

They both declined.

"So how may I help you? You sounded a bit formal on the phone, Des."

"It's a personal matter. We'll try to make it as painless as possible."

Loretta arched an eyebrow at her. "Now you sound ominous. But I'm happy to help, of course. Let's sit in my studio, shall we?"

Loretta meant the space where she practiced her yoga. It was an octagonal-shaped glass sunroom with views in every direction. Exotic cacti and sun-loving succulents grew in colorful hanging pots. There was no furniture in her studio. Just more of that polished bamboo flooring. A wicker basket was filled with rolled-up yoga mats, blocks, and bolsters. Loretta sat cross-legged on the bare floor without needing the use of her hands. She was as nimble as a ballet dancer. Des settled cross-legged on the floor, too, though she for damned sure needed her hands. Yolie, who had balky knees after four years of balling at Rutgers, perched on a bolster, stretching her legs out before her.

Loretta watched as Yolie tried to get comfortable. "Would you prefer a chair, Lieutenant?"

"Nope. I'm good."

"You must spend hours in the weight room."

"When I can."

"You're from the Major Crime Squad, I believe?"

"Yes, ma'am."

"That sounds like homicides, violent attacks, and so forth."

"Yes, ma'am."

Loretta nodded her head sagely. "So this is about Hubie. You found my number on his cell phone and you're wondering why."

"He did call you rather frequently," Des said. "I wasn't aware that you two were such close friends."

"You mean you weren't aware that we were lovers, don't you?"

"Did Gaylord know?"

"We have an open marriage."

"Does that mean yes?"

"It means that he sleeps with whomever he wants and I'm supposed to tolerate it," Loretta replied, raising her chin ever so slightly.

"That sounds familiar."

She studied Des curiously. "You've been down this road yourself?"

"Yes, indeed. I still have the tire tracks all across my back."

"My husband is a womanizer," Loretta declared. "He enjoys being one. That's what makes him happy. It finally dawned upon me that if he was going to find happiness elsewhere then I would have to do the same. I don't believe in feeling sorry for myself. I don't mope or sob into my hankie. I take charge of a situation. But I also believe in being discreet. The Beckwith name means something in Dorset. I have a reputation to protect. So I've been very, very careful."

"Did Gaylord know about you and Hubie?"

"Des, that's the second time you've asked me that."

"You didn't exactly answer me the first time."

"I don't know if he did, but I don't believe so. Gaylord is a possessive man, and he has a temper. If he'd known about us I'm fairly certain he would have bellowed and roared. Lieutenant, you are positively glowering at me, and it's quite a frightening thing to behold. Do you think I'm lying to you?"

"I'm thinking there's another way of looking at this."

"Which is. . . ?"

"That your husband not only knew about your affair with Hubie Swope but actively encouraged it."

"Why would he do that? I don't understand what you're getting at. Do you, Des?"

Des did indeed. Her own thoughts were traveling down the very same path. But this was Yolie's investigation. Yolie's hand to play. So Des stayed silent and let her.

"Hubie Swope was single-handedly blocking your husband's river project, correct?"

"So?"

"So maybe you started getting busy with him in order to help your husband's cause."

Loretta blinked at Yolie in surprise. "Are you suggesting that Gaylord *told* me to jump into bed with Hubie so that Hubie would green-light those houses of his—one of which is for Gaylord's very own mistress?" She let out a humorless laugh. "My God, you must think I have no self-respect. None."

"Not at all, ma'am. I'm just saying that's how it could look."

"Allow me to assure you that nothing could be further from the truth. And I wasn't sleeping with Hubie to 'get even' with Gaylord, either, if that was going to be your next brilliant theory. I genuinely cared for Hubie. He was a dear, sweet man. Spending every Wednesday afternoon at Pure with him qualified as the highlight of my week. We'd have massage therapists come to our suite. It was a slice of heaven. Pure is a wonderfully private place. Also very expensive. I wanted to pick up the tab, since I have money. Hubie wasn't comfortable with that idea so we took turns paying. We'd have an early dinner there before we returned home to Dorset. The food's excellent. All organic."

"How did he manage to disappear from work every Wednesday afternoon?" Des asked.

"He was always booked solid on Saturday mornings. That's when homeowners are available to sit down and discuss whatever permits they're seeking. He'd put in a half-day on Saturday and take off early on Wednesday."

"And how did. . . ?"

"I told Gaylord I was there for a spa treatment and an evening yoga class."

"How long had you and Hubie been seeing each other?"

"About three months."

"You seem like an unlikely couple, if you don't mind me saying so."

"I don't mind. Perhaps we were, on a highly superficial level. Yet I adored that man. And he called me each and every morning just to tell me how much he adored me. Can you imagine that? He was not what I'd call an accomplished bed partner. But that didn't matter to me. He was genuine. And we were friends. I *liked* Hubie. He was easy to talk to, and interested in what I had to say. Gaylord isn't. He just nods and grunts and doesn't remember a thing. Hubie remembered every single word. I'm terribly sad that he's gone, especially in such a horrific fashion. Can you tell me if, was he still alive when the fire. . . ?"

"Those details are part of an ongoing criminal investigation," Des said. "I'm afraid we can't discuss them."

"I understand. I was just hoping that he didn't suffer."

"We don't believe he did."

"I'm glad of that, because he was extremely sensitive to the touch. And so ticklish. The most ticklish man I've ever known."

Des decided that this was not something she'd ever needed to know. She gazed out the window at the lady's view of the river. Watched a Boston-bound Acela cross the river on the stone railroad bridge. Watched a hawk soar over the blue water, wafting on a current of wind. It seemed so idyllic and perfect here in Loretta Beckwith Holland's private yoga studio. And yet, as Des had learned ever since she came to work in Dorset, absolutely nothing was what it seemed to be. "You said that you and Hubie were happy together. Yet you were planning to break it off with him, weren't you?"

Loretta's blue eyes narrowed slightly. "Mitch told you about our little conversation, I gather."

"Yes, he did."

"He's easy to talk to himself."

"Yes, he is."

She took a deep breath in, exhaling slowly. "It's true, I'd decided I had to end it with him. I had to. Gaylord was starting to act suspicious."

"In what way?"

"Oh, asking me for details about Pure's yoga studio. What my teachers' names were. How many people were in my class. Whether

I was taking hatha yoga or ashtanga or what have you. Gaylord's no fool, Des. And he can be very possessive, like I said."

"You also said he has a temper."

"He does," Loretta acknowledged. "But I wasn't suggesting he'd *do* anything to Hubie. Gaylord isn't the violent type. Kindly put that out of your heads."

Des studied Loretta, fairly certain that she'd just made sure to put it *into* their heads. "May I ask how it started between you and Hubie?"

"He stopped by the Fellowship Center one morning," she recalled, a wistful smile creasing her smooth face. "Told me that we needed to discuss our wheelchair access to the Food Pantry. When we stepped outside he confessed that he actually wanted to know how I felt about Gaylord's project."

"Why'd he care about how *you* felt?" Yolie asked.

"I'm a Beckwith, Lieutenant. We're one of the three families that settled Dorset back in the 1600s. Our opinion, *my* opinion, is something that a town employee like Hubie takes seriously when he's making a critical decision about the future of the Historic District. Hubie was genuinely conflicted about Gaylord's project."

Des's left foot had fallen asleep. She shifted the cross of her legs and said, "What did you tell him?"

"That I thought it was a horrible idea for a number of reasons, not the least of which was that one of the homes was intended for Gaylord's mistress. You ladies should have seen the look of disbelief on Hubie's face. It was so sweet. He said, 'Gaylord is *cheating* on you?' I said, 'It happens, Hubie.' He said, 'But it shouldn't happen to *you,* Loretta.' I said, 'Why not?' He said, "Because you're the most beautiful, wonderful woman I've ever known.' I said, 'Why, Hubie, are you making a pass at me?' He got terribly red-faced and said, 'Why, no, never.' And I said, 'That's too bad, because if you'd asked me to have lunch with you I would have said yes.' And so he did. Don't ask me why I coaxed him into taking me to lunch. Although I suppose . . ." Loretta closed her eyes and sat there that way for a moment. Des was struck again by how silent it was in this big house on the hill. Too silent. If she lived here she would start to hear voices. Then the lady opened her eyes and said, "I suppose I needed a sympathetic ear. Hubie provided me with one. We were in bed together one week later."

"Do you know if Mr. Swope was seeing anyone else?" Yolie asked her.

"Another woman, you mean?"

"Yes."

"Why on earth would you ask me that? Hubie's love for me was genuine. *He* was genuine. He wasn't at all like Gaylord, I assure you."

"Your husband told us he was at his Lions Club meeting when the fire broke out. He and Sherm Gant both."

"That's what he told me, too. But please don't ask me to verify it, Lieutenant, because I can't. I wasn't with him."

"Where were you yesterday between, say, five and six P.M.?"

She mulled it over, her lower lip fastened between her perfect white teeth. "I stopped off at the Youth Services Bureau after yoga and stayed there for about an hour. Then I came home. It was about four o'clock by then. Let's see, I went upstairs. I spent some time in the sauna. . . ."

"You have your own sauna?"

"Right off the master suite. It's wonderfully detoxifying. Would you like to see it, Lieutenant?"

"Naw, I'm good. What'd you do after that?"

"I stretched out and took a nap on the sun porch until five or so, then poured myself a glass of Merlot and went to work on my laptop at the kitchen table. I'm supposed to be writing a thousand-word entry about our Meals on Wheels program for the town's annual report. I *hate* writing. My thoughts get all bottled up and I get so frustrated and flustered. I'm just terrible at it. I almost asked Mitch if he had any advice, but I didn't want him to think I'm an airhead. I find smart men so intimidating." Loretta turned her gaze on Des. "Do you find Mitch intimidating?"

Des showed the lady her smile. "At times."

"He's a good man, Des. You should hold on to him."

"I intend to. You were working on your laptop at the kitchen table . . ."

"Yes. That's where I was when Gaylord called and told me there was an awful fire raging at The Pit. I didn't realize that anyone had died in the fire. Not until he got home later and told me that someone had been found and you were pretty certain it was . . . that it was Hubie." Loretta's blue eyes shined at them. "I'm going to miss that sweet little man," she confessed softly. "I adored him, you know. I truly did."

"Is it my imagination or did that wonderfully detoxified bitch just throw her own husband under the bus?"

"Do you mean the part when she went out of her way twice to tell us that he has a temper?" Des replied, easing her Crown Vic down the steep driveway to Elmer's Ferry Road. "Or the part when she told us she couldn't vouch for where he was when The Pit went up in flames? Because the answer is no, that wasn't your imagination."

"Why do you think she did that?" Yolie wondered.

"Wild guess? Loretta divorced John Friday because Gaylord convinced her that she was the great love of his life. Now he's getting it on with a younger woman. He's even building her a damned love nest, or trying to. Loretta is one proud lady. She let herself get royally played by Gaylord. She doesn't strike me as the type to sit still for that. She's the type who gets even—by working on Hubie to block Gaylord's project. I'm sure she was *all* kinds of persuasive once she got naked with him." Des took Elmer's Ferry Road to Eight Mile River Road and started back through the lush green countryside toward town. "Although I do have to admit she came across as genuinely fond of Hubie."

"Are you buying that she doesn't know about his other girlfriends?"

"I am. That's one proud lady, like I said. Not in a million years would it occur to her that little Hubie Swope would feel the need for anyone else."

"But what if she found out the real deal about him? She has no alibi for yesterday between five and six P.M., in case you didn't notice."

"Oh, I noticed."

The cube vans were gone from Sherm Gant's cottage. The Fire and Explosions techies had moved on. But Sheila Enman was still out in the yard of her red mill house hand-raking her flower beds.

"Don't that old lady ever get tired?"

"Never. That would be admitting that she's human."

"I don't understand these people."

"They take some getting used to. When I first started out here I felt like I'd moved to a foreign country. I had to learn new customs, new ways of communicating, new everything. It wasn't easy. Especially the smiling part. I swear, by the end of the day my face would *ache*."

"What about now? Is Dorset starting to feel like home?"

"Dorset will never feel like home."

Yolie's cell rang. She glanced down at it and took the call. "What you got, Sergeant. . . ? Uh-huh. . . . Okay, good. Hold them at Town Hall. What time does Inez clock out. . . ? Perfect. We'll see you then." She rang off and said, "Toni found Petey Neto and Darla Romine at Darla's crappy apartment in Cardiff smoking weed and watching season two of *Game of Thrones*. Inez gets off work at the Big Y in about an hour." Yolie's cell rang again. She took this call, too. "What's up, Lieutenant Latham. . . ? No, no. I appreciate you checking in. I was going to call you. . . . Uh-huh. . . ."

Now Des's cell rang. She glanced at the screen and felt her stomach tighten right away. Pulled onto the shoulder of Route 156, got out, and took the call. "What can I do for you, Daddy?"

"I hear that you're in the middle of a situation down there," he said in that hard-edged voice she knew so well.

"You hear right. I'm afraid I don't have anything solid to report yet."

"Perfectly okay, Desiree. That's not why I'm calling. I was wondering if I could take you to lunch tomorrow."

"Lunch?" Des stood there on the country roadside trying to remember the last time her father had asked her to lunch. She couldn't. He didn't *do* lunch. All he ever did was work. He never socialized. In fact, Des wasn't sure he even had any friends. Just colleagues, all of whom were terrified of him. "Lunch would be great. Absolutely. What's this about?"

"We'll talk about it tomorrow," he replied, sounding uncomfortable.

Her pulse started racing. "Daddy, if this has something to do with your heart I want to know about it right goddamned now."

"It's not about my heart. And watch your language, young lady."

So it was job related. "What have you heard?"

"Like I said, we'll talk about it tomorrow."

"Fine." She rang off and got back in the car.

Yolie was done with her own call. "Everything good?"

"My father wants to have lunch with me."

"That sounds nice."

"Trust me, it won't be." Des eased the Crown Vic off of the shoulder and back onto the road. "Did Latham have any news we can use?"

"Not exactly. Waldo Pepper couldn't find any tangible trace evidence in Sherm's house or truck linking him to the fire. Leland's condo and car are clean, too. Zimmer's still looking for Sid, Sherm Gant's alleged kitchen appliance dealer. That phone number Sherm gave us for him was a burn phone."

"Whoa, there's a surprise." They rode in silence for moment, Des still wondering what the Deacon wanted, before she said, "Do you think you could stand to swing by Hubie's house on Lavender Lane again for a quick second?"

"I'm cool with it as long as you don't make me go back inside." Yolie peered across the seat at her. "Why, what's the deal?"

"A little something's been gnawing at me."

"Can we talk some more?"

"Sure thing, Des." Shannon Burns smiled wearily as she stood there in her front doorway. "Come on in. But *puh-leeze* ignore the mess, okay? I just can't keep up these days."

Loretta's mansion had been so spotless and silent that it seemed devoid of life. Shannon's cramped little house next door to Hubie's was anything but. The smell of soiled diapers, dirty socks, cat piss, and fried chicken assaulted Des's nostrils right away, and a beagle started barking at her when she walked in, and it wouldn't stop. There was a playpen in the middle of the living room, currently unoccupied. The sofa was occupied by three cats that were dozing on a ratty old blanket. The coffee table was heaped with dirty dishes and empty beer bottles. Four different pairs of shoes were scattered on the floor under the coffee table. A television was blaring from somewhere.

"Hush, Normie, you'll wake T.J.," Shannon cautioned the beagle. "I just put him down for his nap," she explained to Des. "I was getting dinner started while I had a chance. Come on in the kitchen, okay?"

Shannon was browning chicken thighs in a cast-iron skillet. Dr. Oz was holding forth about thyroid health on the TV. Shannon flicked it off and cleared a place at the cluttered kitchen table for Des to sit, then went over to the stove and moved the thighs around with a pair of tongs. Through the kitchen window, Des could see Yolie standing in Hubie's driveway talking to her crime-scene techies.

"Shannon, I thought maybe we could do a retake, as my friend Mitch likes to say."

"Do a what?"

"You weren't totally honest with me this morning about Hubie. You said he was a homebody who hardly ever went out."

"Well, yeah."

"Well, no. We're aware that Hubie had several women friends whom he met on a regular basis. So let's try again, okay?"

Shannon looked at her uneasily before she turned off the chicken. Then she wiped her hands on a towel and sat down across the table from Des. Normie promptly flopped over on his back at Shannon's feet. She leaned over and patted the beagle's belly. "Hubie was a good neighbor. He made me that rocking chair, like I told you. And he took such a shine to T.J. He'd wanted kids of his own, I guess. He and Joanie never had any. And T.J.'s such a cutie. Our little blessing, we call him. We had *such* a difficult time conceiving. I'd just about given up hope, to be honest. Wasn't about me. My doctor said I was a baby factory in waiting. It was Tommy. But he refused to go see a fertility specialist. You know how men are."

"I know."

"We were so thrilled when we were finally successful. I'd like to try again. I come from a big family. I want a whole mess of kids."

"You were saying about Hubie. . . ?"

Shannon lowered her eyes. "I don't want to speak ill of the dead. Or spread rumors. That seems wrong to me."

"I understand how you feel. But we're conducting a murder investigation."

"I know, but it still doesn't sit right with me. If I tell you something can we keep it between us?"

"I won't spread it around town. You have my word on that."

Shannon gave Normie a final pat and sat back up, folding her hands on the table before her. "Tommy was always accusing me of trying to make some kind of a soap opera out of Hubie's life. But this was no soap opera. This was real. I'm up and down all night, every night with T.J., okay? Plus Tommy's on emergency call for Ballek's if somebody's furnace seizes up in the middle of the night or whatever. I'm up a lot, is what I'm trying to say. And I saw what I saw outside that window with my own two eyes."

Des leaned forward across the table. "What did you see, Shannon?"

"Hubie coming and going in the night. It was pretty danged hard to believe at first, what with him being so quiet and kind of nerdy, you know? But that man made the rounds, let me tell you. I took to calling him the Lavender Lane Lothario. Fridays and

Saturdays he'd stay out until just before dawn. Pull his car into the garage with his headlights turned off so people wouldn't see him. But I saw him. *And* I saw him when he prowled the village on foot."

"I'm sorry, he what?"

"You heard me. That little man was just like a tomcat making his rounds, I swear. He'd head out after midnight and go strolling down the lane toward Dorset Street. Always wore dark clothing so he wouldn't be real visible. And he always made it back home by about five in the morning."

"How often did he do this night prowling of his?"

"Two nights a week, maybe three. I'm not sure. The only night I'm positive he stayed home was Sunday. He had to sleep sometime, right?" Shannon went back to the stove and turned the burner back on under the chicken. "If you talk to Tommy about this he'll tell you I'm full of bull. He thinks Hubie was just hoofing it over to Town Hall to get in some extra work at the office."

"Maybe Tommy's right."

"Oh, yeah? Then explain this to me: If Hubie was going to Town Hall why did he sneak around so late? Why didn't he walk over there after dinner and come home to bed at a decent hour?"

Des stood up from the table, squaring her big hat on her head. "I can't explain that, Shannon. But I do appreciate you telling me about it."

Shannon swallowed uncomfortably, her eyes avoiding Des's. "I'm sorry I held out on you this morning. That was wrong. I felt super bad about it."

"I know you did. It's okay."

"*How* many more women was he doing?"

"Yolie, I have no idea."

They were parked outside of Hubie's house in Des's cruiser. The techies were poking around in the dead man's garage.

"Just give me your best guess, okay? Toss out a nice round number we can start with and then we'll work our way down."

"Okay, sure. My best guess is that Hubie Swope was sleeping with every woman in Dorset with the exception of Sheila Enman and myself. And Sheila I'm not a hundred percent certain about. She's mighty feisty."

Yolie stared out the car window at his house. "I ain't never encountered a case like this before. You?"

"Never."

"It's like the man fits the working profile of a serial killer, except he wasn't a serial killer. He was a—a . . ."

"Serial lover."

"This is just plain whack."

Des nodded her head. "Whack."

"Shannon told you he went midnight prowling two nights a week?"

"Maybe three. She wasn't positive."

"So that means he must have two more grieving girlfriends we don't know about. Maybe three."

"That was certainly Hubie's pattern. He compartmentalized them very carefully." Des paused before she added, "And then there's also Shannon."

Yolie looked at her in disbelief. "You think he was doing her, too?"

"I think there's a decent possibility that a DNA test will reveal that Shannon's husband, Tommy, isn't her baby's biological father."

"This is just plan whack."

Des nodded her head. "Whack."

"Explain this to me, will you? Toni didn't find any other women on his cell log. If he was doing two or three or four others, then how come he didn't call *them* each and every morning just to tell them how much he adored them?"

"Maybe he didn't have to."

"Why not?"

"Because he saw them in person during the course of his day."

"Maybe," Yolie allowed. "If he visited them on foot, then that means we're talking about women who lived within, say, a mile of here. Agreed?"

"Agreed. I can't picture him hoofing it more than a mile to and fro in the middle of the night. But a mile will take you past a lot of houses in this village. We're talking about the entire Dorset Street Historic District and all of the side streets off of it—this lane, Appleby, Beckwith, McCurdy Road. That must be a hundred or more houses."

"These are women who live by themselves, most likely. Unless their husbands work nights."

"Or are real sound sleepers."

"So we're looking for widows, divorcées, spinsters . . ."

"Most likely."

"How are we going to find them?"

"We could wait for his funeral and see how many unaccompanied women show up with tears streaming down their faces. Short of that, we're not going to."

"So what are we going to do?"

"Yolie, it gives me no pleasure to say it, but this is a job for Mitch."

"How will *he* find them?"

"Don't ask me how. I don't know how. I just know that he's our man."

"In that case you'd better set him loose."

"Will do."

They sat there in silence, watching the techies at work in Hubie's garage.

"Girl, let's say one of Hubie's ladies found out he was dogging her. The truth had to catch up with him eventually, right?"

"Eventually," Des agreed.

"Let's say she told him to meet her at The Pit last night. It was dark and private there. Nobody around. For all we know The Pit could have been where they regularly got it on. Except not last night. Last night she went rage queen on him. Bashed in his head and set the fire to cover it up."

"Where are you going with this?"

"What if Sherm Gant's telling us the truth? What if he *is* a victim here?"

"And what if he's not? Believe me, I'm aware that Hubie's freaky love life raises a lot of questions. I'm right here with you asking them. But it's still way, way possible that this whole thing is exactly what we figured from the get-go—our stickler of a building inspector got done in by Sherm, either acting alone, with Leland, or with Gaylord Holland. We've got to keep our eye on the ball here, because you know what? This whole Lavender Lane Lothario business may turn out to be nothing more than a good story for us to tell late at night when we kick off our shoes and sip wine."

"Do you think that's really the case?"

Des let out a sigh. "Yolie, I honestly don't know what to think."

CHAPTER 12

SOMEHOW, DORSET'S PUBLIC LIBRARY had bypassed the twentieth century entirely. Its main building, a red-brick Victorian with dormer windows and a slate roof, dated back to the 1880s and oozed with cozy charm. It had paneled walls, a wood-burning fireplace, and an ample supply of overstuffed armchairs. The brass lamps on the oak library tables had green-glass shades. The books even smelled the way library books used to smell when Mitch was a kid. The charm-free new wing, which had been added on in 2004, was all-out twenty-first century, complete with Wi-Fi, a dozen computer workstations, a curved, low-slung check-out desk, recessed lighting, and purified air. The old and new buildings flowed into each other but didn't seem to interact. In that sense, they were very much like Dorset itself.

Mitch parallel-parked his truck out front on Dorset Street—hearing a new and really unwelcome groan when he turned its steering wheel to the left—and gathered up the offerings he'd brought. He often received review copies of Hollywood memoirs and biographies from their publishers. Also newly minted DVDs of recent hit movies. Whatever he didn't need he donated to the library, which also gave him an excuse to stop by and chat with Nancy Franklin, the head librarian. Since Nancy happened to make the best soup in town, Mitch tried to stop by around lunchtime. Nancy always had an extra Tupperware container in the fridge for him just in case he hadn't eaten lunch. Today, it so happened he'd already had clam chowder at the Mucky Duck with the Deacon. But Des, much to his surprise, had called and asked him to do some discreet poking around.

"You told me to stay out of the fray this time," he'd pointed out to her. "In fact, you were quite insistent."

"Are you going to make me beg?"

"Okay, I'll do it. But this is going to cost you."

"Oh, God, do I have to watch all eight of those Dracula movies with Christopher Lee?"

"Seven. And no. I was thinking more along the lines of you, me, and a vast quantity of whipped cream. Deal?"

"You drive a hard bargain, wow man. Deal."

And so here he was paying a call on Nancy, who was helping out at the front desk when he arrived with his arms full of books and DVDs.

Nancy had just turned sixty a few weeks back. She was a slender, petite woman with inquisitive dark eyes, a long, narrow blade of a nose, and silver hair that she wore cropped very short like Jean Seberg in *Breathless*. She wore a pale blue silk blouse, dark blue slacks, and a burgundy silk scarf knotted artfully at her throat. Because she was on the small side, soft-spoken, and a librarian by trade, people who didn't know Nancy leapt to the conclusion that she was a timid little mouse. Library board members who tried to push her around quickly discovered that she possessed a spine of steel.

She treated him to a smile. "So many goodies, Mitch! Are you sure you won't be needing them?"

"Positive. Besides, I'm a man with a library card. If I need them I can check them out just like everybody else."

"You're very generous. We appreciate it." Nancy glanced at her watch. "Gosh, it's almost one thirty. Have you had lunch yet?"

"Why, no."

"Neither have I. Let's see what we can find in the refrigerator, shall we?"

He followed her into the employee lounge, where what they found were two containers of her split pea soup.

Nancy popped them into the microwave. "Such awful news about Hubie," she said quietly. "So upsetting. I imagine Des is up to her ears in it."

"I won't see much of her until they figure out what happened."

"Do you think they will?"

"I know they will."

When the microwave beeped, Nancy removed the containers and handed him one. Then she found spoons and napkins and they started out of the lounge toward the older part of the library, where Sunny Breen, the ancient children's librarian, was subbing at the reference desk for Nadine Ambinder, Nancy's newest librarian. Nadine, who was young, bashful, and a bit plump, spent her lunch break every day on a treadmill at the Dorset Fitness Center.

Mitch followed Nancy into the reading room, where two snowy-haired geezers were parked in easy chairs before the fire. One was pretending he was reading *The Wall Street Journal*. The other wasn't pretending he was doing anything at all. Both men were snoring softly.

Nancy unlocked a door that said STAFF ONLY and led Mitch up a steep, narrow staircase to the quirky old attic space that had been the staff lounge before the new wing was built. The old lounge was squeezed under the peaked slate roof, with dormer windows that looked out over Dorset Street. It had lots of bookcases and a fireplace that no longer worked. Hardly anyone went up there anymore unless they were looking for a place to store back issues of magazines. But Nancy liked the old lounge, as did Mitch, so they always ate their soup up there at a nicked-up library table, comfortable with each other's company. Mitch felt tremendously relaxed around Nancy. This had nothing whatsoever to do with the fact that his mom was a small, slender librarian of about her age. There was no need to page Dr. Freud, Dr. Sigmund Freud.

He opened his container and sampled his second lunch of the day. It was a tough, dirty job but Des needed him and he wasn't about to let her down. "This is *the* most awesome split pea soup, Nancy. You have to tell me your secret."

"Well, the ham hock's from Cliff's butcher shop up in Centerbrook. He smokes everything himself, which I think makes a difference. I sauté pancetta and onion in the pot before I add my liquid. And I use chicken stock instead of water. My own chicken stock, not store bought."

"Yum. I'll have to try making it sometime."

"It's really not that hard."

"Sure, that's what all of the great ones say." Mitch had another spoonful, gazing out the dormer window. He could see Nancy's immense gingerbread Victorian two blocks away on the corner of Dorset Street and Beckwith Lane. Nancy had grown up in that house and had lived in it her entire life, except for the brief time that she'd been married when she was just out of college. Mitch knew very little about Nancy's marriage beyond the fact that it hadn't worked out. Nancy didn't talk about her personal life. If indeed she had a personal life. But she seemed to be a contented woman, at peace strolling back and forth every day between the library where she'd worked for the past thirty years and the mansion that her family had owned for several generations. She rented out her guest cottage, which had its own garden-gate entrance. When Des first moved to Dorset she'd almost rented it until she got lucky and found her house overlooking Uncas Lake. Nadine Ambinder was currently living there, which was a nice deal for Nadine. It wasn't easy to find affordable living in Dorset on an entry-level librarian's salary. "Tell me, what's it like, Nancy? Living in the same house that you grew up in. Knowing every single person who you pass on the street. Hardly anyone lives that way anymore."

"I suppose they don't," she acknowledged, sipping a spoonful of soup. "I enjoy it. I wake up every morning feeling as if I belong somewhere. Dorset is home." Her eyes gleamed wistfully. "But I'm going to miss Hubie. This feels like a different place whenever one of the old gang dies."

"So you knew him a long time?"

"Forever. Back when we were kids, he and my younger brother, Milton, were best friends. Hubie practically lived at our house. He was a quiet boy, and even worse at sports than Milton. Since Milton and I were both bookworms we tried to get Hubie interested in reading, but it turned out that he was a born tinkerer. He loved to fiddle with things. By the time he was twelve he could take a broken toaster apart and get it to work again. Hubie had wonderfully adept hands. Patient hands. A lot of people in town thought of him as an uptight little pain in the you-know-what. But he wasn't. He had a sense of humor, and a kind heart. I know he missed Joanie a lot."

"They were a happy couple?"

Nancy pursed her lips primly. "It was a mature relationship."

"Okay, I don't know what means."

"It means they weren't a pair of lust-crazed kids when they took up together. But they cared deeply for one another. Joanie was a gentle person. So was Hubie. I don't believe I ever heard him raise his voice in anger. Hubie was . . . He was a good friend."

"Did you two ever become more than friends? After Joanie died, I mean."

"Hubie and me?" Nancy let out a soft laugh. "No, I never thought of him that way. He was always my kid brother's best buddy. Besides, I have my guy. We've been together for, gosh, going on fourteen years now. Don't look so surprised, Mitch. There *are* men out there who find me not unattractive."

"That's not what I'm surprised about, believe me. I just had no idea, that's all. You keep it under wraps awfully well."

"I learned a long, long time ago that if you want to protect your privacy in Dorset you have to pursue your private life out of town. Besides, we were obliged to keep it a secret at first."

"*We* would be. . . ?"

"Rick Koster. Rick used to be our research librarian here. His wife left him for another man and he and I were coworkers and, well, we didn't want people whispering about us. So he ended up taking a job in Santa Fe, New Mexico. I spend my vacation there with him every year. It's lovely there. The light is absolutely amazing. And he comes here every month or so for long weekends and holidays. His daughter and her husband have a big house up in Avon. He visits with them and then the two of us take little trips to Maine, Vermont, the Cape. We go all over the place. We camp out. We ski. It depends on the time of year. We have a good time together. It's not what other people would consider an ideal arrangement, but it suits us." Nancy had some more of her soup before she added, "Hubie was a dear friend. And he became an avid reader after Joanie died. I got him interested in that Aubrey-Maturin series by Patrick O'Brian. He devoured all twenty volumes and then started right over again from the beginning. He'd stop by here every couple of days to check one out or to fuss over our elevator."

"Your elevator?"

"The one that they installed in the new building. It's never behaved properly. Hubie always made sure he was here when the repairman came because I'm hopeless with anything mechanical. Which can be a bit of a challenge when you live alone in a big, old house like I do, so Hubie would swing by the house after work and fix things for me. A stopped-up drain, leaky faucet, what have you. I'd feed him dinner, since he wasn't much of a cook. I even managed to talk Nadine into joining us a few times. Nadine's not exactly a sociable girl. Spends most of her time alone writing poetry. She's shown me some of her work."

"Any good?"

"I would say that as a form of therapy it's highly serviceable."

"Nancy, that's the most tactful *no* I've ever heard in my life."

She grinned ever so slyly. "Nadine's the best young librarian I've had in years, but she's painfully shy around men. The last time Hubie stayed for dinner, this was maybe two weeks ago, I swear she didn't lift her eyes from her plate once during the entire meal. Didn't say a word, either. Just sat there with her head down twirling a jade ring around and around her finger. The poor girl couldn't bring herself to converse with him. And this is *Hubie* we're talking about. He wasn't exactly a dashing rogue."

"Beg to differ. Did you know that he and Bitsy Peck were involved?"

Nancy looked at him in surprise. "Why, no. He never said a word. Are you sure?"

"Positive. Bitsy told me they spent every Saturday night together at the Mohegan Sun."

"That's not possible. Hubie abhorred gambling."

"They didn't go there to gamble, Nancy."

"I had no idea they were even interested in each other. I guess I'm pretty clueless when it comes to such things. Poor Bitsy must be heartbroken. And that woman has already been through so much. She was the children's librarian here before she and Redfield were married, you know. The two of us started here within weeks of each other. They called us 'the new girls.'" Nancy shook her head. "How odd that Hubie didn't tell me they were involved."

"It gets odder. Please don't repeat a single word of this, okay . . . ?"

She studied Mitch with her inquisitive dark eyes. "Okay . . ."

"Bitsy was sure that Hubie was seeing another woman behind her back."

"You mean he was *cheating* on her? I find that very hard to believe."

"Why is that, Nancy?"

"Because love triangles are messy. Hubie hated disorder of any kind. He liked everything to be neat and exact. I loved to watch him eat. No matter what I served him—meat loaf, pork roast, you name it—he'd carefully cut his entire portion into identical bite-sized pieces before he'd taste a single bite. Little boys do that, not grown men. But that was Hubie. And we . . ." She trailed off, crestfallen. "We told each other everything. Or so I thought. He knew all about Rick. He was the only person who did. I can't believe he never said a word to me about this."

"What *did* he talk about?"

"Gaylord Holland. He thought Gaylord was a two-bit phony, not to mention terribly full of himself for a man whose chief accomplishment in life was prying that bitch Loretta away from John Friday."

"You don't care for Loretta?"

"I've known Loretta since she was a little girl in pigtails and she's an even bigger phony than Gaylord. Always 'generously' serving on this board or that. It's strictly for show. Deep down inside, she's a selfish, nasty person. Plus she's dumb as a post."

"Did Hubie ever talk about Sherm Gant?"

"Of course. The two of them had had that ridiculous feud hanging over them since they were little boys. But he and Sherm got along well enough. And Mary Ellen was an absolute rock when Joanie was slipping away." Nancy pushed her half-eaten soup aside, gazing out the window at Dorset Street. "Mostly, Sherm tried Hubie's patience. Hubie wanted him to be a more responsible landlord, particularly in regards to The Pit. Which I guess is over and done with as a subject of controversy now that it's nothing more than a smoldering pile of—of . . ." She shuddered. "Sorry, I still have trouble thinking of Hubie all burnt up like that. Do they have any idea who did it?"

"They're pursuing every avenue. Which is to say no."

"I'm also having trouble thinking of Hubie as a cheat. I can't believe it. I really can't." She glanced at her watch. "And now, my young friend, I'm afraid I'd better get back to work."

The snowy-haired geezers were still snoring softly away in front of the fire. And old Sunny Breen was still parked at the reference desk.

"Nadine seems to be putting in some serious time at the fitness center these days," Mitch observed as they strolled past the desk.

"Actually, she called in sick today," Nancy said in response. "It seems that there's a stomach bug going around."

CHAPTER 13

CENTER SCHOOL HAD JUST let out for the day. Jimmy Tarasco, the crossing guard, was on duty out in the middle of Dorset Street. The big yellow buses were lined up in the bus lane. Moms were crowded out front on the sidewalk, chatting with one another while their kids came scampering out.

"Our timing's good," Des said as she eased her cruiser over to the curb and parked. "We may as well take advantage of it. Follow me."

"That's what I've *been* doing," Yolie grumbled as they got out. "And you want to know something? I liked this investigation a whole lot better when it just looked like a nice, simple case of a sleazeball torching his own place for the insurance money."

"I know."

"Tiptoeing my way through a minefield of lovesick women? Not my idea of a good time."

"I know."

"You just going to keep saying 'I know' until I shut up?"

"How did you guess?"

"Because that's what Toni always does."

"Smart girl, that Toni. I've always said so."

Center School had been built in 1923 out of granite and white-washed brick. Its roof was slate. Its window shutters were painted Colonial blue. Des and Yolie strode through the double front doors, Des's big leather belt creaking as they made their way down the main hallway. The walls were lined with class photographs and art projects. And the smell in there, a familiar blend of finger paint, glue, and heavy-duty floor cleaner, took her right back to her own elementary school days. She spotted a custodian and asked him where Miss Grossel's room was. The room was empty, however. She'd already left.

They found her in the faculty parking lot marching toward a Honda Civic, her arms full of books.

"Hey, Brianna!" Des called out.

Brianna stopped and turned around. Leland Gant's fiancée was a cute, curvy little thing, barely five feet tall, with shiny auburn hair and big doe eyes. She still had a teenage girl's creamy complexion and soft young mouth, but she also had the determined, authoritative air of an adult who was accustomed to taking charge of a roomful of eight-year-old kids. She was dressed in a tan sweater, dark brown skirt, and pumps.

"Well, hey, Trooper Mitry." She smiled at Des uncertainly. "What can I do for you?"

"This is Lieutenant Snipes of the Major Crime Squad. We want to ask you some questions about Leland if you have a sec."

"Is he. . . ?" Briana's brow furrowed with concern. "He's not in trouble, is he?"

"He's fine, as far as I know."

Brianna dumped her things in the backseat of her car and closed the door. Then she brushed her hair from her forehead with her fingertips and said, "The reason I ask is that he texted me a couple of hours ago to say that a bunch of your people had shown up at our condo with a search warrant. They even brought a bomb-sniffing dog with them."

"Actually, Waldo's trained to detect accelerants, not bombs."

"Who *were* they? And what were they looking for?"

"Those were crime-scene technicians from the State Police's Fire and Explosions Unit," Yolie informed her. "They're looking into last evening's arson attack on The Pit. Master Sergeant Mitry and myself are pursuing a different aspect of the investigation."

Brianna studied Yolie curiously. "Which aspect is that?"

"The attack on Hubie Swope."

"Does that mean they were two different crimes?"

"We don't know. That's what we're attempting to ascertain."

"We're just following routine procedure," Des said. "It's what the higher-ups make us do. Same way they make you fill out forms."

Brianna's big, brown eyes narrowed suspiciously. This was no cupcake. This was an alert, careful young woman. "What is it that you want to know?"

"For starters, where you went yesterday after school," Des said.

"Home," she answered with a shrug. "I stopped off at Walt's market to pick up groceries on my way. Pulled in at maybe twenty minutes after three."

"Do you own your condo or rent it?"

"We own it. Well, technically, *I* own it. My parents gave it to me as a present when I graduated from Trinity."

"Nice present. What did you do when you got home?"

"Went down to the laundry room and put a load of dirty clothes in the washer. Then I got started on my lesson plan for today."

"And how about Leland?"

She raised her chin at Des. "What about Leland?"

"What time did he get home?"

"A few minutes after four."

"How did he seem to you?"

"What does that mean?"

"What sort of a mood was he in?"

"He was real quiet. His shirt was torn, but he wouldn't tell me how it happened. Wouldn't tell me anything, in fact."

"How well does he get along with his dad?" Yolie asked her.

"Not well at all."

"Do they fight a lot?"

"No, it's not like that. It's more like Sherm is nasty and disrespectful to him and Leland's too nice a guy to speak up for himself. He just gets real, real quiet—which pains me to watch because I love Leland so much and I hate to see him suffer like he does. I've known my share of guys. I've been dating them since I was sixteen, and I was in two serious relationships before I met Leland. Or what I would call serious, if you understand what I mean. One was my college boyfriend, a frat boy who turned out to be a real jerk. The other was an older man whom I got involved with when I first started teaching here. Which was a huge mistake, so I ended it. And then along came Leland. He is, without question, *the* most thoughtful, considerate guy I've ever known. Would you believe I've never once had to ask him to put the toilet seat down? His aunt, Mary Ellen, raised him to be a real gentleman. But she failed him big-time in one respect. She didn't teach him how to tell his father to fuck off, if you'll pardon my French."

Des smiled at her. "That's okay, we speak French sometimes ourselves."

"Leland wants to *do* something with his life. He wants to make a real difference."

"He's interested in becoming a physical therapist, I understand."

"That's right. He'd like to work with disabled vets. And there's absolutely no reason why he can't get to do it. He's smart. He's motivated. We can get by on my salary while he's in school. But he feels this sense of obligation to the family business. I keep telling him, 'Sweetie, your father doesn't own you. It's your life to live.' But he just can't bring himself to break free."

"You mentioned that he got home yesterday a few minutes after four," Yolie said. "What happened after that?"

"He washed up and put on a different shirt. Then we drove here to set up chairs in my classroom for parent-teacher night."

"What time did you get here?"

"Around five."

"Was anyone else around?"

"Not for a while," Brianna replied. "Bunny Cherman, who has the classroom next to mine, showed up a bit later with her husband."

"How much later?"

"About five thirty, I guess. Most of the other teachers started showing up around then, too. Leland and a few other men were in the cafeteria setting up tables for coffee and cake when Sherm called him about the fire. Leland came and told me, then went flying out of here."

"Did he seem upset?"

"Super upset. And that was before he found out about Hubie Swope. Which is . . . that's just so awful. Hubie seemed like a real decent person."

Des looked at her curiously. "You knew Hubie?"

"Of course. I grew up here. I know everyone. And I'm genuinely sorry that Hubie died in the fire. But I'd be lying if I told you that I'm sorry The Pit is gone, because I'm not. I hated that place. I hated how it was always hanging over Leland and making him miserable. I'm glad that he's free of it. He can get on with his life now."

"Maybe so," Yolie said. "But Hubie Swope can't."

"I *know* he can't," Brianna shot back, glaring at her. "You really didn't need to say that. Are you trying to get a rise out of me?"

"We're just doing what we do, Brianna," Des assured her. "It's nothing personal. Thanks for your time."

"So we're good?" she wanted to know.

"All good."

Brianna gave Yolie another cold look before she got in her car and headed out.

"Girl's a little touchy, isn't she?" Yolie said, watching her drive away.

"A lot touchy."

"What are you thinking?"

"Same thing you are. Leland had a half-hour window between five and five thirty when Brianna was his only alibi."

"I'm wondering if she'd lie for him."

"Really? I'm not wondering about that at all." A chilly sea breeze picked up as they stood there, reminding Des that it was still April and the nearby waters of Long Island Sound were still frigid. "Then again, maybe we're over-thinking this. Maybe Brianna's just a genuinely nice person who loves Leland and that's all there is to it."

"I don't know many genuinely nice people," Yolie said. "Do you?"

"God, what do you bitches *want* from us?" Darla demanded. "First, that little bitch dragged us out of our apartment for *no* reason. And now we've been sitting here for, like, *ever*!"

"Here" being the auxiliary conference room in Town Hall, where Darla Romine and Petey Neto were seated next to each other at the table. Darla was what Des called a Too Much Girl, as in too much hair, too much eye makeup, too much skanky perfume, and way too much mouth. She was a pudgy, plain-faced girl of twenty-one with a pimply complexion. Wore a hoodie, torn leggings, and a pair of Uggs knock-offs. Petey had on the same overlarge pea coat he'd been wearing yesterday when Des stopped him on Appleby Lane. And he still came across like a clueless, sniffling cheesehead.

"Her name is Tedone," Yolie growled, standing there with her massive arms crossed. "*Sergeant* Tedone. And she's not a bitch."

Toni stood there saying nothing. She looked thoroughly fed up with the pair of them.

"We just wanted to have another chat with Petey," Des explained. "Pleased to meet you, Darla. Thanks for coming."

"Hey, it's not like we had a choice."

"Am I in trouble?" Petey asked Des, his voice quavering.

"If you were in trouble we'd be sitting in an interrogation room at the Troop F barracks in Westbrook. You're simply cooperating with an ongoing investigation. And for that we're extremely grateful."

Darla's eyes widened. "You mean we could have left?"

"Why, yes. You're free to leave anytime you want."

She shoved Petey in the shoulder. "Why didn't you know that?"

"How was *I* supposed to know? The little one told us to stay here. You're supposed to do what they say, right?"

Des sat down at the conference table with them, as did Yolie and Toni. "What do you do for work, Darla?"

"I'm on the courtesy desk at your friendly neighborhood big-box store over in Old Saybrook. Sort of."

"What does 'sort of' mean?"

She shrugged. "Whatev."

"Let's take another crack at that, okay? Because 'whatev' isn't a real helpful response."

"Screw this." Darla got up from the table. "I want to leave. You said we could."

"You absolutely can. But I wouldn't if I were you. I'm told that Sergeant Tedone found a quantity of marijuana in your apartment."

"A couple of lousy joints," Petey protested.

"Still, she can file a possession charge against you if she chooses

181

to. And you do have priors, Darla, if I'm remembering right. Am I?"

"Bite me," Darla snarled.

"Just answer our questions and then you, Petey, and that mouth of yours will be free to go, okay?"

Darla heaved a suffering sigh before she sat back down and said, "I got into a—a thing with my assistant manager, okay?"

"What kind of a—a thing?"

"He accused me of swiping a pair of Lee jeans which I, like, totally didn't. Then he told me he'd keep quiet about it if I'd *do* him in the storeroom."

"He *what*?!" Petey cried out. "I'll beat the living crap out of that asshole!"

"Babe, he outweighs you by a hundred pounds. He'd squash you."

"How did this situation resolve itself?" Des asked her.

"I threatened to report him for sexually harassing me. So now I'm not working there."

"He fired you?"

"Kind of, except I'm sure he'll take me back soon. They have a hard time finding good people at that place, especially on the courtesy desk. Anything else you want to know?"

"Yeah, there is," Yolie said. "Where were you two yesterday between five and six P.M.?"

"Home," Petey said.

"Doing what?"

"Binge-watching *Game of Thrones* from the very beginning. Yesterday we watched season one for, what, the third time?"

"Fourth, babe. Today we were watching season two. Or trying to." Darla glowered across the table at Toni.

"I canvassed the neighbors, Loo," Toni said. "One of them told me that their TV *was* blaring yesterday when he got home from work about twenty minutes past five. He said he pounded on the wall and they turned it down."

"Fair enough," Yolie said. "But how do we know they were *both* there?"

"Because we were," Petey said. "I just told you. Why would I make it up?"

"That's a very good question, Petey," Des said. "You and Sherm Gant aren't exactly on friendly terms, are you?"

He shifted uneasily in his chair. "So. . . ?"

"So you didn't decide to get even with him yesterday by torching The Pit, did you?"

Petey gulped in alarm. "No way! You can't pin that on me."

"Did Sherm pay you to do it for him? Is that how it went down?"

"No!"

"If you're straight with us we'll do right by you," Yolie promised. "It'll be Sherm who does the heavy time. Of course, there's that charbroiled building inspector to reckon with, but if that was just an honest mistake we can understand. Right, Sergeant?"

Toni nodded her head. "Absolutely, Loo."

"Do I need a lawyer?" Petey wondered, sinking lower in his chair. He had a sickly expression on his face now.

Darla reached over and squeezed his hand. "Grow a pair, will ya, babe? They're strictly messing with your head. Just tell them the real."

"The real?" He puffed out his cheeks. "Sherm has it in for me, but I got no beef with him. I'm just trying to get by. I didn't burn his place down, I swear. So do I need a lawyer or what?"

"You're not under arrest," Des assured him. "You're just giving us a hand."

Yolie nodded in agreement. "Thanks for your help. You can go now."

"*How* are we supposed to get home?" Darla demanded, glowering at Toni again. "*She* drove us here."

"We'll make sure an officer gives you a ride," Des said just as Petey's mother, Inez, came bustling into the conference room wearing a pink fleece pullover and black trousers.

"I got here as fast as I could from work," Inez gasped, out of breath. "They said on the phone that this was about . . ." She froze when she noticed Petey and Darla seated there. "What's going on? Are you in trouble, son?"

"Chillax, Inez," Darla said. "They were just hassling us."

"Was I speaking to you?" Inez snapped at her.

Apparently, the love thing was not happening between them.

"Sergeant, why don't you keep these two company in the resident trooper's office while we talk to Inez?" Yolie said.

"Right, Loo." Toni got up from the table. "Let's go."

"When do we get to go home, bitch?" Darla wanted to know.

"Soon," Toni answered. "And if you call me a bitch one more time I swear I'm going to clock you."

Inez stood there with a scowl on her face as she watched them leave the room. "You'll be doing Petey and me both a big favor if you throw that tramp in jail. Darla's a common thief, you know. Got fired for stealing merchandise from her employer. And it wouldn't surprise me if she's a druggie, too. I can't remember the last time that little pig washed her hair. Their apartment is disgusting. She don't wash the dishes. She don't make the bed. And she don't work for a living. Neither of them do. And if you're wondering how they pay the rent, you're looking at her," she informed them sourly. "I'm the big sap."

Not that Inez Neto was big. She stood no more than five feet four. She was a bottle blonde with major boobage. Wore just a bit more blue eye shadow and bubble gum-colored lipstick than was considered socially acceptable in Dorset on a woman who was in her late thirties. Inez had a reputation for acting frisky and flirty with the legion of lonely Mucky Duckers who flocked to her cash register. She was neither frisky nor flirty right now.

"Lieutenant Snipes would like to ask you some questions, Inez. Why don't you have a seat?"

Inez sat, folding her small hands before her on the table. She wore her fingernails long and painted them in elaborate candy-striped designs, each one different from the others.

Des showed her a smile. "I love what you do with your nails."

"Oh, thanks. My customers like them. I'm all about trying to cheer people up. Not many of them seem real happy these days."

"You don't have trouble working the register with your nails that long?"

"Nah, you get used to it." Inez had a slightly nasal voice that Des imagined could wear on you after a while. "Besides, Hubie told me they were . . ." She fought back a sob. "He thought they were sexy."

There was a box of Kleenex on the table. Des slid it over in her direction. Inez took one, dabbing at her eyes.

"We found your phone number on his cell log," Yolie said. "It appears he called you quite a bit."

Inez nodded her head. "Every morning. I—I can't believe he's gone."

"So you two were close?"

"We were going to get married. Hubie didn't get down on one knee and give me a ring, but we had an understanding. He wanted kids real bad. I'm pushing forty but for him I would have had a baby. Two of them if that's what he wanted. I was sick as a dog when I was carrying Petey. Believe me, I wouldn't put myself through that again for just anybody. But Hubie wasn't just anybody. For him I'd have done it. For him I'd have done anything," she said forlornly.

"How long had you two been seeing each other?" Des asked.

"Almost a year. He was one of my regular customers. Always nice. Always polite. I don't know if you girls have noticed but there are an awful lot of creeps out there. Hubie was different. Not the first guy you'd look at in a roomful of men, but a keeper. Not a mean bone in his body. I kept hoping he'd ask me out. Finally, I decided you don't get anywhere in life by being bashful so I gave him my number and told him to call me. He did. We talked on the phone for hours that very night. Made a date to go to Foxwoods and ended up spending the night there together. After that we spent every Friday night there. It was the one night of the week that I looked forward to. We'd take a bubble bath together. He'd massage my feet. That man treated me like a princess. I've never had much luck that way. You might even say I'm a loser magnet. Hubie . . . he was like a dream come true. And not just because he had a good, steady job with benefits. He was *there* for me. I've been carrying the load all by myself for a long, long time. I'm on my feet eight hours every day at the goddamned Big Y. And before and after work I have to tend to my mom. She's confined to a wheelchair on account of she's a diabetic who won't stop drinking or smoking or stuffing her face. She's had three gangrenous toes removed in the past six months. *And* she's just a genuinely nasty, ungrateful person. I work. I take care of her. And I've got Petey and his trampy girlfriend to look after. That's been my life. With Hubie . . ." Inez's voice caught. "With Hubie everything was going to change. We were going to put Mom in a residential treatment facility. And he was going to find Petey a job in the Public Works Department. Petey's not a bad kid. Maybe not the sharpest knife in the drawer, but a good worker. He just needs a chance, that's all." She dabbed at her eyes again. "Hubie was going to make everything better. Except that's not going to happen now. None of it."

"What will you do?" Des asked.

Inez shrugged her shoulders. "Same old same old. I've been slinging groceries for twenty years. I'll sling them for twenty more, I guess. It's not the life I wanted, but it's the life I've got."

"Do you live with your mom?" Yolie asked.

"Who, me? No, I'd slit my throat if I had to live with her in that house. It's in Westbrook. She's lived there forever. I've got an apartment in South Dorset."

"Where were you yesterday at five P.M., Inez?"

"Why are you asking me that?"

"It's a routine question," Yolie said. "I have to ask."

"Sure, okay. I finished my shift at three, same as today. Stopped off at Mom's to make her something to eat and listen to her complain about her gangrenous toes. Got out of there by about half-past four and went straight home. Fed the cat. Fixed myself a wine spritzer. Flopped down in front of the TV and turned on Channel Three news. That's when I saw the story about the fire."

"Did anyone see you come home?"

"No, I don't think so." Inez's gaze hardened. "Why?"

"Like the lieutenant said, these are just routine questions," Des said. "Were there other women in Hubie's life? Was he seeing anyone else?"

Inez looked at her in surprise. "Hubie? Not a chance. This was a nice, sweet guy, like I told you. We'd made plans for the future. He called me every single morning to tell me how happy he was about everything. Would he do that if he was cheating on me?"

Des felt her chest tighten before she said, "No, Inez, I can't imagine he would."

CHAPTER 14

BITSY WAS OUT IN her garden feverishly digging a foot-wide trench between a raised planting bed filled with tulips and a section of lawn that she'd taken out last fall and replaced with native meadow grasses. The meadow grasses had been an experiment. Bitsy was always experimenting.

"What in the heck are you doing?" Mitch wondered, watching her toil away. Des stood by his side wearing her big hat and her stern game face.

"My new carex is *drowning*," Bitsy answered fretfully as she dug and she dug, tossing the soil onto a drop cloth. "It does *not* like to be wet. That's why I put it in—so it would stay green over the summer without watering. But it turns out that I need better drainage, so I'm installing a gravel trench to contain the runoff from my beds. I've ordered a load of gravel from Dorset Landscaping. I'm going to dig all of the way around, lay in two feet of gravel, then cover it back over. *That* should do the trick, don't you think?"

"Makes perfect sense to me," said Mitch, who'd experienced this before with Bitsy. Whenever she got upset she took on a huge, physically demanding garden project. Some people drank. Bitsy dug. "If you need help horsing all of that gravel around just let me know."

"You're a good neighbor, Mitch, but I intend to handle this myself." Bitsy paused to dab the sweat from her brow with a blue bandanna, glancing uncertainly at Des. "I never thought I'd be that person again, you know."

"What person?" Des asked her.

"The dizzy schoolgirl. The silly airhead who's crazy in love all day long. I swear, it wasn't even about the sex, although that was certainly part of it. It was about being *wanted* again. Do you know what I mean? Please tell me that you do, Des, because I'm feeling like such a fool."

"You're not a fool. What you and Hubie had together was real."

"And now he's gone and I'm all alone and I always will be," Bitsy said despondently. "Hubie was my last chance."

"You don't know that, Bitsy," Mitch said.

"Yes, I do. It's never going to happen again. I won't let it. I can't handle the pain. I'm not strong enough anymore."

"You told Mitch that you suspected Hubie was seeing someone else."

"I was sure of it." Bitsy resumed her digging. "But if he'd come clean to me about her I would have taken him back in a second. I would have understood. That's how much I loved that man."

"Any idea who the other woman was?"

Bitsy glanced at her sharply. "What difference does it make now? He's gone. That big idiot Sherm Gant killed him."

"So you think Sherm did it?"

"Of course. Don't you?"

"It seems he was at his Lions Club meeting when it happened. He and Gaylord Holland both."

"Then they both cooked up something clever," Bitsy said with total certainty. "That is to say Gaylord did. Sherm isn't bright enough, but Gaylord is. Gaylord's also a man who's accustomed to getting his way, and Hubie was fighting him. If you ask me, you have your culprits right there. Seems obvious."

"Bitsy, the only thing that's obvious right now is that somebody murdered Hubie. We have to explore every possible reason why."

Bitsy puffed out her cheeks, her gloved hands resting on the handle of her shovel. "You're wondering about the other woman. Do you think she might have a jealous husband?"

"It's certainly a possibility. Are you being straight with me? You really don't know who she is?"

"Oh, I suppose I could find out if I wanted to. But the truth is I *don't* want to, because once I know who she is the mental image of them naked together will stay with me for weeks, months, possibly even for the rest of my life. Every time I close my eyes I'll see them. So if you find out please don't tell me, okay? I want you to promise me, Des."

"I promise you. And I'm genuinely sorry for your loss."

"Thank you." Bitsy went back to her digging.

Des motioned to Mitch with her chin and the two of them walked away from Bitsy's ginormous shingled bungalow down toward the water's edge. They were about to lose their late-day sunshine. Dark storm clouds were approaching over Long Island Sound. A chilly wind had picked up. The water was getting choppy. Rain was expected by nightfall according to Jim Cantore of The Weather Channel, who was one of Mitch's idols. The greatest meteorologist ever.

"I got a very strange call from my dad today," Des told him as they strolled along the narrow strip of beach.

"Is that right? What did he want?"

She peered at him, frowning. "Why did your voice just do that?"

"Do what?"

"Get all high-pitched."

"It didn't get high-pitched."

"There, you hear that? Just did it again."

Mitch breathed in and out, steadying himself. "What did he. . . ?"

"He wants to meet me for lunch tomorrow. When I asked him what was up he got super evasive. This is going to be bad news, trust me."

"What kind of bad news?"

"My guess? He has to go back into the hospital. Either that or I'm being transferred out of Dorset and onto some crap undercover detail that involves me wearing hot pants, spandex, and a whole lot of fake fur."

"You know the man much better than I do, but it seems to me that if he had that kind of news he would have just told you. I wouldn't worry about it. He probably just wants to spend time with you."

"That's what Sunday afternoons are for. No, something's up. He sounded really weird."

"I wouldn't worry about it."

"That's the second time you've said that. Do you know something I don't know?"

"How would *I* know something? Why are you asking me that?"

"Whoa, big boy, you don't have to jump down my throat. I just wondered if you had an educated guess. You usually do."

"Not this time. I have no idea what he wants. None."

"Okay, you have no idea what he wants. None. And, no offense, but I must say you are acting a bit weird yourself right now. When did you last ingest chocolate? Does your body need chocolate?"

A thin strip of low clouds passed in front of the sun. Right away it felt five degrees colder. Mitch was wearing a jacket. Des wasn't. He took his off and draped it around her shoulders.

"What did you do that for?" she demanded.

"You were shivering."

"Was not. And I hate it when you treat me like a girlie girl."

"My bad. Here, I'll take it back."

"Not a chance. I'm freezing." She zipped it up and snuggled inside of it, her hands buried in the pockets. "Woo-hoo, I am loving this fleece lining."

"So how is the investigation going?" he asked her as they made their way past the lighthouse. "Is it still throwing you?"

"I'm afraid so. We have a million possibilities and they all add up to a lot of nothing. Yolie and Toni are having a team meeting right now at Town Hall with Latham and Zimmer. Maybe they can sort it out. Me, I keep thinking we're missing something that's staring right at us. And laughing at us."

"Well, if it's any help I think I know who Girlfriend Number Four is."

"You found her?"

"You asked me to look into it. I looked into it."

"Well, what did you find out? Who is she?"

"Here's the deal. I stopped by the library to drop off some freebies . . ."

"*And* mooch some of Nancy's soup," Des said, nodding.

"It was split pea today. Nancy uses sautéed pancetta in addition to a ham hock. And homemade chicken stock instead of water."

"Mitch . . ."

"I've got to try that sometime, but first I'll have to make a batch of chicken stock. What do you use for that, anyhow? Is it necks or backs or—?"

"*Mitch. . . !*"

"Yes, Des?"

"Nancy's house is an easy walk from Hubie's place. Are you telling me that he was slipping out in the night to visit her?"

"No, I'm not. Because he wasn't. Nancy and Hubie were strictly platonic friends. Besides, she's involved with a guy named Rick who used to work at the library with her. He lives in Santa Fe now."

"So what *are* you telling me?"

"Nadine Ambinder, Nancy's newest research librarian, called in sick today. There's a stomach bug going around, apparently."

"So. . . ?"

"So Nadine is young, lonely, writes bad poetry and—cue the drum roll—lives in Nancy's guest cottage. So Nancy told me that when Nadine joined them for dinner a couple of weeks ago she was so ill at ease around Hubie that she couldn't take her eyes off of her plate. Take my word for it, thin person. Nadine is Girlfriend Number Four."

"Do you have anything genuinely solid or is this just a hunch?"

"I'd call it a genuinely solid hunch. Have I ever steered you wrong?"

"Hell, yes."

"When?"

"That time you made me watch *Abbott and Costello Meet Frankenstein*."

"It's a seminal work. That was an important part of your film education."

"It was stupid."

"It's a seminal work."

"You really like the saying the word 'seminal,' don't you?"

"Is it that obvious?"

"Only to me."

"Nancy told me that Hubie used to spend a lot of time fixing things around her house. He stopped by the library a lot, too. Took a keen interest in the problems they've been having with their elevator. He also got very into the Aubrey-Maturin books."

"Yeah, I saw one on his nightstand. So what?"

"He was hovering around Nadine, that's so what."

Des mulled it over as they walked. "Hubie was old enough to

be her father," she pointed out. "Then again, Shannon and Inez both said that he wanted kids. So he might very well have been interested in someone Nadine's age."

"There, you see? You're already onboard."

"Slow down, cowboy. I wouldn't go that far. But I'll check it out. Shannon told me he went out prowling at least two nights a week. Any idea who Girlfriend Number Five might be?"

"Maybe there is no Girlfriend Number Five. Maybe he visited Nadine two nights a week."

"That doesn't fit his pattern."

"You're right, it doesn't. I'll keep at it. But first I have to run over to Duck River Cemetery. I want to snap a picture of Aurora Bing's tomb to go with my Warren William essay." He glanced up at the darkening sky. "I hope the rain holds off."

"Want to borrow my Nikon?"

"Thanks, but if I use the camera on my super-duper new Batphone I can zap the photo directly to the Web site and Facebook and Twitter with a push of a button. Des, I truly don't know how I lived without this thing."

"Are you getting decent shots with it?"

"Not in the same league as your Nikon, but pretty damned good." He pulled his phone out of the back pocket of his jeans, snapped her picture, and showed it to her. "See. . . ?"

She studied it, scowling. "Is that what I really look like?"

"Kind of. Why?"

"I come across as . . . fierce."

"Fierce happens to be very, very hot right now. I just read all about it in the latest issue of *Cosmo*. Pouty is out, fierce is in. Hell, you're fashionable and you don't even know it. They have a name for that, you know. It's called effortless chic."

Des shoved her heavy horn-rimmed glasses up her nose and said,

"I'm going to take my effortlessly chic self over to Nancy Franklin's house to have a chat with Nadine. I'll catch you later."

"Not so fast. You forgot three things. You didn't thank me for the 411 on Nadine. You didn't give me my jacket back. And you didn't kiss me."

"Thanks, baby." She kissed him, a long, lingering kiss. Then hugged him tightly before she said, "What if he's dying?"

"Your dad's not dying."

"He'd better not be, because if he is I swear I'm going to kill him." She gave Mitch back his jacket and kissed him once more, quickly this time, then went striding back across the sand toward her cruiser.

Mitch watched her go, smiling contentedly. There was no more captivating a sight on the planet than that of his long-stemmed, bootylicious ladylove walking away across a sandy beach. He gazed down at her picture on his cell, continuing to smile—until a thought suddenly occurred to him and he froze, his pulse quickening.

He raced back to Bitsy's garden, where she was still digging away at her drainage trench.

"I meant what I said, Mitch," she gasped, her chest rising and falling. "I don't need your help. I'm fine."

"Bitsy, we're good friends, right?"

"Why, yes. I like to think we are."

"I need to ask you something personal. You don't have to answer me if you don't want to. I'll certainly understand if you don't. But I'd really, really appreciate it if you would, okay?"

Bitsy stopped digging, her eyes narrowing at him slightly. "Okay, go ahead and ask me, Mitch."

And so he asked her.

CHAPTER 15

MOST OF THE LANDMARK houses in the Dorset Street Historic District were center-chimney Colonials, an architectural style that tended toward the spare and unadorned. Nancy Franklin's turreted gingerbread Victorian mansion was done up with so much ornamental trim and scrollwork that Des thought it looked like a giant three-story wedding cake. It was also painted the same exact color as French's mustard.

A light drizzle was starting to fall by the time she and Yolie arrived out in front of it in the Crown Vic. She'd had to pull Yolie out of her team meeting with Latham and Zimmer, although she hadn't needed to pull too hard. Yolie detested team meetings. Toni had stayed behind.

Nancy's house anchored a two-acre plot of land on the corner of Dorset Street and Beckwith Lane. There was a spiked wrought-iron fence around the entire property. A gate opened onto a brick path that led from Dorset Street to the front porch. Around on Beckwith a second gate opened onto another brick path that led Des and Yolie through a formal English rose garden edged with neatly trimmed boxwood. The guest cottage, a miniature replica of the big house, was set at the back of the garden. Des had looked into renting it when she moved to town, but it was too cute for her. Creepy cute.

"Who the hell lives here, the Sugar Plum Fairy?" Yolie groused.

"Dorset's newest librarian. And she's all flesh and blood, according to our source."

"Would our source happen to be a certain doughy film critic of the Jewish persuasion?"

"Hey, we asked him to nose around. He nosed around."

Des knocked. No one answered, though there was a light on inside.

"You sure she's here?"

"She called in sick today," Des replied, raising her voice. "Nadine, it's Resident Trooper Mitry!"

Still no answer. No sound of footsteps inside. Nothing.

Des grew concerned as she stood there with the drizzle falling on her big hat. Pounded on the door with her fist. "Nadine, may I come in, please?"

Finally, she heard the murmur of a voice from inside. Couldn't make out the words but took the response as a yes. The door was unlocked. They went in.

It was teeny-weeny and low ceilinged inside. Suffocating, too. The air was heavy with the cloying scent of that fruity perfume some old ladies wear. Des felt as if she were trapped inside of somebody's dollhouse as she loomed there in a parlor barely big enough for two armchairs and a coffee table. There was a Pullman-style kitchen, a bedroom with a single bed.

Nadine was curled up on top of the bed in a fetal position sobbing her head off. Her red, swollen nose was running. Her red, swollen eyes were streaming tears. Her face was all flushed and blotchy. The poor girl was a hot, snotty mess. The wadded-up tissue she was clutching was thoroughly sodden.

Des found a box of tissues in the bathroom and brought it to her.

Nadine used one to dab at her eyes and blow her nose. Then she sat up with her back against the pillows and chewed fretfully on her lower lip as she gazed up at them. Even at her best, Nadine was not particularly attractive. She had eyes that were a bit too close together and a nose that was more than a bit too broad. Her cheeks were chubby. Her chin was pointy. And the way she wore her mouse-colored hair, pulled back in a tight ponytail, did her no good at all. She had on a shapeless cable-stitched sweater and a pair of mommy jeans. She was decidedly plump through the haunches and thighs.

"This is my friend Yolanda Snipes from the Major Crime Squad," said Des, who'd chatted with Nadine a few times at the library and had come to think of her as Little Miss Strange. Pleasant enough, but also dreamy, childlike and, well, strange. "I understand you told Nancy that you'd picked up a stomach bug."

Nadine didn't answer. Just lowered her eyes.

"But that's not the truth. This is about Hubie, am I right?"

She blinked at Des in surprise. "What about Hubie?"

"You can talk to us about him, Nadine. It's okay."

"We're on your side," Yolie said. "We know all about the pain you're feeling right now."

"I want to die," Nadine sobbed. "I can't go on without him. I don't *want* to. I want to die."

"No, you don't," Des said. "You'll keep on going. You have to."

"How?" Nadine wondered plaintively. "Please, tell me how."

"Do you have family you can be with?"

"My parents don't understand me," she said, her eyes straying over to a notepad on the nightstand next to her. Verses were scribbled on it in pencil. "Besides, they live in Albany and I hate it there. It's cold. I like to be near the beach. The beach is so . . ." She trailed off, her eyes puddling with tears. "I don't know what I'll do."

Des tilted her hat back on her head. "Do you have a good friend?"

"There's Martha, my roommate from SUNY Binghamton. She

teaches first grade in North Carolina now. You think I should I go visit her?"

"Sounds like a good idea to me."

"But before you hop on the interstate," Yolie said, "we need to ask you some questions about Hubie."

"What kind of questions?"

"Why don't you tell us about your relationship," Des suggested.

"He was m-my everything," Nadine said softly. "I'd been waiting my whole life for Hubie. And he'd been waiting his whole life for me. He felt sure of it the very first time he saw me sitting there at the reference desk. Hubie was incredibly open about his emotions that way. I used to read him my poems. He'd brush my hair while I read them. He loved to brush my hair. He was so gentle and understanding and . . ." She smiled at them shyly. "With Hubie it was the first time I enjoyed the sex. There were a couple of boys when I was in school but they were always in such a hurry. Hubie was patient and considerate. He never pressured me. Some nights he'd be perfectly happy if all we did was cuddle. There was a big age difference between us. He was two years older than my father, in fact. But that didn't matter to me." She gazed down at her hands in her lap. Her nails were unpainted and chewed to the quick. "He gave me this," she said, showing them a jade ring on her right ring finger. "Isn't it beautiful?"

"Very beautiful," Des said. "Was he in the habit of visiting you here?"

Nadine nodded. "Two nights a week."

Des and Yolie exchanged a glance. Two nights a week definitely qualified Nadine as more special to Hubie than his other ladies were. Now they were getting somewhere. Maybe.

"He'd get here right around midnight. I kept a candle burning in the window for him. And he'd always leave before dawn."

"Why so much secrecy?" Yolie asked her.

"It wasn't my idea, believe me. I wanted us to be a normal couple. Cook dinner for him at his house. Go to the movies together. But Hubie said that if we were seen together then people would start whispering nasty things about me and I'd lose my job. He thought we should keep our relationship a secret until we were ready to announce our engagement."

Des exchanged another glance with Yolie before she said, "And when was that going to be?"

"Soon. We were planning to start a family right away. We wanted at least two kids. Maybe three."

"How long had you been seeing each other, Nadine?"

"A little over two months. Hubie was always stopping by the library to chat with Nancy. One day he just came up to me at the reference desk and started talking to me. Asked me if I liked my job. Asked me how much I'd seen of Dorset. He told me I just had to take a walk out to the Peck's Point Nature Preserve at sunset sometime because it was really, really special. He offered to take me there that day after work. Since he was a friend of Nancy's and seemed nice enough I said okay." Nadine gazed down at her hands again, swallowing. "It was real cold out and the wind was blowing, but it's incredibly beautiful out at Peck's Point. Such amazing views of the Sound. And the sunset that day was one of those really special ones where the sky's streaked with more shades of red than you ever knew existed. We were totally alone out there, but I felt safe with Hubie. Believe me, that doesn't usually happen when I'm with a man. Especially one who I barely know. I felt like I could say anything to Hubie and he'd understand what I meant. There was this instant *bond* between us. When we were walking back to our cars he told me that I'd been in his thoughts ever since the first time he'd seen me at the desk. When I asked him why, he said,

'Because I think you're beautiful.' Then he put his arms around me and kissed me, and right away I knew that I'd met my soul mate."

"We checked his cell," Yolie said. "Your soul mate never phoned you."

"He never had to. He promised me he'd be here every Monday and Wednesday at midnight, and he always was."

"Nancy is right across the garden in the big house," Des said. "She never spotted him coming or going?"

"Never. She goes to bed early and takes Ambien so she'll sleep."

"How do you know that?"

"She told me."

"Nadine, where were you yesterday between five and six P.M.?"

"On duty at the reference desk. The library stays open until seven o'clock three evenings a week so that people with full-time jobs can stop by after work. And the study room gets a real work-out, too. That's when the high school kids schedule their tutoring sessions."

"Was anyone being tutored yesterday at that time?"

"The Miller boy. His teacher, Ward Tatum, was working with him. Ward's real dedicated. He's there practically . . ." Nadine let out a sob. "Oh, God, what am I going to do?"

"You're going to mourn Hubie," Des told her. "And then you're going to get on with your life."

"I don't see how I can. I—I just don't."

"You have to. Hubie would want you to."

"Do you really think so?" she snuffled, dabbing at her eyes with a tissue.

"I do. We're going to leave you now, Nadine. Thank you for your time. And we're sorry for your loss."

They went back outside into the late-afternoon drizzle.

"Know what I hate the most about this case?" Yolie grumbled as they started back across the garden. "It keeps depressing the hell out of me."

"I know."

"I mean, that librarian in there is just plain pathetic."

"I know."

"Girl, is that all you've got for me?"

"What do you want to me to say, Yolie?"

"I was kind of hoping you'd cheer me up."

"Do you want a lollipop?"

"A lollipop? Yeah, a lollipop would go down pretty good right now."

"Too bad. I haven't got any."

"Wow, you're not very good at the cheering-up thing."

"I never said I was."

As they approached the Crown Vic, Toni pulled up behind it in the turbo-charged Taurus. Yolie got in front with her. Des got in back. The three of them sat there in tired silence for a moment watching two hyperkinetic boys on skateboards fool around on the wet sidewalk outside of the ice cream parlor.

"How did the team meeting go?" Yolie finally asked Toni.

"Not great, Loo," she answered, puffing out her cheeks. "Zimmer found Sid, Sherm Gant's kitchen supply sleaze, drinking beer at a sports bar in West Haven called 744 West. Sherm's story about the exhaust fan checks out, three-thousand-dollar price tag and all. Sid confirmed it."

"And Zimmer believed the guy?"

"He said he was inclined to."

"What's his reason?"

"Sid still had the thing in the back of his truck out in the parking lot."

"Good reason," Yolie conceded, as Des sat there staring out the window at the skateboarders, lost in her own thoughts.

"I don't mean to be a Debbie Downer, Loo, but we're getting *nowhere*. Sherm Gant and Gaylord Holland were both at the Clam House when the fire broke out. Leland Gant was at Center School with Brianna. . . ."

"Actually, we picked up a little something there," Yolie said. "Brianna's the only one who can vouch for Leland's whereabouts between five and five thirty. And that girl would do anything for Leland, including lie for him." She glanced over the seat at Des. "Wouldn't you say?"

Des nodded absently. "I would . . ."

Yolie frowned at her. "You've got something on your mind. What is it?"

"It keeps bothering me, that's all. Seemed odd last evening and still does."

"*What* does?"

"The tailpipe on Hubie's Explorer was cold. So was the hood. Our Fire Chief's pickup was still warm. That means Hubie arrived at the scene an hour or more before the fire started. And that's just plain odd. Toni, what was the tide doing there yesterday afternoon at, say, four o'clock?"

"Hang on . . ." Toni grabbed her laptop and went searching for the tidal calendar. "Okay, here we are. It was peaking. High tide yesterday at Sound View Beach was four seventeen P.M."

"Which means Hubie wasn't out strolling on the beach, because when it's high tide at Sound View there *is* no beach. So what was he doing there?"

"You're not selling us that he torched The Pit himself, are you?"

"No, I'm not, Yolie."

"Good, because that would be too strange—even for Dorset."

"Everybody keeps mentioning how thorough and professional our victim was," Toni said.

"What's your point, Sergeant?"

"Maybe he was having another look around The Pit before he made his final decision about whether to let Sherm reopen it or not. Maybe he happened to stumble upon somebody who was busy squirting lighter fluid all over the damned place. A confrontation ensued. His head got bashed in. Our perp lit a match and *whoosh,* there went The Pit."

"That plays," Yolie had to admit.

"No, it doesn't," Des argued.

"Why not?" Toni asked.

"Because I don't think this case is about the battle Hubie was having with Sherm over The Pit. Or about those two houses on the Lieutenant River that he and Gaylord were fighting over. I don't think it has a thing to do with Hubie's job. This is about Nadine, who thought Hubie was her soul mate. And Inez, who thought Hubie was going to rescue her from that nasty, ungrateful mother of hers with those gangrenous toes—and if you *ever* hear the words 'gangrenous toes' come out of my mouth again I want you to shoot me. It's about Bitsy, who never thought she'd find love again. It's about Loretta, who told us Hubie made her so giddy that Gaylord, who happens to be very possessive, was starting to get suspicious. It pains me to admit this but I'm starting to believe Mitch was right. This case is about Hubie and his women. Or I should say, Hubie and one pissed-off woman. The woman he met up with yesterday afternoon at The Pit for a secret tryst. The woman who'd found out she wasn't the one and only true love of his life. I think she went there intending to kill him. I think she confronted him about his lying ways, bashed in his head, and set the fire to cover her tracks."

Yolie mulled this over for a moment before she said, "You figure she brought the lighter fluid with her?"

"I do. Sherm wouldn't leave a container of it lying around all winter."

Toni raised her hand. "May I ask a stupid question?"

"Just ask it! This ain't no damned classroom!"

"Sorry, Loo. Right, Loo. How'd they get inside? The Pit was all locked up, wasn't it?"

"Sherm probably kept a spare key stashed outside somewhere. Maybe Hubie knew where it was. Maybe she did. Besides, it was no big to get into that place. Kids broke in all of the time to party." Des gazed out the window at the boys on their skateboards, who were playfully haranguing each other and laughing. The drizzle wasn't bothering them. Nothing was bothering them. She wished she could trade places with them right now. "Here's what we know about Hubie. He was a neat, organized little man who kept all four of his women carefully compartmentalized. None of them knew about the others, or so Hubie believed. What he didn't know was that his love train was starting to derail. Bitsy had become positive that he was seeing another woman."

"Bitsy has an alibi," Yolie pointed out.

"A woman who has long fingernails that left scratches on his back," Des went on. "Inez has long fingernails and *no* alibi. Neither does Loretta. That makes two of his ladies who are unaccounted for."

"What about Nadine?" Toni asked. "Where was she?"

"On the reference desk. Or so she claims."

"She wouldn't be dumb enough to lie to us about that, would she?" Yolie said.

"Dumb, no. But she's definitely on the strange side."

"True that." Yolie stuck her lower lip out thoughtfully. "Hubie was Inez's shot at a better life. And she struck me as a scrappy little battler."

"What's your point, Loo?"

"I don't see her killing the guy. If she found out about his other women, I mean. I see her giving him grief, then hunting down those other women and telling them to leave her man alone or she'd claw their eyes out. Inez wanted him for keeps. Unlike, say, Loretta, who wanted to break it off with him. So I don't see her bashing in his skull, either. Why would she?"

"Maybe Hubie refused to go quietly," Toni said. "Maybe he threatened to out her as the town tramp if she tried to end it. He could have made life hard for her around here if he'd wanted to."

"I don't buy it. Hubie would never go public about their affair. He still had three other women on the string, remember?" Yolie looked at Des. "Could Sheila Enman have lied to us about Bitsy being with her when it went down?"

"Sheila's a very moral person. I don't believe she'd cover up a murder. Not even for a friend."

"Which leaves us with strange but not-stupid Nadine. If *she* charbroiled Hubie she wouldn't be waiting around for us to discover that she wasn't working the desk at the time of the murder. She'd be halfway to Florida by now." Yolie shook her head. "I don't see it. I can't picture any of these four women as our perp. It doesn't play for me."

"So where are we, Loo?"

"Nowhere, Sergeant," Yolie growled. "We're nowhere."

Des felt her cell vibrate on her belt. Glanced down at the screen, excused herself, and stepped out onto the sidewalk to take the call. The drizzle was becoming a light, steady rain now. "You were right about Nadine, boyfriend," she said into the phone. "She thought that she and Hubie were going to have a whole houseful of kids together. Did you get your pictures of Aurora's tomb?"

"Afraid not," he mumbled, chomping away on a mouthful of food. "Something came up."

"And now, wait, don't tell me, you're sitting on the love seat in front of the fire scarfing Cocoa Puffs straight from the box."

"What little is left in the box. You practically cleaned me out last night. If you're developing a taste for them I'll have to start buying in bulk at one of those discount stores where they forklift them onto the back of your pickup for you. That's assuming I still have a functioning pickup by next week. Did I tell you that my front end let out a whole new groan when I turned the—?"

"Kind of busy here right now. What's going on?"

"Got a question for you. Do you remember when I got my new Mac Pro laptop a few months back?"

"I do. What about it?"

"Do you remember my techie, Doogie Howser?"

"I remember that wasn't his real name. You just called him that."

"Well, I've been thinking about something that happened when Doogie was transferring everything from my old laptop onto my new one."

"Okay, this doesn't sound like a question. More like one of your stories that'll somehow end up circling all of the way back around to Arlene Francis."

"*Anne* Francis. And hear me out, will you? Doogie was showing me the new dashboard icons at the bottom of the screen, okay? My Contacts, Calendar, Mail, all of that. And he was whipping his way through them, one after another, in that insufferably smug way that geeks do when they're talking about stuff they know all about and we don't. Until he got to the iPhoto icon, stopped cold, and in a super-serious voice said, 'Do I have your permission to access your personal photos?' I thought it was really, really strange the way he suddenly turned so formal. I said, 'Of course you do. Why wouldn't you?' And he said, 'I always have to make sure to ask—because I never, ever know what I might find.'"

Standing there in the rain, Des felt her heart start to pound.

"Are you still there, girlfriend?"

"Still here. You're asking me about the photo album on Hubie's laptop. You want to know if Toni's had a look at it yet. I don't know. I'll ask her."

"Will you call me back?"

"I'll call you back." She rang off and got back in the Taurus. Yolie and Toni both eyed her expectantly. "Mitch has a question for Toni."

"For me?" Toni's eyes widened. "What is it?"

"He wondered if you've searched the photo album on Hubie's laptop yet."

Toni didn't say. Just sat there in tight-lipped silence.

"Well, have you?" Yolie asked her.

"When would I have done that, Loo?" she answered defensively. "I've only had it for a few hours, and you and I both know I zeroed in on the victim's financials, e-mails, and cell log. That's standard protocol and it's super time-consuming and *you're* the one who hates calling in the Computer Crimes people. Which, believe me, I am perfectly fine with. But there's only one of me, Loo. Remember that murder-suicide we caught in Salem last winter? I didn't get to the photo album for two whole freaking—"

"Does that mean no?"

"Plus you ordered me to fetch Petey and Darla and then babysit them. And that skank would *not* shut up."

"Does that mean no?" Yolie asked her again, louder this time.

"I was planning to do it tonight," Toni informed her.

"Maybe you'd better do it now."

"You mean right here and now?"

Yolie nodded her head slowly up and down.

"Sure, Loo. Whatever you say." Hubie's laptop was in a clear plastic evidence bag on the front seat. She removed it from the bag and flicked it on. When it had powered up she logged on with Hubie's personal password and accessed his photo album. "We're in," she said briskly, her little fingers flying across the keyboard. "He's got *tons* of photos of buildings in here. Not a surprise, considering he was the building inspector. He's got construction sites. He's got empty lots, septic tanks . . . Okay, wait, here's a bunch of baby pictures."

"Let me see those." Des leaned forward over the seat for a better look. "That's Tommy Burns, Jr. Shannon calls him T.J."

Yolie raised an eyebrow at her. "That's the neighbor, right? You had a funny feeling about who might have fathered her child."

"And it just got funnier."

Toni continued searching. "Okay, here's a lovely shot of a huge underground oil tank that's being dug out. What is that, a thousand gallons? Let's see, what else have we. . . ?" She let out a gasp. "Oh. My. God."

"What is it, Sergeant?" Yolie demanded.

"Des, how on earth did Mitch know?"

"How did he know what, Sergeant?"

"The man took pictures, Loo," Toni answered in a hushed voice. "He's got hundreds of nude photos of his lady friends on here and, oh, jeez, himself, too. This is way too much information for me. And what *is* it with old people and all of that pubic hair? Don't they know how disgusting it is?"

"How *did* Mitch know?" Yolie asked Des.

"I truly have no idea. The man's instincts are uncanny. I used to think it had to do with how many thousands of movies he's seen.

But I'm starting to come around to the idea that he may simply be an idiot savant."

"Okay, let's see who we've got . . ." Toni began scrolling through Hubie's X-rated photo gallery of his lady friends in bed, on the bed, enjoying bubble baths. The photos appeared to have been taken in a succession of hotel rooms.

"That's Bitsy," Des said, hating what she did for a living at this moment.

"And there's Inez," Yolie said. "*All* of Inez . . . And Loretta. She's got a smokin' bod for a lady her age."

"That she does," Toni said, moving on to another set of photos that had been taken in the bedroom of the dollhouse Des and Yolie had just visited.

"Damn, Nadine sure strips heavy from the waist down," Yolie observed. "I played with a power forward at Rutgers named Natitia who was built like her. When Natitia established position in the low post you could not budge her."

"Wait, wait, we've got somebody else here," Toni said excitedly. "Can you believe it? That horny old goat had himself another one. I *think* I've seen this woman around town somewhere. Do we know who she is?"

"We know," Des said, staring at the photos. Her cell vibrated on her belt. She got out of the car again and stood on the sidewalk in the rain, which was coming down harder. The merry skateboarders had skateboarded on home. "What is it now?" she said into the phone.

"You said you were going to call me back."

"I was just about to."

"Did you find anyone who you weren't expecting to find?"

"As a matter of fact we did."

"Well, don't keep me in suspense. Who is it?"

"Mitch, we're not going to do this."

"Do what?"

"Pull whatever crazy scheme that's bubbling around inside of your brain. We're talking about an individual who has been incredibly careful. That means we've got to handle this a hundred and ten percent by the book."

"Which will get you a hundred and ten percent nowhere. Des, I can do what you can't do."

"Which is. . . ?"

"Get her to show her hand."

"Pull over and stop right now. We've talked about the e-word before."

"It's only entrapment when *you* do it. If *I* do it then it's—"

"Sheer lunacy. Besides, it's not kosher."

"You're so cute when you go Jewy on me, know that? It's a few minutes past five. Our timing couldn't be better. Just leave everything to me and I'll . . . Oh, hell, I have another call. Can I put you on hold for a quick sec?"

"Sure," she sighed, standing there in the rain with her stomach churning.

"Okay, I'm back," he announced when he returned. "Just leave everything to me. I have a plan."

"Baby, you always have a plan. And I always end up having to rush you to the Shoreline Clinic emergency room at ninety miles per hour. You *promised* me you were going to stay out of the fray this time, remember?"

"That's the beauty of this. My plan won't expose me to physical danger of any kind."

"Is that right? How are you going to manage that?"

"You don't really want me to tell you, do you? That would give you prior knowledge."

He wasn't wrong about that, Des had to concede. "All right, then answer me this. Just exactly how do you intend to set your plan in motion when you don't know the identity of the surprise somebody whom we found in Hubie's photo album."

"But I do know her identity."

"You do? How?"

"You told me."

"I didn't tell you. When did I tell you?"

"Besides, it so happens I've already set the plan in motion."

Des drew in her breath. "When?"

"Just now, when I put you on hold."

"Mitch . . ."

"All it took was a simple phone call. The best plans are the simple ones. It's when you get complicated that you run into trouble. I should write a book about it someday."

"*Mitch* . . ."

"Yes, Des?"

"You are *the* most colossal pain in the ass I've ever known in my life."

"I love you, too, you big lug. Here's what the three of you need to do now. And I mean *right* now, because you have to scoot. Where are you?"

"Parked outside Nancy's house."

"That'll work. Leave your cars there and hoof it to Town Hall."

"Town Hall's all locked up for the night. It's after five, remember?"

"Yeah, but you have a key don't you?"

"So?"

"So let yourselves in, go into the auxiliary conference room, and lock the door behind you. That's vital. Be sure to lock the door. Then sit down at the conference table with the lights out and don't make a sound, okay? Oh, and I almost forgot the most important part—bring Hubie's laptop and cell with you."

"You want her to think that we've locked them in there for the night?"

"Precisely."

"We'd never do that. The conference room isn't a secure evidence lockup. We'd take them to the Troop F barracks in Westbrook."

"You know that and I know that. Well, I know it now. But the killer doesn't."

"Mitch, I'm not liking this."

"Not to worry, it'll work. You may have to hang there for a while, but don't lose patience. When the killer shows I'll call you. I'll be staked out on Dorset Street."

"You will not. You'll be tucked safely at home with your cats watching *Mr. Blandings Builds His Dream House.*"

"Relax, will you? I'll park a safe distance away and use my binoculars. That's assuming, of course, my truck doesn't steer itself into a ditch on my way there. We're talking rain-slickened pavement now. But that's a chance I'll just have to take. Des, I have a lot to do right now so I'm going to hang up. I'll call you when the killer shows." And with that he rang off.

Des stood there in the rain staring at her phone and wondering how on earth this maddening blimp of a man had so completely taken over her life. She'd let him, that's how. This was on her. She should have reined him in way back when she had the chance. Or shot him.

She got back inside the Taurus and said, "Somehow, Mitch has figured out on his own who that surprise somebody is in Hubie's photo album. He's concocted a plan, *and* he's already set the plan in motion. "

"Of course he has," Yolie huffed. "It's his case. I'm just here using up oxygen. What does he want us to. . . ? Wait, step out of the car, Sergeant. You'll be better off if you don't hear this."

"No way, Loo. I know the drill. I'm all in."

"You sure about that?"

"Positive. Our job is to close out the case, period. We do whatever it takes. Sometimes that means a no-good snitch gets to walk. Sometimes money changes hands. And sometimes . . . sometimes there's a Mitch."

"I don't think there's such a thing as a Mitch," Des pointed out. "There's just Mitch."

"I'm down with that." Yolie stared across the seat at her. "Let's hear it."

"He wants us to walk to Town Hall, lock ourselves in the auxiliary conference room, and wait in there with the lights out."

"Wait in there for what?"

"For the killer to show up."

"That's it? That's all there is?"

Des nodded. "That's all there is."

"Then let's do it," Yolie said, opening her car door.

"Oh, hey, Toni? Bring Hubie's laptop and cell," Des said. "Leave the cannolis."

Toni frowned at her. "Leave the what?"

"Nothing. Never mind. I have definitely been spending too much time around that man."

"Shouldn't we let Latham and Zimmer in on this, Loo?"

"Yes, but no," Yolie responded quietly as they sat there in the dark with the door locked. They'd been in the auxiliary conference room for twenty minutes now. It was dusk out, and the rain was coming down hard. Town Hall was all locked up for the night. There was no one else in the building. "We're not tight with them. If this goes south they'll burn us to save their own booties. If it works we'll give them a share of the credit and they'll be happy."

"But won't they want to know the details?"

"Who, Latham? No way. He's strictly the 'don't ask, don't tell' type. Wouldn't you say so, Miss Thing?"

"Yes, I would." Des's cell vibrated on the table before her. Mitch. She picked up and said, "What have you got?"

"*Serious* trouble with my front end. I could barely keep this old truck on the road. I sure hope I don't need new tie rods. They may not even make them anymore."

"Mitch . . ."

"She's pulling up outside of Town Hall right now."

"Okay," Des said. "Where are you?"

"Down by the firehouse," he answered as Des heard him fumble with his binoculars. "She's getting out of her car. Closing her door. Standing on the sidewalk in the rain and looking around, still looking around, not seeing anyone. . . . Okay, here she comes. She's starting her way up the path toward the front door of the building. Stay totally quiet now, got it? I'm here in case you need me." And then he rang off.

Des put her phone on the table and whispered, "Don't make a sound."

They sat there in the dark. Heard the front door to Town Hall open and close. Heard brisk footsteps on the polished oak floor out in the main corridor. Heard those footsteps approach closer and closer to the auxiliary conference room. Now the footsteps were right outside of the door. Des drew in her breath. Heard the doorknob being jiggled. Then heard the creaking and snapping of someone trying to jimmy the door open. With a loud *crack* the lock gave way. The door to the room swung open. And there, silhouetted by the night-lights of the corridor, stood the woman who'd murdered Hubie Swope and burned The Pit to the ground.

"Why, hello, Mary Ellen." Des smiled at Dorset's town nurse, who had a key to the building but not to any offices or rooms other than her own.

Mary Ellen Tatum let out a gasp of dismay as she stood there in the doorway, pry bar in hand.

"We were just sitting here trying to figure out who torched your brother's place. Didn't realize the door was locked. Why don't you come in and join us?"

Mary Ellen remained frozen in the doorway for a moment before she glanced furtively in the direction of the building's front door.

"Don't try to make a run for it," Yolie warned her. "You can't."

"It's okay, I won't," Mary Ellen said in a thin, defeated voice. She came in and sat down with them, placing the pry bar on the table with a clunk. "Des, I've discovered something about myself in these past twenty-four hours."

"Which is what?"

"I'm no good at carrying around a load of guilt. I'm . . . tired. I've never felt this tired in m-my entire . . ." Mary Ellen let out a sob and then began to weep.

"Call Latham, Sergeant. Tell him to get over here, ASAP."

"Right, Loo."

"And turn on some lights, will you? I hate sitting in the damned dark."

CHAPTER 16

DES DIDN'T KEEP HIM waiting out there for long.

Mary Ellen hadn't been inside for more than a few minutes when his ladylove came striding out of Town Hall and down Dorset Street toward him in the rain. She got in the Studey and sat there staring across the seat at him in stunned disbelief, beads of water dripping from her big hat.

"Does this mean you got her?"

"We got her. Yolie's reading the lady her rights. She doesn't want a lawyer. Wants to talk. We're just waiting for Latham and Zimmer. We don't want to cut them out of this."

"Sure, I understand."

"Mitch, I *don't* understand. How on earth did you. . . ?"

"I called Mary Ellen up, told her I was feeling dizzy, and asked her if she'd mind stopping by to have another look at me. She said no prob, she'd be right over. While she was shining her light in my eyes I mentioned how tied up you've been with the investigation. She asked me, super casual, how it was going. I told her, super casual, that you people had turned up squat at the crime scene and had moved on to Hubie's laptop and cell. That you'd been poring over his personal finances and e-mails, and that next you'd be searching his photo album for leads. When she asked me what sort of leads I told her you'd spitballed that maybe Hubie had been getting ready to condemn somebody's house or place of business and maybe he took photographs of it. Which sounds believable, doesn't it?"

"I guess, but . . ."

"Mary Ellen knew that Hubie had photographed her naked self. She knew it meant you'd come knock-knocking on her door tomorrow with a whole lot of questions that she didn't want to answer. She had to get her hands on that laptop and cell pronto and destroy them. I give her credit for being reasonably subtle about it. She started marveling about the way computer experts can keep their eyeballs and fingers going all night long. I told her Toni's not like that. She's a normal human being with a normal same-sex love life who'd already clocked out and gone home. Which prompted Mary Ellen to speculate that Toni probably took the laptop home with her to work on after dinner. Which prompted me to school her in how the whole chain of custody thing works when you're dealing with critical evidence. As in you can't take it with you. It has to be kept locked overnight in a designated secure location, which was why you'd asked Glynis for permission to designate the auxiliary conference room as your temporary field headquarters. Town Hall is a secure building, and the door to the conference room can be locked."

"Are you telling me she *bought* that?"

"Girlfriend, you'd be amazed what people will believe if you act like you know what you're talking about. Especially when they're scared out of their wits, which Mary Ellen most definitely was. She suggested I get a good night's sleep and call her in the morning. Then she sped like hell out of there. I made my way here and, sure enough, she showed up maybe five minutes after I did. Had to stop off at home to pick up a pry bar is my guess."

"Your guess is right. But I still don't understand."

"Don't understand what?"

"How you knew that it was Mary Ellen."

"You told me."

"*When?*"

"You said that Nadine Ambinder was on duty on the reference desk when The Pit got torched, correct?"

"Correct."

"And that Mary Ellen's husband, Ward—which, by the way, I still think is a funny name—was tutoring a kid in the study room at the time, correct?"

"Correct."

"That left Mary Ellen, Dorset's tireless angel of mercy, unaccounted for—beyond what little she told you, which was that she and Ward had been sitting down to dinner when Sherm called with the news about the fire. Don't ask me what they were having for dinner because I don't have that information, sad to say. But I do know that she's someone who spent a lot of time with Hubie back when his wife, Joanie, was dying."

"They were neighbors," Des acknowledged. "Mary Ellen had their spare key so she could look in on Joanie when Hubie wasn't home."

"And when he *was* home the two of them had every opportunity to get involved. It wouldn't surprise me one bit if they started sleeping together while Joanie was still alive. Even if they didn't I'll bet you a shiny quarter that Mary Ellen was the first of Hubie's multiple conquests, which means she was involved with him the longest of the bunch and was therefore eligible to be *the* most pissed off when she found out he was a no-good cheating dog."

An unmarked Crown Vic pulled up outside of Town Hall followed by a pair of State Police cruisers.

"Latham and Zimmer," Des informed him as two men got out of the Crown Vic, one middle-aged, one young. "Let's go in. You may as well hear what she has to say."

"You don't mind?"

She smiled at him. "I don't mind."

The door to the auxiliary conference room was wide open, its frame in splinters. Mary Ellen was seated at the conference table wearing her brightly patterned nurse's smock and white trousers, her wiry copper-colored hair glistening from the rain as she dabbed at her eyes with a tissue. She'd been weeping. Yolie and Toni sat across the table from her watching her with stern expressions on their faces. Latham and Zimmer were getting themselves settled there. They both looked mystified.

When Mary Ellen looked up and saw Mitch standing there she cried out, "You *liar*!" And came lunging up out of her chair at him.

Des stepped quickly between them. "Sit back down, Mary Ellen," she said calmly. "Sit back down and behave yourself."

"That man's a conniving bastard! He *tricked* me!"

"Sit back down," Des said once again. "If you don't I'll have to cuff you to your chair. Do you want that?"

Mary Ellen continued to glare at Mitch as she sank back into her chair.

Des took a seat at the table. Mitch sat down next to her.

Latham frowned at him. "Who's he?"

"He's with me," Des answered.

"He's not a reporter, is he?"

"Actually, I do have a master's degree from the Columbia University Graduate School of Journalism," Mitch said.

"But he's not here acting as a reporter," Des told Latham.

Latham shook his head. "*Why* is he here?"

"Leave it alone," Yolie advised him. "Trust me, you'll be much happier if you do." She set a microcassette recorder on the table and flicked it on. Stated the date, time, and the names of the State Police personnel who were present, then said, "Your name is Mary Ellen Tatum. You live at number twenty Lavender Lane in the town of Dorset. You are speaking to us voluntarily and have chosen to do so without the presence of legal counsel. Is all of that correct?"

"Yes, it is," Mary Ellen said.

Yolie folded her big arms before her on the table. "Okay, Mary Ellen, you said you wanted to talk. Let's talk."

"What do you want to know?" Mary Ellen asked, sounding deflated and beaten. Her fury was gone. So was the cheery, bemused voice that Mitch was accustomed to hearing. This was not the Mary Ellen Tatum whom he'd known for so many months.

"For starters, when did you discover that you weren't the only woman in Hubie Swope's life?"

Mary Ellen's mouth tightened to a narrow slit before she said, "Two nights ago. Our place is four houses down the lane from Hubie's, but we're set way back from the road at the end of a long driveway, practically in the woods."

"Which would explain why Shannon Burns saw him stepping out at night and you didn't," Mitch said, nodding.

Mary Ellen blinked at him in shock. "*Shannon* knew?"

"You didn't tell me he was going to speak," Latham murmured at Des.

She elbowed Mitch in the ribs. Hard.

He took this to mean he should be seen but not heard.

"Please continue," Yolie said to Mary Ellen.

"Ward and I were getting ready for bed when I realized that I'd forgotten to get our mail. I threw on my fleece sweats, grabbed a flashlight, and went down to the mailbox to get it. It was late, nearly midnight. I was just about to open the box when I heard footsteps in the road. I couldn't imagine who was out walking that late. I flicked off the light, stepped back behind our arborvitae hedge, and discovered it was *Hubie* heading toward Dorset Street. I started to say hello to him but then I stopped myself. I wondered where he was going at that hour and, well, I decided to follow him."

"So you were suspicious?"

"Not exactly. I had no reason to be suspicious. I was curious, that's all. He led me straight to Nancy Franklin's house and went around to the guest cottage in back where that young librarian, Nadine, lives. Her place was dark but she'd lit a candle. He went inside and . . . there was a gap in the curtains. I could see them through the window, hugging and kissing and *undressing* each other. I watched until I couldn't watch any longer. Ran home as fast as I could. Ward wondered what on earth had taken me so long. I told him I'd been chasing away a stray cat that was trying to sleep in our garage. Then I undressed, got into bed, and lay there with my fists clenched and my insides boiling. I—I felt betrayed and used and stupid beyond belief. I don't do that," she said, gazing around the table at them. "I never, ever do that."

"Do what, Mary Ellen?" Des asked.

"Sleep with other men. But I loved Hubie Swope with all of my heart, and he loved me. He'd told me so a million times. Except now . . . now I knew he hadn't meant it. That what we had together meant nothing to him. He *lied* to me. Can you imagine how much that hurt?" Mary Ellen swallowed, fighting back more tears. "I was a decent person before I got involved with Hubie. He made me into someone despicable. A cheat. A tramp. I'm *not* a tramp."

"And you're not a killer, either," Yolie said. "Except you are. How long were you and Hubie Swope involved?"

"We started sleeping together three weeks after Joanie's funeral. I wouldn't, *we* wouldn't while she was still alive. But we'd been emotionally involved for a long while before that. I sat with him every evening those last months when Joanie was slipping away. We'd talk for hours. He was so alone. I was, too. Alone, I mean.

I'd thought I was happy with Ward but I began to realize that I wasn't, because when Hubie and I talked Hubie *listened* to me. He thought I was interesting. He made me feel special. Ward doesn't. We've just been going through the routine motions for a long, long time. There's no passion. No affection. Ward cares more about his students than he does me. He hardly ever tells me what's on his mind. Hubie did. He was open and vulnerable. He needed me, and I wanted to be needed. I found myself looking forward to stopping by every evening to see Joanie because it meant that I'd get to sit and talk with Hubie. That's all we did. Talk. But we both knew."

"Knew what?" Yolie asked her.

"That we were meant to be together. I found love again with Hubie, and he found it with me. After Joanie passed we had a second chance at happiness together. We had a plan. We were waiting a few more months for Hubie to become fully vested in the town employees' pension plan like I am. Then I was going to divorce Ward and Hubie and I were going to start a new life together somewhere. We'd been talking about Nova Scotia."

"And in the meantime," Yolie said, "the two of you met secretly somewhere on a regular basis and had sex together."

Mary Ellen reddened. "Yes."

"Did Ward know about your affair?"

She shook her head. "He knows that I was being a supportive friend to Hubie, but it would never occur to him that another man would find me attractive enough to want me."

"Why not?"

"Because *he* doesn't."

Yolie's eyes narrowed. "I see . . ."

Mary Ellen gazed at her curiously. "Do you, Lieutenant? I don't think you have the slightest idea what I mean. How could you? You're still young and desirable. Wait twenty years. Wait and see how *you* feel when men start looking right through you as if you're not there. Even your own husband. *Especially* your own husband. And then see how you feel when a decent, kindly man takes an interest in you and tells you he adores you. Then you'll be qualified to sit there and judge me."

"There were no phone calls between you and Mr. Swope on his cell log. How come?"

"Because there was no need for us to speak on the phone," Mary Ellen explained. "We communicated in person here at Town Hall."

"Where did the two of you usually meet?"

"At the Bayberry Motor Lodge just outside of Mystic."

"It didn't show up on any of his credit cards."

"We always paid cash."

"Did you have a regular day and time?" Des asked.

"Not exactly. We'd try to meet whenever Ward had one of his after-school tutoring sessions at the library. Those typically run from five until seven. Some weeks we'd meet twice. Some weeks we wouldn't meet at all. But that was our time. And the Bayberry was our place. It's a dumpy little place," she said fondly. "But it was ours. Just us."

"Just you *and* his camera phone, you mean."

Mary Ellen reddened once again. "I'm no nineteen-year-old swimsuit model, God knows, but Hubie loved to photograph me with my clothes off. It excited him. I could see how it excited him. I wanted to make him happy. I loved him. And he told me that he loved me. Whenever we'd meet that was always the very first thing he'd say to me: 'Have I told you recently that I love you?' Hubie Swope convinced me that I was the great love of his life. I opened up my heart to him. And he—he broke it," she said despairingly. "It shattered into a million little pieces while I stood outside of Nadine's window watching the two of them together. I—I couldn't live with that much pain. I had to let him know that he couldn't treat me that way. I had to—to teach him a lesson."

"You had to do something else, too," Des said. "Didn't you?"

Mary Ellen frowned at her. "I'm sorry, what are we talking about now?"

"Your brother Sherm's place, The Pit."

She sat up a bit straighter now. "My brother is a genuinely horrible person. I grew up in the same house with him, so I'm entitled to say that. He was a cruel, awful little boy and he's a cruel, awful man. He used to beat up his wife, Tess. She was my best friend, you know. She'd come to me covered with bruises. I've . . . never spoken to anyone about this before. I considered it a private matter. If anyone asked I always said Tess took off for Hilo because she was bored with Sherm. But that was never the truth. She left him because he smacked her around. And she left with my blessing. I encouraged her to go. She told me she'd send for Leland once she got settled, but she didn't. When Tess cut ties with Sherm she cut ties with their boy, too. I hadn't anticipated that. To this day I still don't know how a mother could do that to her child. I'm speaking as someone who lost my own little boy, Wyatt, when he was three. Believe me, my pain has never gone away. I felt *so* badly for poor Leland. I did what I could to be a mother to him. He's needed a mother's love over the years. God knows, Sherm was no help to him. So it was up to me. Leland has grown up to become a nice young man. Too nice. He couldn't bring himself to tell Sherm that he wanted to strike out on his own. He needed to be free of The Pit, and for that he needed my help."

"Did you talk to Sherm about it?" Des asked.

"*Talk* to Sherm?" Mary Ellen looked at her in disbelief. "You don't *talk* to Sherm. He doesn't hear you. He's too busy bellowing and roaring. But I've been very fortunate in my choice of careers.

I'm our Town Nurse. That's who I've been for the past twenty-six years. I look after my people. Leland needed his freedom. I gave it to him. Hubie needed to be punished. I punished him. I'm not a crazy person. I know that what I did was wrong. And I meant what I said before—I'm carrying around a huge load of guilt right now. Yet at the very same time I'm *glad* that I did what I did. And I'd do it all over again if I were given the chance."

The room fell silent, aside from the rain tapping against the window. Mitch didn't know what the others were thinking. He was thinking how glad he was that he'd gotten along well with Mary Ellen. Clearly, you didn't want to piss this woman off.

"Let's talk about the events of yesterday," Yolie said to her. "Did you and Hubie arrange to meet at The Pit?"

Mary Ellen nodded. "Ward told me he'd be tutoring the Miller boy, so I asked Hubie to meet me there at five o'clock."

"Had you two met there before?"

"Never. I hated the place. It reeked of stale beer."

"Did Hubie wonder why you wanted to meet there?"

"He did."

"What did you tell him?"

"That it was quiet and out of the way."

"How did you get in?"

"Sherm kept a spare key underneath a brick outside the kitchen door," Mary Ellen said. "I got there first. Brought a plastic bottle of charcoal lighter fluid with me that I'd found in our garage. I put it behind the bar before Hubie got there. I also brought a change of clothes that I left in the car."

"Just to be clear . . ." Yolie said. "You're telling us that you went to The Pit fully intending to kill Hubie Swope. Am I hearing you correctly?"

"Yes, you are," Mary Ellen responded without hesitation.

"What happened when he got there?"

"I was good and ready for him. Hiding in the kitchen with the kitchen door propped half-open. I was just waiting for him to turn his back toward me, that's all. I'd already grabbed one of those heavy glass beer pitchers that was on the bar."

Yolie glanced at Des before she said, "And. . . ?"

"And I whacked him over the head with it," Mary Ellen said calmly. "I came at him so fast that he never knew what hit him. He sank to his knees, dazed, and I whacked him again. And again. I whacked him until he toppled over onto his back and lay there, blinking up at me in disbelief."

"Then what did you do?"

"I smiled at him and told him he was a lying son of a bitch. I assured him that there was a very, very special place in hell waiting for him."

"And then what happened?"

Mary Ellen shrugged. "And then he was gone."

"He wasn't gone," Des said.

Her eyes widened. "Excuse me?"

"He was still alive when you left him there. The ME found soot in his lungs. It was the fire that killed him."

"Well, he wasn't *conscious*," Mary Ellen said. "I can assure you he felt no pain."

"Would it bother you if he had?"

"Of course. I loved him."

"What'd you do after you bashed his head in?" Yolie asked her.

"I squirted the lighter fluid all over him and then those picnic tables that were stacked in the middle of the room. Then I went to the door, lit a match, and tossed it inside. Got in my car and drove my way back to Old Shore Road. I didn't make a left turn back toward town because I didn't want to drive past the Citgo. Someone

229

might see me. So I made a right toward South Dorset and kept on going for a couple of miles until I reached that park they have there with the basketball courts and baseball fields. It was getting dark by then. The park was completely deserted. I pulled into the parking lot and changed my clothes in the car. I thought that the ones I'd been wearing might smell of lighter fluid. I wrapped them around the empty bottle of the lighter fluid and tossed them into the woods out behind the baseball field. Then I drove home. I got there before Ward made it home from the library. Washed my hands and face, and dabbed a bit of perfume on my neck just in case my hair smelled. Dinner was already taken care of. I'd started it in the slow cooker that morning."

"What did you make?" Mitch asked her.

"A brisket. Well, sauerbraten, really. It's my mother's recipe."

"I find that so hard to imagine."

"Making sauerbraten in a slow cooker? Why, it's as easy as—"

"No, that you had a mother."

"Who *is* this guy?" Latham demanded. "And why are words coming out of his mouth?"

Des elbowed him in the ribs again. Even harder.

"We were just sitting down to eat it," Mary Ellen went on, "when Sherm called to tell us what had happened. We drove straight to Pitcairn Avenue. And there you have it. That's the whole story."

"I know I'm just a dumb little girl from Glastonbury," Toni said. "But I'm totally confused about something, especially because you sound like you were being so careful and thorough. Mr. Swope's laptop and cell were locked in his car right outside of The Pit. You knew he'd taken photos of you. You had to know we'd find those photos eventually. Yet you left his devices behind."

"That's a really good point," Zimmer said, nodding his buzz-cut head.

"If you'd snatched his car keys from his pants you could have taken the devices with you and destroyed them," Toni said. "Didn't that occur to you?"

"Not until I was halfway home," Mary Ellen confessed with a sigh of regret. "By which time it was too late to go back. You're absolutely right. I should have taken them, but I was in such a hurry to get out of there that I panicked a little. Once the thought *did* occur to me it distressed me greatly because, as you say, it was only a matter of time before you people found my pictures."

"Which explains why you just broke in here," Latham said, scratching his head.

"What was Plan B?" Yolie asked her. "If you weren't able to grab the laptop and cell, I mean. What then?"

"Admit to you that Hubie and I had been lovers. How could I not? But that didn't necessarily mean I killed him and burned down The Pit, did it? Every sign pointed toward Sherm, after all. It was Sherm who was at war with Hubie over the damned place. It was Sherm who was flat broke and staring at foreclosure if Hubie didn't let him reopen it. I was fairly certain that you'd think Sherm was responsible."

"But you played it cagey anyway, didn't you?" Des said. "You started muddying the waters yesterday morning when you checked up on Mitch by tossing out the names of those Casserole Courters whom Hubie might have gotten mixed up with, knowing that Mitch would mention them to me and that we'd have to give a good, hard look at them. You didn't dare mention Nadine Ambinder because there was a chance Nadine knew all about you and Hubie. He might have told her. But you did mention Nancy Franklin, even though Nancy and Hubie were never anything more than friends. You also mentioned Inez Neto."

"As if Hubie would ever get mixed up with *that* cheap bimbo," Mary Ellen said, her face hardening.

The room fell into strained silence. Mitch was waiting for Des to tell her that Hubie had, in fact, been boinking Inez, not to mention Bitsy, Loretta, and possibly Shannon Burns. But Des kept quiet about it. So did Yolie.

"We considered every possibility," Des went on. "We looked good and hard at Sherm and Leland and Gaylord. We talked to Leland's fiancée, Brianna, who told us she'd made the mistake of getting involved with an older man a while back. It did occur to me that Hubie might have been that older man, but we didn't find any pictures of Brianna on his computer. We talked to Inez and Inez's son, Petey, and Petey's delightful girlfriend, Darla. We talked to Shannon, whose husband, Tommy, comes and goes at all hours in his Ballek Oil service truck, which is chock full of flammable liquids. We talked to Nadine, who thought that she was going to start a family with Hubie. Two kids, maybe three."

"She was quite mistaken about that," Mary Ellen stated emphatically. "Hubie hated children. He complained about them to me all of the time."

"We've run ourselves ragged these past twenty-four hours, Mary Ellen, and yet here we are with you," Des concluded. "It all comes back to you."

"Only because your boyfriend is a big, fat liar," she said bitterly.

"He's not a liar and he's not fat. He's thick."

Mary Ellen glowered across the table at him. "You are one conniving bastard, Mitch Berger. If I ever get my hands on you . . ."

"Never going to happen," Yolie informed her coolly. "Everything you're telling us indicates that Hubie's death was the result of a premeditated assault with intent to kill. We call that first-degree murder. You won't set foot outside the walls of a prison for the rest of your life."

"I know that," she acknowledged. "But I did what needed doing. I took care of Hubie Swope for what he did to me. And I gave Leland a chance at a better life. The boy's free of that place now."

"Not necessarily," Latham said. "If we determine that the arson was the result of a criminal act by a third party—that would be you—then Middlebury Mutual will be obligated to make good on your brother's rebuilding costs. I'm afraid you didn't accomplish a thing in that regard."

"All you did was murder your boyfriend," Des chimed in, nodding.

Which pretty much lowered the curtain on Mary Ellen's show of defiance. She crumpled right before their eyes. "H-He promised he was going to m-marry me," she sobbed, fresh tears spilling down her cheeks. "Not Nadine. *Me*."

"He's not going to marry either one of you now. You made sure of that." Yolie reached over and flicked off the microcassette recorder. "Sergeant, would you please ask those two troopers who're out in the hallway to escort Mrs. Tatum to the Troop F barracks?"

"Right, Loo," Toni said, gathering up Hubie's bagged laptop and cell.

"Would you like us to call Ward for you?" Des asked Mary Ellen.

She looked at Des blankly. "Why on earth would you want to do that?"

"No reason. Just thought I'd ask."

Dorset's Town Nurse had nothing more to say about that or

anything else. She reached for a tissue and dabbed at her eyes, then got up from the table and went quietly out the door with Toni.

The rest of them remained at the conference table.

"There's one thing I still don't understand," Latham told Yolie, his brow furrowing. "How did it come about that she attempted to break in here, *did* break in here, while you, Sergeant Tedone, and Master Sergeant Mitry were all sitting here—with the door locked?"

"She was hoping to destroy the victim's laptop and cell," Yolie answered.

"But why did she think they were locked in here?"

"Sometimes you get lucky. We got lucky."

"Is that what you call it?" Latham studied Mitch with intense curiosity for a moment before he turned back to Yolie and said, "Okay, we'll call it lucky and leave it at that." He got to his feet with a tired groan. "Ladies, it was a pleasure working with you. Or at least I think it was. I'm still not sure I understand what in the hell just happened here."

Yolie raised her chin at him. "Is that going to be a problem?"

"Nope. Not as far as I'm concerned. But let's touch base before we file our paperwork, okay? I want to make sure we're all on the same page."

"We will be, Lieutenant," Yolie promised him.

"Make it 'Jocko,' why don't you?"

"Fair enough. Catch you on the flip side, Jocko."

"C'mon, Zim, let's hit the road before it hits us."

"Right, boss."

Latham and Zimmer went trudging through the doorway of the auxiliary conference room and out into the rainy night.

Yolie started out of the room herself, cell in hand. "It's been real, Miss Thing," she said, flashing a grin at Des.

Des grinned back at her. "Yes, it has."

"Mitch, take care of my girl, hear? Or you'll have *me* to answer to."

"Now I'm afraid."

"Good. Be afraid," she barked at him. Then she left them there at the conference table.

A trooper with an evidence bag came in and retrieved Mary Ellen's pry bar from the table. After that, Mitch and Des were alone in the room.

"Why didn't you tell Mary Ellen about Hubie's other women?"

"Didn't have the heart to," Des confessed. "Yolie didn't, either. We're a pair of marshmallows, I guess. No matter. She'll find out about them before long." Des studied him with those pale green eyes of hers. "Are you okay?"

"I guess so," he answered quietly.

"No, you're not. What is it, baby?"

"I just think this whole thing's kind of sad, that's all."

"You think I don't?"

"I think I don't know how you do this, day in and day out."

"It's a snap. I stay up half the night at my easel drawing portraits of dead people. I run ten miles a day. I rescue feral kittens. And I've got you, remember?" She squared her big hat on her head and said, "I have to head over to the barracks to file my paperwork. I can stop by later, if you'd like."

"I'd like."

"What are you going to do?"

"Cook up a giant batch of my famous American chop suey. There's nothing better on a cold, rainy night than a hearty bowl of my American chop suey. And then I'm going to do exactly what you suggested—watch *Mr. Blandings Builds His Dream House*. The Dude's never seen it. Unless I decide to watch *The Bachelor and the Bobby-Soxer.* He hasn't seen that, either. I haven't made up my mind yet. It's a tough decision. These are the hard ones."

Des brushed his lips with hers, smiling at him. "Yes, they most certainly are."

EPILOGUE

(THE NEXT DAY)

DRAW WHAT YOU SEE, *not what you know.*

The late-afternoon sunlight over Uncas Lake came slanting right into her living room thanks to the floor-to-ceiling windows Des had installed when she remodeled her cottage. The living room had become her studio the day she moved in. A cluttered, charcoal-smudged mess of a studio with sketches and sketchpads always scattered about. Right now, dozens of photos of Hubie Swope were taped to every wall. Crime-scene photos of Hubie's charred remains as well as every photo of the living, breathing Hubie that Des was able to lift from the town's Web site and online newspaper, *The Gazette.* Hubie seated behind his desk at Town Hall with a tight, grim look on his face. Hubie standing at the groundbreaking for a new office complex on Big Branch Road with a tight, grim look on his face. It was still so hard for her to believe that Dorset's building inspector, the persnickety little man who cut his breakfast sausages into identical bite-sized pieces, had wooed and won over five different women at the same time. One of whom had murdered him when she found out the real deal.

And yet it was all true.

Des stood before her eighteen-by-twenty-four–inch Strathmore 400 drawing pad, graphite stick in hand, and drew gesture sketch after gesture sketch, using her whole arm, staying light on the balls of her bare feet as she bopped to Les McCann and Eddie Harris's joyful rendition of "Compared to What" from their *Swiss*

Movement album. She drew, trying to find the truth of who Hubie Swope had been.

Draw what you see, not what you know.

Her involvement in the case was over and done. Mary Ellen Tatum was over and done, being held without bail on charges of first-degree murder and arson. Earlier that day, Des had driven down to the end of Pitcairn Avenue and discovered two huge Dumpsters there. A workman was clearing away the charred remnants of The Pit with a backhoe.

Chuck Ranberg and Sherm Gant were both there watching him work. Ranberg stood in the middle of Pitcairn Avenue with his hands in the pockets of his Armani leather jacket and the breeze off of the Sound ruffling his glossy black hair. Sherm was watching the final demolition of his beloved family business from the front seat of his pickup truck.

"Jocko worked this case good," the man from Middlebury Mutual said to her. "You all did."

"We got it done," Des said, tightening her hat against the wind.

"We're still not absolutely convinced that Mr. Gant's innocent of any criminal association with this fire."

"Sherm had nothing to do with it. You know that."

"No, I don't, actually. And I won't until it's been established in a court of law. Some people think he was involved in the arson with his sister."

"By 'some people' you mean *you,* don't you?"

Ranberg showed her his nice, white teeth. "We honor our commitments. But we've stayed in business for a hundred and forty-seven years because we always make sure, understand?"

"I understand." Des also understood that this meant it would be many, many months before Sherm would see so much as a nickel from Middlebury Mutual. She strolled over to his pickup and said, "How are you, Sherm?"

"Mad as hell," he growled at her. "That bastard's going to stonewall me until the cows come home. You know what I ought to do? I ought to hire me a lawyer."

"Our First Selectwoman's a lawyer. Damned good one, too."

Sherm let out a sour laugh. "I'm the mayor of Pitcairn Avenue. You honestly think high and mighty Glynis Fairchild-Forniaux would help *me*?"

"I do. She told me herself that Dorset isn't Dorset without The Pit. But you'll have to be straight with her about all of the facts."

"Facts? What facts?"

"Why Tess left town."

Sherm's face darkened. "There isn't a day goes by I'm not sorry about the way I treated her. I've never laid a hand on another woman since. Not once, I swear to God. You believe me, don't you?"

"What I believe doesn't matter, Sherm."

"Yeah, it does. It matters." He sat there behind the wheel watching the backhoe pick up a shovel-load of blackened debris. "I had no idea Mary Ellen was mixed up with Hubie. I thought everything was fine between her and Ward. So did Ward."

"You've spoken with him?"

Sherm nodded. "Poor bastard's shell-shocked." He looked back at Des, his gaze troubled. "Leland wants to become a physical therapist."

"I know."

"You do? How come I didn't?"

"You haven't been listening to him."

"I guess you're right about that," he allowed glumly. "I've been sitting here thinking about things. I keep wondering if this whole thing's been my fault. Like if I'd just been a better husband and father and brother—a better person—none of this would have happened. Like maybe I'm the one who ought to be in jail. Does that sound crazy to you?"

It did and it didn't. There was never a simple yes or no answer when it came to murder. Legally, Sherm wasn't responsible for the fire that had taken Hubie Swope's life. And, yet, if he hadn't driven his wife, Tess, away by beating the crap out of her, and if he'd been a more tolerant and understanding father to Leland, then maybe he was right. Maybe he was partly to blame. But not completely. Because Sherm had zero to do with Mary Ellen falling in love with Hubie and then bashing his head in when she discovered he was dogging her.

Draw what you see, not what you know.

Des drew, one sketch after another. She drew with her eyes open. She drew with her eyes closed so as to awaken her other senses. She awakened them, all right. Summoned up the smell of Hubie's burnt flesh. The bilious taste in her mouth. But for some reason Hubie himself continued to elude her. There was a fundamental truth about the man that she was missing.

She was still searching for it when Mitch arrived with the fixings for their dinner. He'd volunteered to bring a chicken to roast. But first he got busy uncorking a bottle of Chianti Classico.

"Sorry I'm so late," he called to her from the kitchen. "I stopped off at All Pro Automotive so Jeff could take a look at my Studey. It turns out that the left tie rod is, in fact, partially cracked. He told me not to drive it anymore because if it gives way that could lead to a catastrophic crash, which he didn't recommend."

"I'm right there with him."

"He's going to surf the Internet for a supplier who still carries parts for a 1956 Studebaker."

"Does he think he can find one?"

"He does. But it'll take a few weeks, not to mention many, many hundreds of dollars." Mitch joined her in the studio with two glasses filled with wine. Her three live-in cats, Christie Love, Missy Elliot, and Kid Rock, escorted him, bumping his legs with their heads. "For now, he's loaned me a flatulent Mercedes diesel wagon that has two hundred and fifty-six thousand miles on it. I feel like a for-real Dorset geezer now. All I need are some egg yolk stains on my sweater and a splash of that special cologne they wear, Eau du Goat." He handed her one of the glasses. They sipped, Mitch eye-balling her from head to toe.

"Why are you checking me out that way?"

"I haven't seen you in your flannel artist's smock in a while. I forgot how insanely erotic you look. Just exactly how long are those legs of yours?"

Draw what you see, not what you know.

She sipped the Chianti, her eyes straying back to the photos of Hubie, searching, searching. The truth was there. It had to be. So why wasn't she seeing it?

Frustrated. Mitch's ladylove was most definitely frustrated. He was pretty sure he knew why, too. He came around behind her to have a look at the sketch she'd been working on. A gesture sketch. Plenty of raw emotion. No insight. "How is it going?"

"It's not," she answered. "As you can see."

"I had a cup of tea with Bitsy this morning."

"Is she okay?"

Mitch nodded. "Bitsy's been through a lot in her life. She's a sur-vivor. Nadine will have a much harder time. Nancy told me that she's gone home to Albany to be with her folks. Wouldn't surprise me a bit if she never comes back. Inez didn't show up for work at the Big Y today. I'm guessing she'll go on a forty-eight-hour toot, then return to her cash register and keep on keeping on. She's used to disappointment."

"How about Loretta?"

"Serene as can be at yoga today. Acted as if nothing had happened."

Des stood there staring at the sketch on her drawing pad. "I don't get Hubie."

"Really? I think I do."

"Then kindly explain him to me, will you? This was a careful, methodical man. A man who repaired cuckoo clocks. Yet here he was juggling five love affairs at once. Six, if you want to toss in Shannon."

"Have you asked Shannon if Hubie was the father of her baby?"

"I'm officially no longer involved, so it's officially none of my damned business. Besides, I really don't want to know." Des continued to stare at her drawing pad. "He'd plunged himself so deep into debt that he was going to lose his house. And there was no way he could keep all of those affairs a secret much longer. The truth had to come out, didn't it?"

"Yes, it did."

"So what in the hell was he thinking? Did he honestly believe that he was going to get away with it?"

Mitch went over to the big windows that looked out over Uncas Lake. It was nearly dark out now. He could see the reflection of the half-moon in the inky blackness of the lake. "He didn't care. Hubie Swope was living the dream."

"Dream? What dream?"

"This was a plain little nebbish who lived a plain little nebbishy life. Then his wife died and the Casserole Courters came a-courting and, to his great astonishment, Hubie discovered that he'd some-how become an object of desire. For him, this whole thing was a schoolboy fantasy come true, and he was loving every minute of it. He loved making all of those women happy. He loved being the Lavender Lane Lothario. And he was going to keep right on be-ing the Lavender Lane Lothario for as long as his money and his prostate held out. Sure, he would have come crashing back down to earth before long. But, trust me, that charbroiled man in those photos there, that man died with a smile on his face."

Des studied the photos of Hubie's blackened remains. "You really think so?"

"I know so. Believe me, I don't have any trouble at all channel-ing my inner Hubie Swope. I'm a screening room nerd. I've had weight problems my whole life. And I've been . . ." Mitch broke off, feeling that familiar heaviness in his chest. "I know what it's like to be married to a dying woman. And what it feels like after she's gone. I was a total wreck after I lost Maisie. Hell, I was practically a dead man walking the day you and I met, remember?"

"I remember," she said softly.

"Me, I got lucky."

"We both got lucky."

"Hubie didn't."

She furrowed her brow at him, lost in her thoughts for a mo-ment, then flipped the page on her drawing pad and began to draw. She used her whole body when she drew, dancing on the balls of her feet just the way Muhammad Ali used to, back when he floated like a butterfly and stung like a bee. She was into it now. She had it.

"I'll get our chicken into the oven," he said.

"You're awfully handy to have around sometimes, wow man."

"I'll bet you say that to all of the men who cook for you. Oh, hey, did you meet up with your dad?"

"I did. And, let me tell you, I have *never* seen that man so ill at ease. It turns out he has a lady friend named Marcia who he wants me to meet."

"No kidding? Hey, that's great!"

She stepped back from her easel, gazing at him. "Your voice just did it again."

"Did what?"

"There, hear that? It went all falsetto."

"So . . . how do you feel about it?"

"Me? I couldn't be happier. My mom moved on years ago. It's time he did, too. He's been alone too long. Marcia's going to spend a weekend out here at the Frederick House. He'd like us to join them for dinner there."

"Heck with that. We'll do dinner at my place."

"Yeah, that's what he told me you said. When the two of you had lunch yesterday."

"Damn."

"You held out on me, boyfriend," she said sternly.

"I know, I know. And I apologize. But I gave him my word that I'd let him be the one to tell you. I can't *believe* he ratted me out. The Deacon and I need to have a serious talk about the Man Code."

"Don't sweat it. I understand."

Mitch peered at her. "You do?"

"I do. He's way out of his comfort zone. He needed someone to confide in, man to man. He needed *you*. Just promise me one thing."

"Sure, what is it?"

"Don't ever tell me what else the two of you talked about."

"Not to worry, thinny. These lips are sealed."

He was starting for the kitchen when her doorbell rang.

"Would you mind seeing who that is?" she called out. "I'm not exactly dressed for company."

Mitch went to the front door and opened it, flicking on the porch light.

Standing out there, puffing impatiently on a cigarette, was a short, chunky black woman in her fifties wearing a too-tight purple sweater with a plunging V-neck, even too-tighter dark wash jeans, and a pair of pointy, canary-yellow stiletto heels that matched her pointy, inch-long canary-yellow fingernails. Parked in the driveway behind her was a dented, mud-splattered white Nissan Altima. A very hyper Jack Russell terrier was barking its head off in the front seat. The backseat was crammed to the roof with suitcases and garment bags.

"May I help you?" Mitch asked her.

"That all depends." She looked him up and down with keen-eyed disapproval. "Who might you be?"

"I'm Mitch Berger."

"Uh-huh. You would be, wouldn't you?" She took one last puff on her cigarette before she flicked it into the driveway, where it landed in a cascade of sparks. "Tell Desiree I'm here, would you?"

"Okay, sure. And you are. . . ?"

"I'm Zelma," she replied, her pale green eyes flashing at him. "Just tell her Mommy's home."